At the Little Brown House

Ruth Alberta Brown

Complete & Unabridged

Tutis Digital Publishing Private Limited

First published in 1913 as *At the Little Brown House.*

This edition published by
Tutis Digital Publishing Pvt Ltd, 2008.

All rights reserved. No part of this publication may be reproduced, stored in a retrieval system, or transmitted in any form without the prior written permission of Tutis Digital Publishing Private Limited.

This book is sold subject to the condition that it shall not, by way of trade or otherwise, be lent, resold, hired out or otherwise circulated without the publisher's prior consent in any form of binding or cover other than that in which it is published and without a similar condition including this condition being imposed on the subsequent purchaser.

CHAPTER I

A Morning Caller

It was a glorious morning in early June; the dew still hung heavy on each grass blade and leaf, making rainbow tapestries that defy description, as the waking sunbeams stole into the heart of each round drop and nestled there; the fresh, cool air was sweet with the breath of a thousand flowers; a beautiful bird chorus filled the earth with riotous melody as the happy-hearted songsters flitted from tree to tree saying, "Good morning," to their neighbors. Through a mass of rosy clouds in the east, the sun struggled up over the hilltop and smiled down on the sleeping village of Parker as if trying to coax the dreamers to arise and behold the beauties of the dawning day. In the barn-yards of the little farms scattered around about the town roosters were crowing, hens were clucking, cattle lowing, and horses stamping and neighing, eager for their breakfast.

Old Towzer, from his bed on the porch of the little brown house, almost bidden by tall maples and wide-spreading elms, stretched and yawned, perked up his ears, listened intently, then rose stiffly, shook his heavy coat and leisurely descending the steps, circled around the place to see whether anyone was yet astir. The door slammed at the green house on the farm adjoining, from the little red cottage across the fields came the sound of a busy ax, and down by the creek some early riser whistled merrily as he went about his morning work. All this old Towzer heard, and strolling back to his place on the porch, he looked up at the chamber window above him and barked sharply. The drawn curtain flew up with a flirt, a small, tousled head appeared behind the screen, and a childish voice in a loud whisper commanded, "Keep still, you old Towzer! It isn't time to wake Gail yet. We've got to get those flowers and she wouldn't let us if she knew."

A second small face joined the first at the window, followed by still another, all blinking sleepily, but eager with excitement. "Oh, Peace," whispered the oldest of the trio, in an awestruck voice, "isn't it a beau – ti – ful day? I've a notion to call – "

"Don't you dast!" quickly interposed the first speaker. "You know Gail never'd let us go. Just see how wet everything is!"

"Did it rain?" asked the third child, the youngest of them all, critically examining the trees and porch-roof, and then lifting her great, blue eyes to the bluer sky above as if expecting to see her answer there.

"No, goosie, it's just dew, but it must have been awful heavy. Get your clothes on, Allee, or Gail will wake before we are started. Aren't you ready, Cherry?"

"'Most," came the muffled reply from the corner where a struggling tangle of clothes, hands and feet proclaimed that Cherry was hurrying.

"Then come on; we will have to fly. I'll button your dress when we get outside, Allee. Never mind your other shoe, Cherry; you can put it on downstairs. Have you got your basket?" Giving her directions in sharp, imperative whispers, Peace led the way into the hall, leaped onto the banisters, boy-fashion, and slid quickly, quietly to the floor below, where she waited in a fever of impatience for her less daring sisters to creep backward down the creaking stairs. "Skip that one, it squeaks like fury – oh, Allee, what a racket! There, I knew you'd do it! Gail's awake. Sh! Girls!"

They held their breath, huddled close in the darkest corner of the hall, and waited.

"Peace!" again came the call from above.

A happy inspiration seized the small culprit, and she snored vigorously. Cherry and Allee clapped both hands over their mouths to stifle their giggles, but Gail was evidently satisfied, for she did not repeat her summons; and after another moment of hushed waiting, the half-dressed, dishevelled trio tiptoed down the hall, cautiously unlocked the kitchen door and slipped out into the sweet freshness of the early day.

There was a quick scampering of little feet down the walk, a subdued click of the gate, and the three children, holding hands, raced madly along the dusty road until a thick hedge of sumac and hazel bushes hid them from the little brown house. Then Peace slackened her gait somewhat, but did not cease running, and kept looking behind her as if still fearing pursuit or discovery.

"Oh, Peace," gasped Allee at last, stumbling blindly over sticks and stones as her older sisters dragged her along between them, "my dress is coming off, and my breath is all in chunks. Do we have to run the whole way?"

Peace looked back at the small, perspiring figure, saw the plump shoulders from which the unbuttoned dress had slipped, caught a glimpse of flying shoestrings, rumpled stockings and naked legs, as the little feet were jerked unceremoniously over humps and hollows of the rough road-way, and stopped so abruptly that her companions were thrown headlong into the dust, creating such a commotion that a weary slumberer on the opposite side of the thicket was rudely startled out of his nap, thinking some great catastrophe had overtaken him. As he sat up and rubbed his eyes, looking around him in bewilderment for the cause of his sudden awakening, he heard an angry voice sputter shrilly, "Well, Peace Greenfield, I must say – "

"Don't stop to say it now," interrupted another childish voice. "I never meant to dump you over like that. You shouldn't have been running so fast. S'posing you had been a train and tumbled into the ditch! Reckon all your passengers would have got a good jolt. I stopped so's we could finish dressing. Cherry, where is your other shoe? You have run all the way down the road with only one on. Just look at your stockings!"

"Where's yours? You haven't any stockings at all," retorted the first voice, still sharp with indignation.

"In my pocket. I was afraid Gail would hear as 'fore we got gone. There, Allee, your dress is done. Fasten up your shoes while I put on my stockings. We'll have to hurry like mischief, 'cause I don't think Gail will go back to sleep again."

There was a subdued rustling for a moment or two beyond the dense hedge, and then the listening man heard the sound of hurrying footsteps in the road, and the children vanished without his having caught a glimpse of them. But he was now thoroughly awake, and as soon as the steps died away in the distance, he rose from his bed among the leaves, shook out his gray blankets, rolled and strapped them into a bundle, threw them under the overhanging shrubbery, and slowly made way through the trees to a wide, sparkling creek, whose tumbling waters made sweet music in the woods.

"What a glorious scene this is," he murmured aloud, gazing in rapt admiration at the wooded hills, the singing stream, the bright flowers. "Why can't we be content to live in such places instead of building great, smoky, sooty cities? You little creek, you sang me to sleep last night. Wish I could take you back home with me. What a pretty flower! Little bird, you will split your throat if you try to pour out all your melody at once. Better give us a little at a time. Of course you are happy! Who wouldn't be on such a wonderful day? Oh, what sentiments for a tramp! Campbell, have you forgotten what you are?"

He was near the road now, and suddenly a baby voice piped shrilly, "Yes, here is the bridge and there is the sun. Oh, just look at the sun! It's way up high now. Ain't it big and fiery?"

"S'posing it was a frying-pan," spoke up a second voice, which the startled tramp recognized as belonging to Peace; "and we could have all the buckwheat cakes it would cook. My! wouldn't that be nice?"

They came slowly into view through the shrubbery, – three queer, dripping little figures, with hair flying, dresses wet and rumpled, shoes soaked and muddy, but literally loaded down with masses of late columbine and sweet wood violets. And they made a pretty picture with their bright, rosy faces and excited, sparkling eyes.

The tramp, in the shadow of the trees, caught his breath sharply, then laughed to himself at Peace's supposition and Cherry's horrified exclamation, "Why, Peace Greenfield, what ever put such a crazy idea into your head? – supposing the sun was a frying pan?"

"I bet it would make a good one, and I'll bet the cakes would be dandy, too! Um – m – m! I can smell 'em now. I am starving hungry, and it does take so long for the girls to cook pancakes in our little frying pan. Hurry up! It must be breakfast time already. I wish I had wings to fly home with. S'posing we were birds, we would be there in a jiffy."

"Let's play we were," suggested Allee. "That will make the way seem shorter."

"All right," the sisters assented; and with their great bouquets flapping wildly in the wind, the trio sped swiftly out of sight up the road, leaving the tramp again to his thoughts.

"Pancakes! Makes me hungry, too. Guess I better wash and be moving on in search of a breakfast. I wonder if those youngsters live near here."

He knelt beside the clear stream and ducked his head again and again in the cool water, finally drying his face on a clean handkerchief, and running his fingers through his bushy gray hair in place of a comb. His toilet done, he set out briskly down road the children had taken, whistling under his breath, and keeping a careful lookout for farmhouses on the way.

At the first place he approached, the watchful housewife had loosed a vicious-looking bulldog, and the tramp wisely passed by without stopping. The next house was deserted, the door of the third place was slammed in his face before he could even make known his wants, and he was beginning to wonder if he must go breakfastless when a shrill, childish treble rang out clearly on the still morning air:

> "'The Campbells are comin' Oho, Oho,
> The Campbells are comin', Oho, Oho.'"

So sudden was the discordant burst of song, and so close by, that the tramp stopped in his tracks and stared in the direction of the voice.

"Well, of all things! That announcement quite took my breath away!" he ejaculated, hurrying forward once more. "The voice sounds like 'S'posing Peace.' I wonder if it can be she."

It was, indeed. Another rod and he found himself in front of a gate, on the high post of which was perched a diminutive, bare-legged girl in a soiled, damp frock, superintending the drying of three pair of mud-covered shoes arranged in a row on the picket fence, while she issued orders to the two sisters sitting in the middle of the gravel walk busily sorting flowers.

"As true as you live, I don't believe these shoes will ever be dry by school time. S'posing we have to go barefooted, and this the last day of the term! Cherry, you've got too many columbines in that horn. They look pinched. Put some in Allee's boat."

"Allee's boat?"

"Well, she is fixing it for Miss Truesdale, even if she ain't a sure-enough scholar yet. Don't make such little, stingy bunches of violets. We picked plenty. I can't coax your toes to shine, Cherry. I'm scared that the blacking won't do any good. You shouldn't have worn your best ones."

"I haven't any others. My old pair is all worn out, and – Why, who – "

Cherry had caught sight of the shabby figure at the gate, but before she could finish her sentence, Peace, following the direction of her eyes, wheeled about on her perch, surveyed the man with big, almost somber, brown eyes, and poured forth an avalanche of questions: "Are you a tramp? Do you want some work, or are you just begging? Can you chop wood? Do you know how to hoe? Are you hungry – "

"Yes, miss, I'm hungry," the tramp managed to stammer. "Could you give me a bite to eat?"

"Not unless you will work for it," was the firm reply. "We don't b'lieve in feeding beggars, but we are always glad to help the deserving poor."

The man's shrewd, deep-set eyes twinkled with amusement at her grown-up tone and manner, but he answered with seeming meekness, "I will be only too glad to do anything I can for a breakfast – "

"There's wood to be chopped. Gail ain't strong enough to do such work, and our man is lazy. Reckon we'll let him go as soon as the garden is in shape. There's a heap of vines to be trained up on strings 'round the porches, and there are all the flower beds to be weeded, this grass needs cutting, and the roof of the hen house has to be fixed so's it won't leak, the hoop has come off the rain-barrel, the back step is broken, and – oh, yes, there are three screens that we can't get on the windows, and Mike never finds time for them."

Peace stopped for breath, and the tramp took advantage of the pause to say, "Which one of those jobs will you have me do?"

"Which one?" echoed the child in round-eyed amazement. "Why, all of them, of course! You don't expect us to give you breakfast unless you do something to earn it, do you, after I've told you we never feed beggars?"

"No, miss. I am willing to work. But you better find out what your ma wants me to do first, so I can begin."

"Mamma's a ninvalid," Peace responded promptly. "But I will ask Gail. She will know, and, besides, she is cook here."

She leaped nimbly to the ground and disappeared within doors, where some sort of an argument evidently waged warm and furious for a time, judging from the sound of voices heard in the garden. Finally Peace put in appearance again; not the jaunty, self-reliant young lady who had interviewed the tramp a few moments before, but a very sober-faced, dejected-looking child, who twisted her dress into knots with nervous fingers, and at length stammered in embarrassed tones, "Gail says you can have some breakfast if you will split a little wood for her first, but she says it is a nimposition to expect you to do all I said you should. I don't see why. There's a heap of work around here to be done and no one but Mike to do it. There! Faith told me not to say anything about not having any men on the place. Mike is only a boy, you know, and he doesn't b'long here. We haven't got any – "

"Peace Greenfield!" The voice was sharp with exasperation, and Peace retired hastily indoors once more, calling back over her shoulder, "You'll find the ax by the woodpile, if Mike hasn't got it in the meadow, or it isn't in the shed or the barn. I'll come out and tell you when to quit. Yes, Faith I am hurrying! Be sure you cut a lot, 'cause – " The voice trailed away into indistinctness, and the tramp, with a smile on his lips, went to hunt up the missing ax; and soon sharp, ringing blows told the occupants of the house that he was hard at work.

Rapidly the huge pile of heavy knots diminished in size, and just as rapidly the heap of split stove-wood grew, while the perspiration rolled in great beads down the worker's crimson face. At last he paused a moment to rest his back and wipe the moisture from his hot forehead, and as he drew his handkerchief down from his eyes he saw Peace standing before him, holding a platter in her extended arms while she surveyed the result of his labor with approving eyes.

"You've done splendid!" she breathed, enthusiastically. "The last tramp who cut wood for us piled it up so it looked like there was an awful lot, but after he was gone we found he had heaped it around a big hole in the middle and there wasn't hardly any split. Faith said she bet you would do the same way, but I watched you from the window, while Cherry and me were washing the dishes, and you never tried to hide a hole in the middle at all. Here is your breakfast. Gail cooked it, else you wouldn't have got much. It is Faith's turn to get the meals today, but she is baking a cake for the minister's reception tonight, and is crosser'n two sticks, so Gail fixed it.

"You see, we were all through breakfast when you got here, or you might have had more. I don't know, though, – Faith says if she had her way about it, she'd send every single tramp who comes here marching down the street with the enemy in pursuit. That means Towzer, but he wouldn't bite anyone. Faith is cross every time she makes a cake. You might have eaten in the kitchen if it hadn't been for that. She sends us all out-doors when she is baking, so's we won't make her cakes fall. She does make fine things, though! Um! but they are good! Never mind, the kitchen is hot anyway, but it's nice and cool out here under this maple. This is my maple. Papa built that bench for me and Allee before he went to heaven. You can sit on the ground and play the seat was your table, or you can sit in the seat and hold this platter in your lap. Which'll you do?"

The tramp smiled broadly, relieved the small maid of her heavy load, and dropped wearily onto the wide bench, saying gratefully, "This will do nicely, thank you. What a fine breakfast you have brought me! Gail must be a good cook. Is she your sister?" As he spoke, he picked up an egg and carefully broke it on the edge of his plate.

"Yes, Gail's the oldest of us – Oh, Mr. Tramp, just see what you have done! I was afraid Gail hadn't given you breakfast enough and that you might get hungry before noon, so when she wasn't looking I put on a whole lot of extra toast and four eggs and some matches to cook them with, and you've gone and smashed a raw egg all over everything!"

He stared in dismay at the broken yolk streaming over his creamed potatoes, and then, seeing the consternation in the big, brown eyes of his small hostess, he laughed heartily and said, "Never mind, little girl! I'm hungry enough for even raw eggs this morning. Doctors often make their patients eat such things. Here goes!"

Peace watched him in silence a moment and then observed, "You don't look like any tramps we ever had here before. They always shovel in their food with their knives, but you use your fork. You can work, too. Why don't you get a job somewhere and earn some money instead of loafing around begging for your meals?"

The man paused, with his fork half way to his mouth, surprised at the child's keen observations. Then he answered, lightly, "I do sometimes, but a feller can't work all the time, can he?"

"Well, most folks have to, though I never could see why they all can't have vacations like we do at school. This is our last day until next fall."

"Is that what you and the kids gathered the flowers for?"

"Yes, and for the minister's reception tonight. We went early this morning 'fore the rest of the folks were up; and mercy, but didn't Faith scold when we got back! She said we ought all of us to be whipped and sent to bed. Faith is real ugly when she's making cakes. We did get awfully wet, – I had no notion it would be so bad. But we got the flowers anyway. We made some baskets yesterday out of birch bark and moss. Here comes Allee with them now. She doesn't go to school yet, but sometimes she visits with Cherry and me, and today is one of the times. Ain't the baskets pretty?"

"Scrumptious!" was the admiring answer, as the man clumsily lifted one of the dainty boats filled with dog-tooth violets and drank in its perfume with the delight of a child. "What wouldn't city people give for these little nosegays from the woods! They would go like hot cakes."

"What do you mean?" asked mystified Peace, failing to understand what connection her beloved flowers could have with hot cakes.

"Why, in big cities, at almost any of the important business corners, you will see little boys and girls selling sweet peas and daisies and – yes, they sometimes sell cowslips and wood violets, but only in bunches – never in such cunning little baskets. Why, tucked down in that damp moss, your flowers will keep fresh for hours; while a bunch from a city flower-seller's stock withers as soon as it is taken out of water."

"Would folks in Martindale buy them?"

"Yes, indeed! They are a breath from the woods, and lots of people would be glad to get them. You see – "

"Peace Greenfield, it's time to start! Do you want to be late the last day of school?"

"That's Cherry. I must go. I wish I could stop and talk some more. When you finish your breakfast, just take the dishes around to the kitchen steps, and – if you have time and want to do it – you might weed those flower gardens in the front yard and the onion patch behind the shed. If you don't, I'll have to, and you 'member I gave you some extra lunch that you wouldn't have got if it hadn't been for me – and a few matches. Promise you won't light a fire till you get a long way from our house, will you? Gail won't give tramps matches for fear they will set the buildings on fire. And say, the lawn-mower is right beside the front porch, if you should happen to want to cut the grass – just the little piece fenced in, you know. The rest is for hay. And the ball of twine for stringing up Hope's vines is stuck in the hole of the porch railing nearest the door – you can find it easy enough. The rain barrel is behind the house, and – yes, yes, Cherry, I am coming this very minute! I hope you have liked your nice breakfast, and will come some other time and split more wood for us. Good-bye, Mr. Tramp, I've got to go."

CHAPTER II

The Minister'S Reception

"Are you ready, Cherry?"

"Almost," came the muffled reply from the stiffly-starched little figure sitting on the floor struggling with a broken shoe-string. "Why, Peace, where are you going?"

"Where do you s'pose? To the reception, of course," answered that young lady, who had just entered the room, rigged out in an ancient, faded pink gown which had once been pretty, but was long since outgrown so that several inches of petticoat hung in display the whole way around the skirt, and the ruffs on the sleeves reached almost to the elbow. How she had ever squeezed herself inside the small garment was beyond comprehension, but there she stood, buttoned up and breathless, ready for the evening's social event.

"Did Faith say you could go, and where in creation did you find that ridiculous old dress?" demanded Cherry, after an astonished survey of the grotesque figure in the doorway.

"Faith doesn't have anything to say about it," was the emphatic retort, as the brown eyes snapped indignantly at her sister's criticism. "Didn't mother promise I could go to the next reception that the church had, and ain't this the next? Faith kept me home from Mr. Kane's farewell, but she can't make me stay away tonight."

"Gail isn't going – " began Cherry, scenting the storm which was sure to follow this declaration from her younger sister; but Peace interrupted, "I am going just the same. Mother said I could!"

"Have you asked her about it today?"

"No, I haven't. She promised a long time ago, but it was a sure enough promise, and she always keeps her promises."

"But – "

"There ain't any 'but' about it. I'm going even if I have to walk all by myself. I'm 'most as big as you. Two years ain't much difference! Faith never kicks about your going, but she always tries to make me stay at home. She won't this time, though." The shapely little head shook so vigorously that each tight ring of short, brown hair bobbed emphatically.

"But you can't go in that dress," remonstrated Cherry, still staring at the abbreviated gown and neglecting her own preparations. "It is hardly big enough for Allee any more. You've had that for three or four years."

"It's the only thing I could find. My white one is all worn out, and that ugly green gingham has a long tear on the side which Gail hasn't mended yet."

"But what will Faith say when she sees that rig? Why, Peace, it looks awful!"

"I should say it did!" exclaimed a second voice from the hallway, and Faith, a tall, brown-eyed girl of about fifteen years, entered the door. "What in the world do you think you are doing, Peace Greenfield?"

Peace blinked her somber eyes vigorously, for tears were very near the surface, but she swallowed back the lump in her throat and calmly answered, "I'm getting ready for the reception, same as you."

"Indeed you're not! Gail isn't going, and you can stay right here at home with her and Allee."

"That's what I did the last time, but you don't play that trick on me tonight. Mother said I could go to the next reception, and I am going."

"She didn't mean this kind of a reception, and you can't go."

"I will, I will! Oh, you are the crossest sister!" cried poor Peace, with tears of vexation streaming down over her cheeks. "You always spoil my good times! You never make Cherry stay at home – "

"She is older – "

"Two years ain't much!"

"She knows how to behave herself."

"So do I! I'll be as good as gold – "

"I've taken you on that promise before."

"Oh, Oh, Oh! I will go! I'm going straight to mother and ask her now."

"Mother is worse tonight and can't be bothered. Stop your yelling, or she will hear you."

"I want her to hear! I shall go! She said I might!" The storm was on in all its fury.

"Hush!" interposed Cherry, running to her sobbing sister and trying to soothe her wild rebellion with gentle caresses. "I will stay home with you, Peace. I don't care much about going, anyway."

"You can stay at home if you want to," declared the small rebel with emphasis, "but I am going!"

"Children, children, what is all this racket about?" asked a gentle, grieved voice, suddenly, and the shamed-faced trio wheeled to find the pale, little, invalid mother standing in their midst.

"Oh, mother, mayn't I go? Faith says I can't, but you promised me when Mr. Kane went away that I could go to the next reception if I would make no more fuss about not going to his."

"So I did, dear – "

"But a reception for a new minister is no place for such little girls, mother," broke in Faith, petulantly.

"The 'nouncements said to bring the babies" – involuntarily the mother smiled and the other sisters giggled. "I am lots bigger than a baby – "

"You don't act it – "

"Faith!" The mother's face was as reproving as her voice, and the older girl's cheeks flushed crimson as she murmured humbly, "I am sorry, mother; but really, she does say such awful things. She is always talking. And just look at that dress!"

"I thought it would be pretty – " began Peace, but at that moment she caught sight of her reflection in the mirror, and stopped so abruptly, with such a comical look of dismay and despair in her eyes, that the whole group burst out laughing. Peace joined in their merriment, and then soberly said, "I look like a chicken when the down is turning to feathers. What can I do about it? I can't stay at home!"

"Where is your green dress?"

"Gail hasn't mended it yet."

Faith saw her opportunity and immediately compromised. "Peace, if I mend your dress for you so you can go, will you sit perfectly still all the evening and never say a word until you are spoken to?"

"Yes, oh, yes, I'll promise!"

The mother opened her lips to speak, but thought better of it, and with a smile in her eyes, withdrew, leaving the children to their final preparations.

At length the torn dress was neatly mended and buttoned on the wriggling owner, the bright curls were given a second brushing and tied back with a band of pink ribbon from Faith's own treasures, and the sisters were on their way to the mother's room for a good-bye kiss when a fourth girl, looking very sweet in a fresh, blue gingham, rushed excitedly up the stairs and demanded, "Where did you say you put the cake, Faith? Gail can't find it."

"Why, it's on the wash-bench under the pantry window, covered up with the big dishpan."

"There is nothing under the dishpan but an empty plate."

"Hope! You are fooling!"

"Cross my heart and hope to die," was the solemn answer. "Gail looked and I looked. She says somebody must have stolen it."

"The tramp!" cried Faith and Cherry in one voice.

"Bet he didn't!" declared Peace, who had stood open-mouthed and silent during Hope's recital. "I gave him a great big lunch and – and some matches to make some more with – "

"Yes," said Faith, bitterly grieved over the loss of the cake, "and kept him hanging around here all the morning, till we thought he never was going. I suppose he took the cake for his dinner."

"I don't believe it! But he did weed those flower beds beau – ti – fully!" cried Peace, championing his cause. "And he strung Hope's vines just as even! And the lawn is all mowed, and there ain't a sprill of grass left in the onion patch, and the rain barrel is fixed up and the back step is mended, and – did he stop up the leaks in the hen house? I told him just where they were."

"Perhaps you told him to pay for his breakfast, too," suggested the older girl, sarcastically. "We found a half dollar under his cup after he was gone."

"A sure-enough half dollar?" asked Peace, too astonished to believe her ears.

"Yes, a sure-enough half dollar!"

"Where is it? I want to see it for myself."

"On the pantry shelf. Gail thought he might have left it there by mistake and would come back after it. But I don't."

"Maybe he left it to pay for taking the cake," suggested Allee, who had joined the excited group in the hall.

"He never took the cake," Peace asserted stoutly. "But I don't think he will ever come back for his money, either. He wouldn't have left it in the dishes if he hadn't meant it for us. His clothes had pockets in them, same as any other man's, and if he had any money, he would have kept it there and not carried it around in his hands. Wish he would come back, though. I'd ask him about the cake, just to show you he never took it."

"See here, Peace Greenfield," cried Faith, with sudden suspicion, "do you know where that cake is?"

"No, I don't! How should I know? But I don't believe that tramp took it. So there!"

"I don't believe he was even a tramp. Suppose he was a bad man, who had done something terrible, and the police were after him – "

"Yes, or s'pose he was a prince," Peace broke in, remembering her conversation with the gray, old man. "He might be one for all we know, but he didn't look like a bad man."

"Suppose we stop supposing," laughed Hope, "and all hunt for the cake. Someone may have hid it just for fun. We've half an hour before we really must go to the church."

"I don't care to go at all if that cake is gone," declared Faith, crossly. "Mrs. Wardlaw will begin to think I am lying to get out of helping with refreshments if I have to make excuses again tonight."

"But you're on the program," protested the smaller girls.

"I guess maybe we will find it somewhere," said Hope. "Come on and help." And they scattered in their search for the missing loaf.

But, though they looked high and low, indoors and out, not a trace could they find of it, except the clean, empty plate under the dishpan; and in despair Peace climbed to her gatepost to ponder the question of whether tramp and cake had disappeared together or whether some local agent was the cause of its vanishing. "If it had been a nanimal," she said, thoughtfully, "it would have knocked the dishpan off the bench and broken the plate. It must have been a person. I'd think it was Hec Abbott, only – mercy! What in the world is this? Money! Sure as I'm alive!" Scrambling down from her perch, she raced for the house, shouting, "Gail, Faith, look what I've found, hitched to the gatepost!"

The five sisters ran to meet her, and into Gail's hand she thrust a crumpled, green scrap.

"Ten dollars!" gasped the astonished girl, examining the dingy bill with excited curiosity. "Someone must have lost it – "

"And pinned it to the gatepost so's we could find it?" demanded Peace. "Well, I guess not! Bet that tramp left it. He surely must be a prince. What shall you do with it, Gail?"

"Show it to mother and ask her advice," promptly answered the oldest girl, smiling down at the excited group of sisters; and they hurried away to the house with the precious find – all but Peace.

A wild, daring thought had suddenly sprung into her active brain, and as her sisters vanished within doors, she flew madly up the road through the summer twilight towards the little village, clasping a shining half dollar tightly in her fist. In a surprisingly short time she returned, breathless but triumphant, bearing a huge paper sack in her arms, just as an anxious group came around the corner of the house.

"Peace! Where have you been?" cried Gail in relief, as the panting form flew in at the gate.

"We've been hunting all over the farm for you," added Faith, severely.

"Thought you might be searching for some more money," laughed Hope.

"What's in that big bag?" demanded Cherry.

"Cakes!" gasped Peace, proudly. "Faith said Mrs. Waddler would be nasty if we didn't take something to eat this time, so I spent the tramp's half dollar for some of those marshmallow cakes with nuts on top. They are dandy good, and they cost a lot, but they weigh light, so you get a big bag full for fifty cents. Not many people have money enough to buy them very often, and Mrs. Waddler can't say a word about our bringing them instead of a cake. Have one, Gail and Allee, 'cause you aren't going to the reception. And take one up to mother. Maybe she'd like them, too."

"But, Peace," Faith began, sharply, then stopped at a warning glance from Gail, and with sudden gentleness she took the bulky sack from the small sister's arms and started off for the church where the reception was to be held.

They were somewhat late in arriving, and the little building was already well filled with a laughing, light-hearted crowd, gathered to welcome the new minister into their midst. Glancing hastily about her, Faith saw one empty chair in a dim corner, and pointing it out to Peace, she said, "Sit down over there, and remember not to talk except when you are spoken to. Above everything else, don't get to romping. Hope and Cherry are to help Miss Dunbar pass the cake, so they are needed in the kitchen. Remember, now!"

"Yes, I will," was the unusually meek reply, and Peace obediently curled herself up in the corner to watch proceedings, thankful to be one of the gay company, but wistfully wishing that she might join in the merrymaking. It wasn't so bad when the program hour came, for everyone sat down then and listened quietly to the music and speeches, but it was very lonely in the dim recess, where Peace was almost hidden from sight, and she longed to have someone to talk to. Everyone was so busy introducing themselves to the young minister and his pretty, sprightly little wife, or gossiping among themselves, that no one paid any attention to the somber, brown eyes peering so eagerly from the corner.

"Oh, dear," sighed Peace at length, "I might as well have stayed at home like Faith said, for not a single soul has said a word to me since I came in, and I don't s'pose I will even get a chance to speak to the new minister. My, but he's got an awfully pretty wife! Wish she would smile at me like that. There come the 'freshments. Like as not they'll skip me, off here by myself. If Cherry forgets, I'll shake her good when I get home. A piece of cake is dry eating when all the rest have lemonade, but I'd rather have that than nothing. There, that man is going to play again – Faith is pulling out the stops of the organ. Doesn't he look funny?"

She laughed aloud at a sudden ludicrous fancy, and her laugh was echoed so close beside her that she nearly jumped out of her chair. Recovering herself, she whirled around to find the strong-faced young pastor looking down at her.

"What do you find so funny to laugh at, hid away here in this dark corner?" he asked, in a cheery, hearty voice, as he drew up an old stool and sat down beside her.

And, forgetting her fright in the friendly glance and tone of this new preacher, Peace giggled out, "I was just thinking s'posing we were all grasshoppers, how funny we'd look hopping around here instead of walking. We'd have to shake feet instead of hands, and if we wanted to go across the room all we'd have to do would be to take a big jump."

For a fraction of a second the minister was dumb with amazement at the unexpected answer; then he threw back his head and laughed uproariously, as he gasped, "What ever put such a thought in that little noddle?"

"That man with the big fiddle," was the prompt reply. "Doesn't he look like a grasshopper with that long-tailed coat and all that shirt front? If he just had feelers on his head, he'd be perfect. Don't you think so?"

Again the young man laughed, for Peace's picture was not overdrawn – the tall, angular cellist in evening dress certainly did resemble a grasshopper. But, of course, it would never do for him to say so, and he sought to turn this unusual conversation by inquiring, "Aren't you one of the Greenfield girls? You look amazingly like two or three who have been introduced to me this evening. Isn't the organist a sister of yours?"

"Yes, that's Faith."

"And the blue-eyed one just coming in the door?"

"That's Hope."

"And there is a third one here somewhere, is there not?"

"Yes, Cherry. Her real name is Charity, but that is such a long name for a little girl that we call her Cherry."

He smiled at the diminutive maiden with her grown-up air, and said musingly, "Faith, Hope and Charity. Then you must be Mercy."

"Oh, mercy, no!" was the horrified exclamation. "That would be worse than ever! I am Peace. Faith says I ought to have been called 'War and Tribulation' – it would have been more 'propriate; but I am not to blame for my name, if it doesn't fit. I would have been something else if I'd had my way about it. Unless babies are named pretty names I think their folks ought to wait until they can pick out their own names. Grandpa named me – all of us but Gail and Allee. If I just hadn't been born for two weeks longer maybe I'd have had a pretty name, too, for grandpa died when I was only thirteen days old. You see, grandpa was a minister – papa used to be a minister, too – and he never had any other children but papa, so he didn't get a chance to do much naming in his own family. Papa named Gail; her real name is Abigail. And then grandpa came to live with us. He liked Bible names, so the rest of us were picked out of the Bible – except Allee, and she wasn't born then. Mamma named her."

She paused for breath, and the amused, amazed preacher found opportunity to murmur, politely, "But I am sure you all have good names – "

"Oh, yes, they are good enough! The trouble is, they don't fit, except Hope's. She is our sunbeam, always doing and saying something pretty, and meaning it, too. Now, Gail isn't a gale at all, but just the bestest kind of a sister; while Faith is usu'lly cross as two sticks unless things go just as she wants them; and Cherry doesn't stand around on corners d'livering tracks and worn-out clo's to the needy poor, like Charity always does in the pictures. But mine is the worst misfit. Still, I'm thankful it isn't any worse. Just s'posing I had Irene for a middle name – that's my favorite, and Olive is Hope's choice – then my 'nitials would have spelled P. I. G. and hers H. O. G.; and the school children would never have called us anything else. I know, 'cause they call Nort Thomas Nettie. His whole name is Norton Edwin Thomas, but he always signed his 'nitials on his 'rithmetic papers, and the boys took to calling him Nettie. It makes it all the worse 'cause he is a regular sissy boy. Have you got any children?"

"No."

"Well, I s'pose you will have some day, and if I was you, I'd name them something pretty, or else wait till they got big enough to choose for themselves. And whatever you do, don't let your church people raise 'em."

"Wh – at?"

"That's just what they'll try to do. They did with our family, and when they got us all spoiled, they said we were the worst children in town – that ministers' children always were. Why, Mrs. Waddler – her name is Wardlaw, but she is so big and fat that I call her Waddler – that's her over there feeding cake to that scrap of a man – he's her husband – well, she told Mrs. Grinnell once that I was possessed of seven devils. I asked mother what that meant, and she was dreadfully mad. It takes a lot to make mother mad, too. When we first moved here to Parker, Mrs. Wardlaw thought I was the cutest little girl she had ever seen – she told me so lots of times – but she doesn't any more. Now she says I am a hoy-ena – no, that isn't the word. It means tomboy, anyway. That is what Mr. Hardman calls me, too. He's the imbecile who lives on the farm next to our place."

"The wh – at?"

"Well, he is! He says so himself. He doesn't b'long to any church, and hardly ever goes, and he says r'ligion is all tommyrot."

"Oh, you mean infidel," suggested the pastor, trying hard not to laugh again.

"Maybe. His name is really Hartman. I nicknamed him 'cause he won't let us have the hazelnuts in his pasture, and he stole my pet chicken, – leastwise, he let it stay in his flock so now I can't coax it back; and he chased us out of his apple trees one day when we were just climbing after one pretty red one way up high out of reach. We did knock off quite a few, but we never meant to carry them off with us. He doesn't like girls, and says if he had a family of six like us, he'd – "

"Are you six girls all there are?"

"Isn't that enough? Seems to me it's a pretty big family. When I was little, Cherry and me used to pray that the angels would never bring any more babies to our family, 'cause the pieces of pie were getting awfully little, and, of course, they got littler every time there was another baby. But they brought us Allee anyway. That was just after mother's onliest uncle died and left her some money, and she made papa take it and buy our farm and bring us out here to live after he had been sick a long, long time with tryfoid fever, and had lost all his pretty hair."

"Didn't you say your papa was a minister?"

"I said he used to be."

"What is he now?"

"An angel."

"Oh!"

"You see, papa went right on acting like a preacher even after the bad people in Pendennis made him sick; and when Old Skinflint – I mean Mr. Skinner – most folks call him deacon, but I guess it's just 'cause he is so different from a truly deacon, and is always blaming the Lord for everything that happens – well, when he got cold and had pneumonia, papa helped take care of him. The deacon is so ugly that hardly anyone else would have anything to do with him; and one rainy night papa was soaked going up to Skinner's house, and he had to sit up 'most of the night in a cold room, 'cause the deacon wouldn't have anyone in his room where the fire was. So papa caught cold, too, and he never got well. The angels came and carried him away."

"Oh!"

"Yes, and I heard Mrs. Abbott tell a lady one day that she thought mother would soon be an angel, too. Do you s'pose she will?" The big, brown eyes had suddenly grown wide with fear, and Peace piteously searched the strong face above her for some comforting assurance.

Just a moment he hesitated, and then answered, tenderly, "We shall all be angels some day if we are good."

"Oh, mamma is good as gold! But two sure-enough angels in one family is too many, 'specially when it's the mother and father. Don't you think so?"

Poor man! What could he say? But at that moment came a timely interruption in the shape of Miss Dunbar with a huge platter loaded with glasses of lemonade; and as she spied the two figures in the little recess, she exclaimed, "Why, Mr. Strong, we've been hunting all over the building for you. What an effective screen those brakes and columbines make! None of us thought of finding you here. Peace, you are very quiet this evening. Would you like some lemonade? Have you had refreshments, Mr. Strong? The committee is looking for you to make arrangements for Sunday's meetings."

"I will be there in a moment, Miss Dunbar. Good-night, little Peace, I see your sisters beckoning to you. When the parsonage is ship-shape I want you to come and see us. Will you?"

"You bet!" was the prompt and emphatic reply, as Peace skipped happily away to join her sisters, forgetting, in her gladness, that neither Hope nor Charity had brought her any cake to eat with her lemonade.

CHAPTER III

Shoes and Strawberries

"Cherry! Cherry Greenfield!" called Peace, imperatively, flapping a newspaper vigorously, as if to add emphasis to her summons.

"Here," drawled a lazy voice from the great elm by the road. "What do you want? I am busy."

"You are reading, that's what!" exclaimed her sister in disgust, as she came within sight of the slender, brown legs swinging among the thickly-leaved branches. "Shut up that book and listen to me. I've got some portentious" – she meant important – "news. Cameron's Shoe Store advertises shoes at forty-nine cents. That means a pair, doesn't it? They wouldn't sell them separately, would they, – 'cepting to one-legged people? And the sale lasts the whole week."

"Well, what of it?" asked Cherry, impatiently opening her book once more; but Peace had scrambled up into the leafy retreat by this time, and she thrust a ragged newspaper page into her sister's hands, crying, "What of it? Why, Charity Greenfield, you were saying just this morning that you'd have to have some new shoes pretty quick or go barefooted on Sundays. How would you like that? And mine are 'most worn out, too."

"Well, I can't help it if we must have shoes. Gail says there won't be any extra money this month. It took all she had to pay up Mike, so she could let him go. Besides, this paper says they are canvas shoes. Those wouldn't last us any time. Faith says we ought to have cow-hide – "

"Yes, that sounds just like her. She is always saying something cross. She ought to be thankful that we don't wear our shoes out any faster. S'posing we didn't have any summer so we could go barefooted, or s'posing we had as many legs as a spider, and had to buy a dozen pair of shoes each time. I guess that would take money! Aren't canvas shoes the things Nellie Banker had? Hers wore an awfully long time and she put them on every day, too."

"Well, I don't see how that helps us any if we haven't got the money. Cameron's Shoe Store is in Martindale, too. Where did you get this paper?"

"I've been helping Mrs. Grinnell shell peas, and she dumped the pods onto this scrap. When I saw 'shoes forty-nine cents,' I asked her if it meant sure-enough shoes for that little, and she said it did, and that any time we wanted to get things in town at a sale when she was going in, we could drive along with her."

"But the money – "

"Can't we earn it? I heard Mr. Hardman tell the butcher that he needed someone to help pick his late strawberries, and he'll pay five cents a quart. We've often picked strawberries, and it isn't very hard work – just hot and mon-mon – I can't think of the rest of that word."

"It's just as well," answered Cherry, with unconscious sarcasm. "'Twas likely wrong anyway. Do you mean to say you would pick berries for Mr. Hartman, when you hate him so?"

"Why not – if he will have us? His money is just as good as any other man's, ain't it? Only he's mighty stingy."

"That's just it! I don't believe you heard him right. He'll never pay five cents a quart for picking berries, Peace. Now, if it was Judge Abbott or Mrs. Grinnell – Why, strawberries are cheap!"

"Not now, when they are 'most gone. And, besides, he told the butcher that one of the big hotels in Martindale pays him twenty cents a quart for all he will bring them. It's a special kind, you see, splendid big ones, that only rich folks can 'ford to eat."

Cherry swung her feet thoughtfully as she read the alluring advertisement once more, and pondered the question of such importance to both little girls, but she ventured no reply.

"Well?" said Peace, sharply, after some moments of impatient silence.

"It's awfully hot to pick berries in the sun all day," yawned Cherry, fingering her book longingly.

Peace snorted in disgust, and seizing the precious paper from her sister's lap, she swung nimbly to the ground and started off across the meadow on the other side of the fence.

"Wait, Peace! Where are you going?" cried Cherry, scrambling off her perch, thoroughly awake now.

"To pick me a pair of shoes in Mr. Hardman's strawberry patch," answered Peace, quickening her pace.

"Oh, don't hurry so fast. I'll go, too. But s'posing he won't let us pick berries for him?"

"I ain't s'posing any such thing. We've picked strawberries before. Why, Allee knows how. Anyone with sense can do a thing like that!"

"Is – are you going to take Allee along if he should give us the job?"

"No, her shoes will last a long time yet. She doesn't need any new ones."

By this time they had reached the long, low, green house on the farm adjoining theirs, and almost bumped into Mr. Hartman himself, as they dashed breathlessly around the corner in search of him.

"Highty, tighty!" ejaculated the startled man, leaping aside to avoid a collision. "What are you young rapscallions doing over here? You better make tracks for home."

"Ramscallion yourself," Peace burst out hotly, nursing a stubbed toe and winking rapidly to keep the tears back. "We've come to pick your strawberries."

"You have, eh? Well now, what if I won't let you?"

"Then we'll go home. Come, Cherry!" Grabbing her sister's hand, she marched angrily toward the road, but he called after her, "What will you pick berries for?"

"Five cents a quart," she replied briefly, not looking around or slackening her gait in the least.

He chuckled. "Huh! Your price is pretty steep."

"'Pends upon how you look at it," she flung back at him. "You pay that to other folks, and we can pick as good as anyone. Mrs. Grinnell always – "

"Mrs. Grinnell's berries are only scrubs."

"Scrubs have to be picked carefully so's not to squash them."

He laughed outright, and Peace marched on with head high and cheeks aflame with anger.

Before she had reached the road, however, he stopped her by saying, "What do you want to pick berries for this hot weather?"

"For money. We want some shoes. Cameron's are selling canvas shoes for forty-nine cents a pair all this week, and Mrs. Grinnell is going in town Saturday, and we could drive with her – s'posing we could earn enough for the shoes."

"Why don't your ma buy some?"

"Mother's sick and Gail hasn't any money."

"You've got a pretty little farm there – "

"We can't wear farms on our feet," snapped Peace, moving off once more, but again he stopped them, for he was really in need of pickers in order to harvest his big crop of berries before they spoiled on the vines. "Well, now, I'll tell you, kids, I will try you at picking, and – "

"Pay us five cents a box?"

"Yes, if you are good at the job. Come tomorrow morning."

"We'll begin now. This is Thursday, and that sale lasts only till Saturday. It might rain tomorrow, and 'sides, it might take us more'n a day."

"Well, suit yourselves," chuckled the man. "But be sure you do good work and don't eat up the berries."

So the two small sisters were soon busily engaged in picking the luscious red fruit and packing it in quart boxes, while the sun poured mercilessly down upon them. But they pluckily stuck to their post until the day was done, trying to forget the heat and dust in planning their trip to the big city, which they had visited so seldom. However, two long, thankful sighs escaped their dry lips when at length Gail's horn tooted out the summons to the evening meal, and they hurried homeward as fast as their aching backs and tired feet would carry them, exultant though perspiring.

"Gracious!" murmured Cherry plaintively, as she bathed her hot face at the pump, "I never knew before how many berries it took to make a quart."

"It would take lots more if we were picking wild strawberries. They ain't bigger'n peas, but these are whoppers."

"And covered thick with spiders – ugh! I feel them crawling all over me now. I believe I killed a million just this afternoon."

Peace laughed. They didn't bother her. "Just s'posing those strawberries were bugs really, and when the hotel people ate them the bugs would bite. My, wouldn't you like to hear them holler?"

"Why, Peace Greenfield!" cried Cherry in a shocked voice.

"Well, Hope was reading yesterday about some place where snakes coil up and look just like springs of water, and when thirsty people bend over to drink, the snakes bite them. There might be bugs somewhere that looked like strawberries so folks would try to eat them. Course I wouldn't want them to hurt the people bad – just enough to make them jump good."

"I would rather have strawberries look like pennies – "

"I'd rather have them be pennies. Just think, if we could pick money off from strawberry vines! Everyone would start to raising strawberries, wouldn't they? And how rich we would be! Never mind, we picked ten boxes of berries this afternoon – that means a shoe apiece. We surely ought to get that many more by noon tomorrow. Let's begin early so's to pick as many as we can before it gets hot."

So the morrow found them early in the field again, and by noon the second ten boxes were filled to the brim.

"There!" breathed Cherry in relief, mopping her crimson face on her sleeve as she surveyed the fruit of their labor. "We are done. Now we can get our shoes all right tomorrow. Why, what are you doing, Peace? Are you crazy?" For Peace had snatched up some empty boxes from another crate and was making her way between the green rows again.

"Nope," answered the perspiring little maid. "I am just going to pick some more."

"Well, I'm not!" was the emphatic reply, as Cherry started after the dusty figure plodding down the field. "I am nearly cooked now, and hungry as a bear. Come on home! We have picked enough to pay for our shoes, goosie. Or do you want two pair?"

Peace lifted her somber eyes from her self-appointed task and said briefly, "Yep – for Allee."

"For Allee?" echoed astonished Cherry. "You told me yourself that she didn't need any new shoes."

"Well, I didn't think she did, but last night I 'xamined her only pair and they look awfully scrubby. There isn't any more blacking in the house, and the ink I sopped onto them made them worse than ever. Besides, I – it would look mean to get us some shoes and not any for her."

Without another word, Cherry gathered up an armful of empty boxes and dropped down by a new row of vines, picking silently, ploddingly until at last the third ten had been filled. Then she spoke, "Is this all, or are you going to earn shoes for Hope and Faith and Gail? Because the afternoon is pretty well gone and – "

"Three pair of shoes is all I am going to pick," interrupted Peace somewhat sharply, for she was hot and tired, and Cherry's tone seemed to imply criticism. "Help me tote these crates up to the house now and we'll get our pay."

Mr. Hartman met them as they tugged the second crate, only half filled, up to the berry shed, and the spirit of mischief suddenly took possession of the usually stern, business-like farmer.

"So you have picked all you want to, have you? Well, I am surprised to think you would give up so soon. Here, hand me that box! I want to see what kind of pickers you are." He hoisted the two crates to the corner of the fence surrounding one of his brooding pens, and pretended to examine each box critically, while the girls waited in anxious silence for his word of approval. "Hm!" he said at last, trying to frown, and succeeding so well that both little faces paled with misgiving. "Just as I expected! You don't know how to pick strawberries. You don't deserve a cent of pay. How much were you to get? Five cents a box?"

"Yes, sir," whispered Peace, with lips so dry they could hardly form the words.

"Well, I oughtn't to give you a penny, but I will be generous and live up to my part of the bargain. Five cents a box, was it? And there are two boxes and a half of fruit."

His eyes were twinkling, but this Peace failed to notice, and she cried indignantly, "There are thirty boxes! We picked ten last night and twenty today."

"Oh, those little boxes! Five cents a big box, I meant. That would be ten cents and half a nickel over; but I will be good and give you fifteen cents for your work." He drew three battered coins from his pocket and dropped them into Peace's damp, dirty hand.

She drew in her breath sharply, stared at the money for a moment in dumb amazement, then let it fly with all her might straight at Mr. Hartman's head, screaming in a frenzy of anger and disappointment, "You numscullion of a cheat! Do you s'pose you will ever get to heaven? There are your old berries! You can hire your chickens to pick them up! I'll never work for you again!" One shove of the crates, and the beautiful, tempting fruit lay in a scattered heap inside the chicken yard! And Peace, blinded by the hot tears of rage, was flying for home with dismayed Cherry close at her heels.

It was Mr. Hartman's turn to stare, and stare he did, first at the spoiled fruit and then at the flying girls, too stunned to understand. The hot blood mounted to his forehead, he shook his fist in unreasoning anger and yelled, "Drat your pesky hides! Come back here and I'll tan you good! What do you mean by spoiling all that high-priced fruit? Oh, if I just had my hands on you now!"

"You got only what you deserved, Dave Hartman," said a quiet voice behind him, and he whirled angrily toward his wife, who had come upon the scene unnoticed.

"All I deserved! Twenty quarts of fruit spoiled! Four dollars' worth, Myra Ann!"

"You should have been fair to the children and it never would have happened. They have worked hard and earned their money."

"Fair! I meant to be fair. I was just fooling with them. If she hadn't been quicker'n greased lightning she would have got all that was coming to her."

"How was she to know that? You looked so ferocious I don't wonder she took you at your word. The best thing you can do now is to rescue that fruit before the chickens have spoiled it entirely, and let me wash and can it. Then you better go over and pay the children for their work."

"Pay the children a dollar and a half for spoiling four dollars' worth of strawberries? Well, I should say not! They will never get another cent out of me, no matter if they go barefooted all the rest of their days."

CHAPTER IV

Little Flower Girls

In the hot room, high up under the eaves of the little brown house, Peace sobbed out her anguish of soul, and then faced the problem of shoes with a dauntless spirit.

"We'll have to have new ones when school begins again, and if we could just get some of these canvas things to wear during the summer, our old ones would last quite a while longer. Mercy, where does the money go? Seems as if there never was any to buy things we need with. Wish my tramp would come back and leave us another bill. Wish – why didn't I think of that before? The woods are full of flowers yet. I'll get Hope and Cherry to help me make a lot of birch bark baskets and then Allee and me will sell them in the city. My tramp said lots of folks would buy them if they got a chance. Oh, Cherry, let's go down to the creek and get some more bark. Tomorrow's Sunshine Club day and we will take Miss Dunbar some baskets for her flowers."

Glad to distract Peace's thoughts from her great woe, Cherry agreed, and the two made a hurried trip to the woods for material, getting not only a big armful of bark, but also quite a bunch of moccasin flowers and tiger lilies, which they had chanced upon in an unexpected nook.

"These will be lovely for tomorrow, and ought to sell better than the violets would, 'cause they aren't so common," said Peace, as she looked lovingly down at the mass of red, gold and pink.

"Ought to what?" asked Cherry.

"Oh, dear, what have I said?" thought Peace in dismay; but quickly concealing her confusion, she replied, "They ought to look nice – make better dec'rations, 'cause these are the first I've seen this year."

"Oh! I thought you said sell, and I wondered if you thought Miss Dunbar would pay us for them."

"Oh, mercy, no!" laughed Peace, and Cherry questioned no further.

But she would have been surprised had she seen this young sister stealing out of the house the next morning with baskets and flowers in her arms, headed in the opposite direction from Miss Dunbar's village home. Once out of sight of the house, Peace broke into a wild run and never stopped until the old stone bridge was reached. Here Allee was waiting for her – a queer little figure in a faded blue gown of long, long ago, hatless, barefooted, but looking oh, so sweet, with her sparkling blue eyes and her mop of tangled yellow curls crowned with a wreath of fragrant clover blossoms. "How long you've been!" she greeted Peace. "I thought you would never come. Where's Cherry?"

"I came as soon as I could," was the panting reply, as Peace dropped her burden on the grass and smoothed out a rumpled pink dress of as ancient a style as Allee's. "I had to help with the dishes, and then Faith made me take the milk to Abbott's so's Hope could do something for her. I didn't want Cherry. It takes such a long time to knock any sense into her head that we never would get into town today if she had to be coaxed. Besides, I thought if there were three of us, folks might think the whole family was out peddling, and maybe wouldn't buy like they would of just two. There, don't those boats look lovely? The only thing is, our basket won't hold as many as I hoped it would. I couldn't jam in but fifteen. That will be enough, though, if we can sell them at ten cents each. Oh, I've got a scheme! We will lay our flowers in the basket on the moss and hitch these horns on our dresses. I've got as many as ten pins in my dress which I don't need for anything else." While she spoke she emptied the birch bark boats of their brilliant cargo again, and deftly pinned the quaint devices to their gowns, so they dangled fantastically from their ribbon handles.

"Now are we ready?" asked Allee, as the last flower was tucked carefully away in its bed of moss, and covered over with newspapers.

"Yes, and well have to hurry or miss the car. It's quite a ways through the woods to the track. I wish they would run clear into Parker, don't you?"

They scrambled down the bank of the creek and scurried away through the trees to the little clearing where the city cars stopped at the end of the line.

"There's a car just ready to start," panted Peace, and she waved her hand frantically at the conductor who was lustily shouting, "All aboard!" and jangling the bell to hurry up any belated passengers.

"Nearly missed it, didn't you, kids?" he said genially, as they clambered up the steps and the car moved slowly away toward the city.

"Yes," breathed the older girl, settling her luggage on the seat and sitting down beside it. "I am very glad you waited for us. We're anxious to get down town while our flowers are fresh."

"Going to sell 'em?"

"Yes. You better buy a basketful. You can have a horn or a boat, and choose your own kind of flowers. We've got pink and yellow lady's-slippers, tiger lilies, Johnny-jump-ups, baby's tears, and a few Jack-in-the-pulpits."

As she made her explanation, she drew aside the paper protecting her precious blossoms, and the man exclaimed in delight, "The woods! My, aren't they scrumptious? I'll take a boat. What is your price?"

"Ten cents."

"Ten cents? Why, child, that isn't enough! Here's a quarter. Gimme lady's-slippers. And say, the motorman would like one, too. He's got a girl. Give him something swell – a little of everything. There, that's right! Stick a tiger lily right in the middle and plaster up the edges like you did mine. Whee! ain't that gorgeous? I'll bring you the dough right away." Snatching up the mass of vivid colors, he dashed up the length of the car, thrust his head into the motorman's vestibule, and after a moment's conversation came back and dropped a half-dollar into Peace's trembling hand, saying, "That's his contribution. It's worth it. Why, there ain't a florist in the city who can show such beauties!"

"Mercy!" exclaimed the bewildered Peace, looking at her money and trying to figure out how much more was needed for her wants. "That means a pair of shoes and one over. Why, Allee, if everybody would just pay like that, we will get through quick, won't we? But I 'xpect lots of 'em will try to make us take only a nickel. Just s'posing we get enough money to buy shoes for the whole family! Wouldn't they be s'prised? Thank you, Mister Conductor, and thank the motorman, too. We would like to know his girl. Does she ever ride on his car and do you s'pose he would bring her over to play with us some day? We'd meet her at the end of the line. Or maybe she is too big for us."

The conductor laughed in boyish delight, "Yes, I am afraid she is too big. In fact, she is quite a lady – " Here the car stopped for passengers, and their new friend went out on the platform where he stayed most of the time until they reached the heart of the city. But as he helped them off the car at the busy corner nearest Cameron's Shoe Store, he said, "If

I was you, I would go right over there in the door of that big building. I think you can sell all the flowers you have."

So they took up their stand as he had suggested, and waited for customers; but though many passers-by idly wondered at the odd little figures so overhung with birch bark trifles, no one stopped to inquire their business until a big, burly policeman, who had been watching the wistful, almost frightened little faces, strolled up to them and kindly asked, "Are you lost, little girls?"

"No, sir," promptly responded Peace, jerking aside the cover of her basket and briskly beginning to fill one of the birch bark canoes hitched to Allee's dress. "We are selling flowers. Would you like a chance to buy some that grew in the real woods? We've got money enough now for three shoes, but we need three more to have enough to go around. They are only ten cents each unless you want to pay more, but we won't sell them for a nickel."

Seeing the blue-coated officer talking with such odd little waifs, a crowd had quickly gathered about the trio, and a host of friendly voices echoed the policeman's hearty laugh at the jumbled recital.

"I'll take one," shouted a fashionably dressed man, elbowing his way to the front. "Give me a horn and fill it up with those little pansies. I haven't seen any of them since I was a kid."

"Those are Johnny-jump-ups," responded Peace gravely, detaching a horn from Allee's gown and heaping it up with the tiny flowers. "It's ten cents or more."

He laughed. "How much does 'or more' mean?"

"Much as you think they're worth. They came from the woods, you know."

"And you think that makes them more valuable – worth more, I mean?" And he dropped a shining dollar into the small, brown hand.

"Oh, yes! City folks can't often get wild flowers, my tramp says, and they ought to be glad for a chance to pay high for them."

The crowd shouted, and the policeman ventured to ask, "So you think lots of the woods, do you?"

"You bet!" was the emphatic reply. "It's next best to heaven. Just s'posing the whole world was made up of these great, high, dirty houses, without any woods or flowers or trees anywhere. Wouldn't it be dreadful?" The dismal picture she painted was singularly effective, and other purchasers gathered around, clamoring for her wares.

"I will give you a dime for one of those pink lady's-slippers," said a bent, old man.

"Here's a quarter for a spray of those white blossoms," another voice broke in; and very quickly the fresh, beautiful, woodland flowers changed hands, while the pile of coins in Peace's lap grew amazingly.

A little, ragged, wan-looking bootblack edged through the crowd, and stood with wistful eyes fixed on the rapidly diminishing bouquets, drinking in their beauty, and wishing with all his heart that one of them might be his. He fingered the few pennies in his pocket longingly, and finally, unable to curb his desire longer, he touched Peace's arm and timidly faltered, "Say, lady, will ye gimme one o' them red fellers for a cent? I – I'd like one mighty well, and I ain't got no more money to spare."

Peace lifted her big eyes to the pale, drawn, wistful face of the boy, possibly as old as Cherry, but no older, and a great wave of pity swept through her heart. "You can have it for nothing. Here, take this whole bunch," she said, emptying her basket and thrusting the last handful of gorgeous bloom into his trembling hands. "I am sorry all the birch bark is gone, but I am sold out. You haven't any shoes, either. Cameron's are selling canvas shoes today at forty-nine cents a pair. We've got lots more'n enough money for Cherry and Allee and me – you can have this to get yourself some with." And before her interested audience could realize what she was doing, she had selected a silver dollar from the jingling mass in her apron, and pressed it into the bootblack's grimy fist, while he stood like one turned to stone, staring at the money, unable to believe his senses. Then he took a step toward the little flower girl, but a gentleman in the throng, deeply touched by the unusual scene, said, "Keep it, sonny, and thank the good God for such sweet spirits as hers. Here is another dollar to keep it company. Better run home now and take a little vacation. You are sick."

Then how the men cheered! And to Peace's utter bewilderment, one tall, dignified old gentleman, whose face looked strangely familiar, slipped a shining gold coin into her hand and another into Allee's, saying reverently, "For the Peace which passeth understanding!"

She sat in puzzled silence for a moment, gazing first at the glittering heap in her lap, and then at the sea of friendly faces about her, while the crowd waited in curious expectancy to hear what she had to say. Her lips opened once or twice as if to speak, then closed again; but at last she said simply, "You've paid lots better'n I thought you would, and not a single once has anyone tried to buy a boat for a nickel. I – I wish we could have brought you the whole woods, birds and all. You would have liked it better. I b'lieve I said 'thank you' to every one who has bought any flowers, but if I did forget, Allee hasn't. That was to be her part – just to say 'thank you,' so folks would know we had some manners and were glad to have you buy. But somehow, it feels here" – putting her hand over her heart – "as if that wasn't enough, and so we will sing you a little song – that is, Allee will sing, and I'll whistle. I can't really sing anything, Faith says, 'cept the tune the old cow died on. But Mike taught me how to whistle, and our minister says I do real well for a girl. I tried to think of some thankful song to sing, but I can't remember a one just now, so we'll sing a lullabye. Are you ready, Allee?"

"Yes."

"Then begin!" Peace puckered her rosy lips, Allee opened her baby mouth, and this is the song they sang:

> "Baby-bye, bye-oh-bye,
> Baby-bye, baby-bye,
> Mother's darling, don't you cry,
> Close your eyes for night is nigh;
> Baby-bye, oh, baby,
> Baby-bye, oh, bye."

"Amen," said Peace reverently. "Now we are going to Cameron's Shoe Store for canvas shoes. What size do you s'pose a girl two years older'n I would wear? I forgot to ask Cherry."

"The clerk will know," suggested someone; and the crowd went their separate ways with smiles on their lips, while the two odd, childish figures trudged around the corner to Cameron's Shoe Store to make their important purchases. An obliging young man fitted the little feet with the precious canvas slippers, and sent them away rejoicing with a pair for Cherry, promising to exchange them for others if they failed to fit.

"Now we'll go home," said Peace, as they stepped out onto the sidewalk again. "Won't Gail and Faith be s'prised? I guess we've got 'most money enough left to get shoes for the whole family after all. Well, sir, if they haven't changed those cars since we went into the shoe store! We came down on a big yellow one that said, 'Twentieth Avenue North' on it, and here they are running two little bits of cars hitched together that say, 'Onion Depot!'" Peace employed the phonetic method of pronouncing words, and to her young eyes u-n-i-o-n was easily onion.

"What are you going to do about it?" asked puzzled Allee.

"Sit down here on the sidewalk and wait till they change them back again," was the reply; and Peace plumped herself down in a bunch on the curbing to watch for the yellow car which did not come. One hour dragged by, – two, three. Allee was getting restless. Dinner hour had long since passed, and she was very hungry. "It's getting pretty late, I guess," she ventured at last. "When do you s'pose the car will come?"

"I s'pect there's been a fire somewhere and stopped it. That happened once when Gail was in town."

"Maybe we better start to walk, then," quavered the little voice. "I am tired of sitting here, and Gail will fret if we don't come pretty quick."

"Well, perhaps we better – "

"Peace Greenfield! What on earth are you doing here?"

The two children flew to their feet with a cry of relief, "Oh, Mrs. Grinnell, our car is never coming!"

"No, I guess it won't on these tracks," she replied grimly, guessing from the children's appearance something of the truth. "Does your mother or Gail know you are here? Pile in and ride home with me. Like as not your folks are half crazy with fright."

So the weary duet climbed thankfully into the buggy and were driven safely back to Parker, where they were met by four white-faced sisters and a swarm of anxious neighbors.

"Got shoes for the whole outfit!" cried Peace by way of greeting; "and if Cherry's don't fit, the clerk said bring 'em back and he'd change 'em. We've sold all our flowers, and one man gave each of us some funny yellow quarters – or I guess they are half dollars. It says on one side, 'Five D.' and I suppose that means five dimes, doesn't it? Why, Gail, what are you crying for? I sh'd think you'd laugh to think there are three pair of shoes already bought, and money enough for the rest of you."

CHAPTER V

Sackcloth and Ashes

Just at dusk one cold, rainy night late in August, a shabby, weary, wet, old man plodded through the dripping woods, across the stone bridge, and up the road toward Parker. He had come a long way through mud and moisture, and was very tired, yet the first three farmhouses he passed by with scarcely a glance. But as he neared the fourth one, he eagerly scanned the place as if familiar with its surroundings, and listened intently for the sound of voices, seeming disappointed at the result, for apparently not a creature was stirring indoors or out. Not even old Towzer came to challenge him as he unlatched the gate and approached the house, and not a ray of light shone out into the darkness from window or door, though it was yet early evening. The place was as silent as a grave. Puzzled, the man made a circuit of the cottage, but neither saw nor heard anything of the occupants.

"I wonder what has happened," he thought to himself. "Guess I won't knock, it might scare them if they have gone to bed. Maybe they are away visiting. I will just slip into the barn and go to bed in the hay. Lucky I had a big dinner, I am not in the least hungry now, and if they are at home I can get breakfast here in the morning – I guess."

He had tramped many long miles since dawn, trying to reach this town before nightfall, and was so worn out with his exertions that he fell asleep almost as soon as he had burrowed a comfortable bed in the sweet-scented hay, nor did he awake until the new day was several hours old. The sun was shining – he could tell that from the bright light in the barn, but it was not the sunshine which had awakened him.

The first thing he was conscious of as he opened his eyes to unfamiliar surroundings was the sound of voices close by, and the patter of feet on the loose boards overhead. Cautiously he lifted himself on his elbow and looked about him, but at first he saw only an untidy confusion of garden tools, boxes, bags and other truck, piled promiscuously about wherever space would accommodate them. Then as his eyes became more accustomed to the light, he discovered a slender, brown-haired girl in a faded, dingy, calico gown huddled on top of a pile of empty grain sacks in the darkest corner of the barn. Her face was turned from him, but from her attitude and the sound of an occasional sniff, he judged that she had been crying. Her companion on the rafters overhead was out of range of his vision; but as she scrambled noisily over the loose board floor, which extended only half way across the building, he could catch a glimpse of red now and then, and once a bare, brown foot appeared in view, but that was all. Not daring to make his presence known for fear of frightening the two sisters, he drew silently back into his hiding place to await their departure.

Sniff, sniff, sniff! The slender shoulders of the girl in the corner began to heave, and she buried her face deeper among the grain sacks. Silence on the rafters for a brief moment; then a voice said severely, "'F I was you, Faith Greenfield, I'd stop crying and go into the house and help Gail. She is trying to do the washing herself so's to save money."

"'F I was you, Peace Greenfield," was the tart reply, "I'd try to mind my business once in a while, and not be forever poking my nose into other folks' affairs."

"Guess this is my affair as much as 'tis yours!" answered Peace sharply, and the listener in the hay below fancied there was the suggestion of a sob in her voice.

"It's none of your affair if I want to come out here by myself, but you can't even let me alone here. You are always snooping around to see what I am doing."

"I am not snooping!" was the indignant denial. "I'm hunting eggs for breakfast, and I was here first, 'cause I saw you come in bawling."

"Bawling!" Faith leaped to her feet in wild fury. "You know well enough why I am crying. You would be crying, too, if you cared like I do."

"I can cry with my heart without stopping to cry with my eyes," Peace answered soberly. "I haven't time to sit down and bawl. Someone's got to run errands and help Gail. S'posing we all sat up and cried all the time like you are doing. Who would get breakfast and dinner and supper, I'd like to know? And who would 'tend to the work?"

"Who wants any breakfast or dinner or supper? I am sure I don't! I haven't the heart to eat. I can't eat!"

"Dr. Bainbridge told us we must, and so did Mr. Strong; and he told us to keep busy, too. It helps you to forget the ache if you work."

"Forget! You don't care; that's why – " There was a sudden movement on the rafters above, and an egg came hurtling through the barn, smashing on the wall close by Faith's head – so close that a shower of little yellow spatters flew over her face and dress. "Peace Greenfield!"

"You haven't got half what you deserve," said a tense, hard voice from above. "I ought to have slung the whole batch, even if we'd had to go without breakfast. I'd like to know how you can tell whether you care more than the rest of us. You think you are the only one that knows how to be sorry."

There was a sudden silence – deep, ominous, it seemed to the man in the hay, and he ventured to peep out at the combatants, but all he saw was Faith standing rigid and white-faced in the corner. When she spoke, her voice was frigid in its intensity.

"Come down from those beams, Peace Greenfield, and take the rest of those eggs to the house!"

"I am coming down as fast as I can," began Peace's voice, equally frigid. Then there was a sound of ripping, a dreadful clatter, a dull thud, and Faith rushed forward with the agonized scream, "Oh, Peace, Peace, are you hurt? I am sorry I was ugly! You do care! Open your eyes, Peace! Oh-h-h-h!"

The tramp started up in dismay, to behold Peace huddled in a heap at the foot of the ladder, with frantic Faith bending over her. Before he had stepped from the haymow, however, there was a rush of feet from without, and four frightened girls dashed into the barn, followed by a tall, young man in clerical garb; and the shabby figure slunk back into his hiding place without making his presence known.

"What's the matter?"

"How did it happen?"

"Is she dead?"

"Run for the doctor!" cried the excited voices.

"Oh, Gail, I've killed her, I've killed her!" sobbed Faith.

"Stand back, girls," quietly commanded the minister, pushing the trembling quartette almost roughly aside. "Let me examine her. Perhaps she is only – "

"I'm every bit all right," exclaimed Peace crossly, winking her brown eyes dazedly. "The fall stunted me, I guess. I lit on my head. So did the eggs. Mercy me! What a mess!"

"But look at her face!" wailed frightened and penitent Faith. "She has turned black, and so have her hands!"

She certainly had changed her color.

At Faith's despairing cry, the victim of the fall raised one of her brown hands and looked at it fixedly; then said briefly, "That's ashes. It's on my face, too. It will wash off, won't it?"

Without reply, the minister lifted her to her feet and drew her into the doorway where the sunlight fell upon her. The sisters looked at the grotesque picture, and exclamations of horror and dismay burst from their lips.

"Peace, what have you done to yourself?"

"Are you sick?"

"What have you got on?"

She presented a strange appearance, truly, draped in dirty, ragged burlap, with face, hands and hair covered with ashes, and smeared from head to foot with broken eggs and bits of eggshell.

The tramp hid his face in the hay to stifle his chuckles, the minister covered his twitching lips with his hands, but the little group of sisters gazed at the apparition with only horror in their eyes.

Then, to everyone's amazement, Peace began to cry. In an instant Gail had slipped her arms around her, and had drawn the brown head down on her shoulder, where for a moment the child sobbed heartbrokenly. Then, with a mighty gulp, she swallowed back her grief and explained, "I heard Hope reading about the people who put on ash-cloth and sashes – I mean sackcloth and ashes whenever any one of their family died, so's the angels would let the soul into heaven. No one did that when papa died – and we don't know whether he ever got to heaven or not – but he's a man and could take care of himself, s'posing he didn't get in. With mother it's different, though. She's a ninvalid, and I couldn't bear to think of her outside the gates all alone with none of us to take care of her – so I put on potato sacks – that's sackcloth, ain't it?

– and ashes. The eggs got there by mistake. They were whole when I began to climb down that ladder."

The picture was so ludicrous, the explanation so piteous, that between their wild desire to laugh and the stronger desire to cry, it was a hysterical group who closed in once more about the grotesque little figure, while the earnest-hearted, sympathetic young preacher swept away Peace's fears, and gave her the comfort and assurance she sought.

"Sackcloth and ashes were merely outward signs of mourning for nations in ages past," he told her. "It didn't help anyone get into heaven. It didn't even show how great were their sorrow and grief; and when people came to realize that, they ceased to follow the custom. God knows how sorrowful we are, for He can read our very thoughts. It doesn't need sackcloth and ashes to carry our loved ones home, dear. They lived good, noble, true lives in His sight while they were here on earth, and now He has taken them home – inside the Gates – to live with Him always."

"You are sure?" hiccoughed Peace.

"Perfectly sure! The Bible tells us so."

"Where? I want to see for myself."

He drew a worn Testament from his pocket, turned to the Fourteenth Chapter of St. John, and slowly, impressively read those beautiful words, "In my Father's house are many mansions," explaining his understanding of the passage so clearly, so comfortably that finally the tears were dried and the aching hearts soothed.

At length the grief-stricken company repaired to the house for their belated breakfast, while the tramp, touched to the quick by the pathos of the scene he had just witnessed, made his way across the fields and through the woods, leaving only a crumpled ten-dollar bill among the grain sacks to tell of his visit.

CHAPTER VI

Thanksgiving Day at the Brown House

"Gail!"

"Yes, dear."

Peace stood at the kitchen window looking out into the winter twilight, heavy with falling snow, but as she spoke, she turned her back on the scene without, and walked over to the table where the oldest sister was busy kneading bread. "Are we going to have turkey for tomorrow? It's Thanksgiving Day, you know."

"We can't afford turkey, Peace."

"Chicken, then?"

"No."

"But we keep chickens ourselves, Gail! I'll kill one for you if it's just 'cause you can't chop its head off."

A smile flashed across Gail's sweet, care-worn face. "It isn't that, dear. We can't spare any. All our extra roosters we used for broth when – "

"Yes, I know," interrupted the smaller sister hastily. "But haven't we got a tough old hen that isn't good for anything else?"

Again Gail smiled, but answered patiently, "I am afraid not, Peace. All our hens are laying now, and eggs mean money. We can't afford to kill them."

"Can't we buy one?"

"There is no money."

"Have you used up all we made selling flowers?"

"That went long ago."

"And the bill we found in the barn?"

"No, dear. We don't know whose that is, or where it came from. Someone may come along and claim it one of these days."

"I don't see how anyone could have lost that money in the barn, Gail. It was pinned down to the grain sacks with a real pin. Folks don't carry bills around in their pockets with pins in them; and s'posing they did, if the bills dropped out of their pockets, they wouldn't up and pin themselves onto gateposts and grain sacks. Someone must have left them for us to use. First I thought it was my tramp, and that maybe he was a prince in disgust" – she meant disguise – "but now I think it was Mr. Strong, even if he did say he had nothing to do with it."

"Peace! Did you ask him again, after I told you not to mention it?"

"N-o, not ezackly. I just wrote it on a piece of paper and he did the same. You never said I mustn't write it, Gail."

"What did you write?" asked Gail, faintly.

"I just said – well, here's the paper. I kept it 'cause he is such a pretty writer."

She drew a crumpled scrap out of her pocket, smoothed it out carefully, and passed it over to Gail. At the top of the page in Peace's childish scrawl were scribbled these words, "Didn't you reely put that muny in our barn?" Below, in Mr. Strong's firm, flowing handwriting, was the answer, "I reely didn't." "Are you purfickly shure you aint lying just to be plite?" was the next question. "Purfickly shure." "Cross your heart?" "Cross my heart."

Silently Gail dropped the slip back onto the table and fell to moulding her biscuit vigorously, biting her lips to hide a telltale smile.

Peace watched her for a time and then began again, "Are we going to have meat of any kind tomorrow?"

"I am afraid not, dear."

"What – what do you 'xpect to have?"

"Just potatoes and cabbage and beets, I guess."

"It will seem kind of hard to be thankful for such a dinner as that, won't it?" sighed Peace.

"There are lots of people in the city who won't have that much – unless the churches and Associated Charities give them dinners."

"I wish someone would give us a turkey. I could be lots thankfuller over a drumstick than over a cabbage leaf or a beet pickle."

"That isn't the right spirit, dear," remonstrated Gail, wondering how she could clinch her argument with this small sister. "Thanksgiving Day was created so we might have a special day to thank the Lord for the blessings He has given us during the year – food and clothing and home and family."

"Yes, teacher told us all about that, but seems to me people ought to give thanks every day instead of saving them up for a whole year and praying them all in a lump."

"Oh, Peace! I didn't mean that. People do thank Him every day. Don't we always say grace when we sit down at the table? But Thanksgiving Day is a special time for giving thanks. It is in the fall after the crops are all in, and the barns are full of hay and grain, and the cellars filled with vegetables; and we thank Him for the good harvests."

"S'posing the harvests ain't good? We didn't get much off from our farm this year. I am tired already of turnips and carrots."

"What if we had no vegetables at all?"

"Well, that would be worser, wouldn't it? I s'pose we ought to be glad for even that."

"Yes, dear; there is always something to give thanks for. Suppose you take a piece of paper and write out all the things you have to be thankful for this year."

The idea was a novel one to Peace, and after a moment of debate, she searched out pencil and tablet, drew up an old hassock beside a chair, which she used as her table, and laboriously began to compile her list of thankfuls. She finished her task just as Gail announced the supper hour, and dropped the sheet, scribbled full of crooked letters, into the mending basket, where Gail found it that evening when the three little sisters were fast asleep in their beds. Hope was busy with her lessons and Faith sat listlessly in front of the wheezy organ, idly playing snatches of melody. So Gail spread the paper out on the table and read with reverent eyes what Peace had written from the depths of her heart:

"I am thankful cause my tramp didn't burn us up with his matches.

"Dito (dito means I am thankful and its lots shorter to rite) cause of the muny pined to the gatepost and granesaks in the barn, but I'd be more thankful if Gale would spend it.

"I am thankful cause Mr. Strong says our 2 angels got inside the gates all right.

"Dito cause there ain't any more of us angels.

"Dito cause Hector Abbott got licked for teezing lame Jenny Munn – his name just fits him.

"Dito cause Mr. Strong is our preecher – he's got some sense.

"Dito for his wife.

"Dito for Towzer. He's a good dog.

"Dito for all the rest of our family.

"Dito cause we have some shoes to wear this winter.

"Dito cause for carrots and beets and turnips and cabbige and potatoes. They don't take the place of turkey, but they are good vittles.

"Dito for the hens that lay eggs so we cant kill them for Thanksgiving dinner.

"Dito for the eggs. They meen muny, Gale says.

"Dito for the hot biskits we are going to have for supper.

"Dito cause this paper wont hold any more. My hand akes.

"Amen. Peace Greenfield."

For a long moment Gail sat with tear-dimmed eyes fixed on the queer list before her; then she reverently tucked the badly-written sheet away among her treasures, and in her heart offered up a little prayer of thanksgiving for the blessed gift of so many sisters.

Thanksgiving Day dawned clear and cold upon a world of dazzling whiteness, and with the first ray of the sun, Peace flew out of bed, scrambling into her clothes with such eager haste that Cherry opened her eyes and demanded, "What are you hurrying for? The house is cold as a barn. Gail slept late this morning, and the fire can't be more than beginning to burn."

"Huh, I don't care! It snowed last night, and I'm going out to shovel," was the scornful reply. "If you want a chance to help, you will have to hurry."

Allee scrambled out from the warm blankets, but Cherry snuggled down closer in the pillows with a contented grunt, and was soon lost in slumberland again, so the two youngest sisters had the whole snow-covered world to themselves when they stepped out into the winter morning with shovel and broom.

"Whee! Isn't this fine!" cried Peace, whirling a cloud of feathery flakes off the porch with one sweep. "We won't need the shovel at all, the snow is so light."

Beauty-loving Allee stopped awestruck on the threshold to drink in the glory of the winter dawn, saying slowly, "It is – it looks like – "

"Ice-cream," finished Peace. "S'posing it was ice-cream and we could have all we wanted. Wouldn't we be a sick crowd by night?"

The startled sister pulled on her mittens and trudged down the steps to work, and in a few minutes, the porches and paths were swept clean.

"Wish there was more to do," sighed Allee, when they had finished their chosen task, unwilling to go indoors even for breakfast.

"Tell you what," cried Peace, from her perch on the gatepost. "Let's go down to the village and sweep paths for money. Perhaps we could earn enough to buy a chicken."

"All right! Where will we go?"

"Judge Abbott will pay us, I'm sure, and Mr. Strong would hire us, too, if he hasn't swept his own walks. Maybe Lute Dunbar isn't home yet and we can get their paths."

Without further discussion they sped away to town, dragging their brooms behind them. But here disappointment awaited the small toilers, for at nearly every house some enterprising soul had already cleared away the light snow.

"Lute Dunbar must be at home, I guess," sighed Peace, when she beheld the neat paths circling that house; "and Mr. Strong has swept his whole yard, looks like. Well, Judge Abbott's porch is all covered yet. Hector is lazy. We will try him."

Marching up to the door, she knocked timidly, but to her dismay, no one answered, though three times she repeated the summons.

"What shall we do, go back home?" asked Allee, visibly disappointed, for visions of roast chicken were very alluring to her.

"No," answered Peace with sudden decision. "We'll sweep his paths and collect our pay when it is done."

So again they fell to work making the snow fly briskly, and in a short time had cleared steps and walks, but apparently no one was yet stirring within doors.

"Guess they are still in bed," suggested Allee. "We will have to come back later."

"If we are going to have chicken for dinner we ought to get it as soon as possible, so's Gail can fix it, 'cause it takes hours to cook. I'm going to knock again and see if I can't wake someone. It's time they were up anyway. Rich folks do sleep an awful long time in the morning."

Mounting the steps once more, she knocked loudly, with no result. A happy inspiration seized her, and picking up her broom, she tapped on the door with the handle. No one came.

"I don't b'lieve that is loud enough," whispered Allee. "You'd better pound."

"I think so myself," answered Peace, clutching the broom like a battering ram and giving the door three resounding thumps that shook the house from cellar to garret, and sounded like the booming of a cannon.

"Try it again," urged impatient Allee, and again the broom struck the panels with thunderous force, once, twice –

The door burst open with sudden fury, and an angry-faced man in a long bathrobe confronted the paralyzed children with the fierce demand, "What in creation do you want?"

"It – it's time to get up," stammered Peace. "I mean, it – it snowed last night. I mean, we've swep' your walks off. We s'posed you'd be glad to pay us for our trouble."

"Well!" ejaculated the man, too much surprised for further speech.

"We've swep' real clean – better than Hector ever does."

"Well!" repeated the Judge, an amused gleam in his eyes chasing away the angry frown. "How much do I owe you, Peace? You are Peace Greenfield, are you not?"

"Yes, sir. A quarter will do, I think. The snow was very light, but you've got lots of porch and walk."

"That's a fact, we have. Here is a quarter for you, and many thanks for your good work."

"You are much obliged," she answered gravely, mixing her pronouns in her haste to slip the coin inside her damp mitten. "I wish you a merry Thanksgiving."

With a whoop of delight she bounded down the steps, snatched Allee's hand, and rushed away up the street to the butcher shop for their chicken, never pausing for breath until she had dropped the money onto the counter before the astonished proprietor, who was making ready to close his shop for the day. "A quarter's worth of chicken, Mr. Jones," she panted. "I was afraid you would be gone before we could collect from the Judge."

"Sorry, Peace," answered the astonished man, "but I haven't any chickens as small as that."

"Haven't you a cheap old hen?" she faltered, almost too disappointed to speak.

"No, I am afraid not."

"And you can't sell me a piece of chicken?"

"No, we never do that, either."

"Oh, dear," sighed Allee. "We swep' that walk all for nothing!"

But Peace's bright eyes had caught sight of a tall, wooden bucket on the counter, and now she demanded, "Is that oysters?"

"Yes, jimdandies."

"That's next best to chicken. I'll take a quarter's worth of them. We will have a Thanksgiving after all, Allee."

Bearing the precious burden carefully in her arms, Peace was hurrying down the street toward home, followed by the happy Allee trailing the two old brooms, when they were halted by an excited, boyish voice, screaming lustily, "Peace, oh Peace! Wait a minute! I've got something for you."

She stopped short in the snow and waited impatiently for the boy to overtake her, more interested in her bucket of oysters than in the prospect of a gift from him; but as he drew near, she saw he carried two white, furry bundles, and her eyes grew bright with anticipation.

"Surely not your bunnies, Bryan?" she gasped.

"Yep! We are going to move back to the city on Monday, and papa said I must leave these here. They will starve with no one to take care of them, and you always thought they were so pretty, I decided to give them to you – that is, if you want them."

"Want them? Oh, Bryan, they are the cutest things! I like pets and never have had any all of my very own, 'cept the chicken Mr. Hardman stole. Give one to Allee, and I will carry the other. Tuck your broom under your arm, Allee, and give me mine. There! I'm awful glad you brought them to us, Bryan. We will take real good care of them."

Once more the sisters trudged on their way, happily excited and eager to show their new possessions to the family at home.

"Gobble, gobble, gobble!"

Allee screamed, dropped her broom and almost let go of the little white rabbit in her fear. "Oh, Peace, he's after us again and we can't run!"

"Maybe he won't touch us if we don't look at him," began the older sister; but the old gobbler, with ruffled feathers and wattles flaming, came straight toward them, and Peace stopped with a jerk.

"Drop your bunny in my skirt, Allee, grab that broom and hit the gobbler over the head. Mr. Hardman said to do that whenever he bothered us and he would soon get tired of it." As she spoke she gathered her skirt up apron-fashion, and thrust both rabbits within the folds, while Allee snatched up the broom, according to instructions, and made ready for the attack.

"Gobble, gobble, gobble!" The enemy advanced rapidly, but before he could strike either child the blue-eyed baby let the hard-wood stick fly with all her might over the fierce old head, and without another sound the monstrous bird crumpled up in the snow.

"Mercy!" screamed Peace. "You've killed him! There, don't cry! Hold your coat for the rabbits while I tote this thing up to Hardman's house. I told you to hit him, but Mr. Hardman told us, too."

Laying down her own burdens, she seized the heavy turkey by the neck and dragged it up the path to the door of the green house. "Here's your old bird," she chattered, when Mr. Hartman answered her knock. "He'll never gobble again! We hit him over the head, just as you told us to, and he laid right down and died. But we never meant to kill him. If you chop his head off right away, he will be good to eat yet, for we just now finished him. 'F I had the money, I'd pay for him, just so's we could have a Thanksgiving dinner over at our house, but I spent all I had for oysters, and, besides, I s'pose likely you would charge more'n a quarter for him. You told us to hit him, you know."

With never a word of reply, the dazed man dragged the carcass into the house and shut the door, leaving Peace glaring indignantly after him. "Well, that's manners," she finally sputtered, and stamped angrily away to help Allee home with her load.

"Here are some oysters," she announced, depositing the paper bucket on the kitchen table.

"We earned them shoveling Judge Abbott's porches off. And here are Bryan Tenney's rabbits. He has given them to us for keeps."

"Well, you can march them straight back," declared Faith, with energy. "Where do you expect to keep rabbits on this place?"

"In a box of hay in the barn. We may keep them, mayn't we, Gail?"

"They will die of cold," protested Faith.

"We won't let them. There are lots of gunny sacks we can cover over the box until it gets warmer."

"They will dig the whole farm up and spoil the garden when spring comes."

Gail was perplexed. How could she refuse the children's eager eyes? Yet clearly they could not keep the little animals. There were scarcely enough vegetables in the cellar to last the family until the winter months were over, let alone feeding a pair of hungry rabbits.

While she hesitated, Hope entered the room, and with a cry of rapture, she snatched up one pink-nosed bunny and hid her face in its fur, exclaiming, "Oh, you darlings! Are they yours, Peace? We will fix up that old, big box in Black Prince's stall and they will be as cosy as babies. What shall you call them?"

"Winkum and Blinkum," was the prompt answer. "Their noses are never still. Shall we fix up the box right now?" The four younger sisters gathered up the rabbits and departed for the barn. The question was settled to their satisfaction, at least.

In the meantime, at the Hartman house the gentle little wife was busily plucking the mammoth gobbler, while Mr. Hartman stood idly by the kitchen window, gazing out into the winter sunshine. But his thoughts were not idle, and when at length the great bird was stripped clean, he turned to the woman and said, "What are we going to do with the thing? If they had just killed it before we dressed one for ourselves – "

"Better take it over to them. It's too late to dispose of it to the butcher, and I am afraid they will have a pretty slim dinner. Mrs. Grinnell thinks they are badly pinched for money."

"Sho, now, Myra Ann! It's just because they don't know how to manage. They've got one of the best farms in this part of the country."

"It's mortgaged, and you have the mortgage."

"Yes, but with proper handling they ought to clear that off easily."

"They had to sell Black Prince – "

"And got a fancy price for him, too. That alone would pretty nearly have paid the mortgage. If they are hard up, it's their own fault."

"Mrs. Grinnell is in position to know if anyone does. The mother's sickness must have been terribly costly, and now they are orphans. They are in a bad way, I feel sure, and this turkey would come in mighty handy."

He offered no further arguments, but a few moments later, when Gail answered a knock at the kitchen door, she found their neighbor standing there with the turkey in his arms. Almost too surprised to understand, she accepted his offering, and he was gone before she could stammer out her thanks.

Then how they bustled in the little brown house, preparing such a dinner as they had seldom eaten before, oyster dressing, creamed carrots, mashed potatoes, gravy, and – the height of extravagance – cake and custard, such as only Faith could make. Oh, but that was a dinner! Nevertheless, as the six hungry girls gathered around the table full of dainties their faces were sober at the sight of the two empty chairs in the corner, and each heart bled afresh for the mother who had left them only a few short months before.

Seeing the shadow in the eyes of her sisters, and feeling depressed by the abrupt silence, Gail sought to make the sun shine again by remarking, "I am thankful for so many things, I hardly know which to put first; but I think I will call it friends. That will include them all."

Faith dropped her eyes and made no attempt to speak.

Perceiving this, Hope, with hardly a pause, began, "I am thankful for this beautiful day. The world was so spotless and white when we woke, it seemed like angels' wings had covered up all the sin."

"I'm thankful we have enough to eat and wear," said Cherry. "There is a family with seven children just moved into that tumble-down old house on the next road, and they look starved to death, to say nothing of the rags and patches they wear."

Peace was busily engaged in "being thankful over a drumstick," but as Cherry ceased speaking, she lifted her round eyes from her plate, and stopped chewing long enough to say, "I am thankful my nose doesn't twitch all the time like my rabbit's, that my ears don't grow out of the top of my head, and that I don't have to hop with both feet wherever I want to go."

Five knives and forks fell to the table with a clatter, five napkins flew simultaneously to as many faces, and five voices shrieked out a chorus of mirth.

It was Thanksgiving Day at the little brown house.

CHAPTER VII

Peace Surprises the Ladies' Aid

"Girls, here are some eggs to be delivered," said Gail one snowy December day as Cherry and Peace came stamping in from school. "One basket goes to Judge Abbott's, and the other to Dr. Bainbridge's."

"Oh, Gail," cried two protesting voices, "this is the afternoon we were to gather evergreens in the woods for decorating the church. The bazaar begins tomorrow. You promised we might go."

"I had forgotten," murmured Gail. "I am sorry, but the eggs must be delivered before night."

"Why can't Hope go this once?"

"She is taking care of the Edwards baby."

"Where is Faith?"

"In bed with a headache."

"She always has a headache when there are errands to be done."

"Peace!"

"Those houses are the furthest apart in town. Dr. Bainbridge lives at one end of the street and the Judge at the other."

"I am sorry, but eggs mean money, you know, and Christmas is coming."

"Well, I s'pose we must," sighed Cherry.

Peace's face brightened suddenly. "I'll tell you – let's each take a basket and see which can get there first. Then we'll meet at the church and go to the woods from there."

"All right," agreed Cherry. "You take the Judge's and I'll take the Doctor's."

So they snatched up their burdens and hurried merrily away, much to gentle Gail's relief, for she found it hard to disappoint these small sisters in their gala days.

As far as the church the two went the way together, but here their paths divided, and they parted, calling back warnings to each other.

"Be sure you wait at the church until I get there."

"Be sure you hurry, for there isn't much time before dark, and the women have to finish dec'rating tonight."

Then how they scampered down the snowy street, regardless of the frailty of the loads they bore!

Peace's errand was soon done, and she was back at the little church in a surprisingly short time, but no Cherry was in sight anywhere; so she sat down on the steps to await her coming. It was snowing quite hard now, and the wind grew cold as the afternoon waned.

"Seems 's if I should freeze sitting here," said the shivering child to herself after stamping her feet and flapping her arms like a Dutch windmill, in her efforts to get warm. "What can be keeping Cherry? She's an awfully long time tonight. I s'pose Mrs. Bainbridge has got a gabbing streak on and will keep her there the rest of the day listening to her. Cherry never can get away when folks begin talking to her. I ought to have gone there myself. Bet it wouldn't have taken me this long. My, but it's growing cold! I wonder if I can't get inside someway. I thought sure the ladies would be here before now, but I don't see anyone about."

She jumped to her feet and tried the door. It was locked fast.

"Maybe Mr. Strong is in his study and will let me stay there awhile." But the study door was also secure. "Well, the basement window ain't fastened, I know, 'cause 'twas only yesterday that Hec Abbott broke it with a snowball. I can crawl through that and go upstairs into the church."

Scurrying around the building to the broken window, she crept cautiously through the sash, just big enough to admit her body; and dropped to the cement floor below. Considerably jarred – for the window was high in the wall – she gathered herself up and felt her way up the dark stairs to the main floor, relieved to find the hall door unlatched so she could step out into daylight once more.

"Must have been someone here already," she exclaimed in surprise, "'cause the booths are all up and trimmed. Maybe they don't want any more evergreens. Well, I'll wait for Cherry and we will see then. P'raps some of the ladies are coming back, for the furnace is still burning."

She made a tour of the church, admiring the pretty decorations, and amusing herself by climbing over the seats like a squirrel, while she waited for Cherry, who did not come. At length she grew tired, the rooms were warm and dim, and before she knew it she was becoming drowsy.

"I'll just curl up in this old coat and rest a bit," she thought. "Cherry will make noise enough so I will hear when she comes." But before the belated sister reached the church Peace was fast asleep, and her ears were deaf to the trills and whistles outside. Thinking the younger girl had grown impatient at waiting and, regardless of her promise, had gone on to the woods, Cherry stopped only long enough to make sure that Peace was nowhere about the grounds before she hurried away to join her mates in evergreen gathering.

How long Peace slept she did not know, but the sound of voices in heated debate roused her from her nap, and she heard Mrs. Wardlaw's sharp tones saying, "Well, I, for one, don't believe in getting her a suit for Christmas. She dresses better now than most of us can afford. We never had a minister's wife before who paraded the clothes she does."

"But she came here a bride, practically," remonstrated a less aggressive, but just as decided a voice, which Peace recognized as Mrs. Bainbridge's. "They haven't been married two years yet. Brides always have more clothes than any other women. Nevertheless, they wear out, and it doesn't stand to reason that hers will last any longer than ours do."

"She has worn at least three cloth suits since she came, besides all her summer finery, and two or three separate skirts. I suppose that is where all Brother Strong's salary goes. Stylish! Why, she is a veritable fashion plate!"

"I don't see how you can say that, Mrs. Wardlaw. She certainly looks very neat and up to date in everything she puts on, but I can't see where there is any fashion plate about her. I call her a very sensible little woman, just the kind of a wife Brother Strong needs."

"Well, I am not disputing how much sense she has, but I still declare that she has clothes enough now, without our furnishing her any more for Christmas."

"That's all you know about it!" cried an indignant voice behind them, and both startled ladies turned hastily around to find a pair of flashing brown eyes glaring out from under the janitor's old coat in the corner, "If Mrs. Strong didn't know how to cut and sew, she would be a pretty ragged looking minister's wife by this time."

Peace crawled out of her warm bed and shook an angry little finger accusingly at the women, who exclaimed in unison, "Peace Greenfield, how did you come here, and what do you want?"

"I don't want anything. I clum in the window so's I wouldn't freeze while I was waiting for Cherry, and I guess I went to sleep. But I heard what you were saying, and it ain't so, Mrs. Waddler! Mrs. Strong hasn't got a lot of clothes. The parsonage burned up where they were last time, and 'most everything they had to wear was burned up, too. That pretty gray suit she had when they first came here she dyed brown after you upset a pot of coffee on it at the church supper that night. But the brown didn't color even, so she ripped it to pieces and dyed it black. It was all wearing out, too, so she had to put some trimming on the skirt to cover up the holes. I was over there and saw her do it myself. She cut over her wedding dress to have something nice to wear last summer, and all those sep'rate skirts you talk about are some of her sister's old ones. She hasn't spent a cent for clothes since she bought her straw hat, and that cost two dollars and a half. Mr. Strong told me so, himself. He says she's a jewel of a wife and if there were more women like her in the world there would be more happier homes. That's just what he said. Ministers don't get paid enough to keep them in victuals, hardly. I know, 'cause I am part of a minister's family, if papa's church in Pendennis hadn't starved him out so he got sick and had to stop preaching, he might not be an angel now.

"S'posing you was a minister's wife, how would you like to have folks be so stingy mean to you? Wouldn't you like nice clothes to wear and good things to eat? I was there for supper one night last week when you lugged in a jug of buttermilk, Mrs. Waddler, you know you did, when you had promised her fresh milk. I heard you promise. Do you s'pose she could use buttermilk in her coffee or make custard pie out of it? She had told Mr. Strong that she was going to make one for his supper, and he was 'most as disappointed as I was when she couldn't do it.

"Deacon Skinflint sent her some fresh eggs, too, that were so old you could smell 'em before the shells were broken. I told her 'twas a mercy he hadn't sent her chiny nest eggs, and she laughed! If it had been you, Mrs. Waddler, you'd have jawed good!"

Peace paused for breath. Mr. Strong and his adorable little wife were her idols, and she could not bear to hear them slandered in any way, but she had forgotten herself, her manners, everything, in the defense of her friends; and now, realizing how rude she had been to one of these women confronting her, she dropped her head in shamed silence, and nervously twisted the skirt of her coat about her trembling hands, waiting for the lecture she felt that she deserved.

To her surprise, none came; but after an awkward pause, during which both women were doing some hard thinking, Mrs. Wardlaw said humbly, "Wouldn't you like to go to Martindale with us some day next week and help us select material for Mrs. Strong's new suit? Maybe you would know what she likes better than we do, Peace."

Peace's eyes shone with delight, but she answered mournfully, "I can't, I am afraid, 'cause there's school every day but Saturday, and that's our Sunshine Club afternoon. I know what she likes best, though. I asked her once what kind of cloth made the prettiest suit, and she said she thought longcloth did – navy blue longcloth."

"She means broadcloth," murmured Mrs. Bainbridge under her breath.

"Of course," smiled Mrs. Wardlaw amiably. "So you think navy blue is what she would prefer?"

"Yes, she likes blue, and it just matches her eyes. Hasn't she got the bluest eyes and the goldest hair? Just like Hope's and Allee's. A silk waist would be nice, too. She never had but one in her life."

At this juncture a head was thrust through the hall door and an imperative voice called, "Mrs. Bainbridge, the children have come back just loaded down with greens. Come show us where you want them and we'll hang them before supper time."

CHAPTER VIII

A Mysterious Santa Claus

"Merry Christmas, Gail, Faith, Hope, Charity, Allee! Merry Christmas, everyone! My stocking has something in it, I can see from here. Wake up! Wake up! I want to look at my presents!"

A drop of something hot struck the tip of Gail's nose, and she opened her sleepy eyes to find a white-robed, shivering figure shaking her vigorously with one hand, while in the other was a tiny, flickering candle, which dribbled hot wax prodigally as it was tipped about with reckless abandon by the excited pleader.

"What are you doing with that lighted candle?" demanded Gail, digging the wax off her nose and dodging another drop. "Put it out before you set the house on fire. It isn't morning yet. It can't be! I have hardly slept at all."

"The clock struck a long time ago," insisted Peace with chattering teeth, "and I counted much as five."

"Five o'clock!" protested Gail. "Oh, surely not! Well, if it is that time, I suppose you can get up. Seems awfully quiet for that hour, though." The older sister began the process of dressing, and in a few moments all six girls were gathered around the roaring fire in the kitchen, excitedly examining the contents of their stockings, which Gail had painstakingly filled with homemade gifts and a little cheap candy from the village store, – her one Christmas extravagance.

"Mittens!" cried Peace, investigating the first package her excited hand drew forth. "You knit them, didn't you, Gail? I saw Mrs. Grinnell teaching you how. Mine are red. Have you got some, Cherry?"

"Yes, blue; and Allee's are pink. Aren't they pretty?"

"Just see my lovely knit slippers," cried Hope, throwing her arms about Gail's neck and hugging her with a vim. "Where did you get all the yarn, sister?"

"I found a lot in the attic," replied the oldest girl, smiling happily at the children's appreciation of her labor; but she did not explain that a gorgeous, moth-eaten, old afghan had been raveled to provide all those pretty things.

"What is in your stocking, Faith?"

The girl held up a dainty white waist, but said never a word, for she recognized that Gail's patient fingers had re-fashioned for her one of the dear mother's hoarded treasures, and her heart was too full for utterance.

"I've got some handkerchiefs," called Peace again, "and a ribbon – if I only had some hair to tie with it! It's too wide for a band, and that's all I can wear – here's an apple, a penwiper and some candy. You've got pretty nearly the same c'lection, haven't you, Cherry, and so have Hope and Allee. I wonder how Mrs. Grinnell happened to give me a hair-ribbon when she knows that my hair ain't long enough to tie back."

"How do you know Mrs. Grinnell gave it to you?" demanded Gail, too astonished to reprove her.

"I was in there one day when she had been to Martindale, and the ribbons happened to be on the table all unwrapped. This was one of them. Now, Gail, see what Santa Claus has brought you. There's at least one thing, 'cause – "

Cherry clapped her hand over her younger sister's mouth, and began to giggle. So did Gail, when she drew forth from her stocking a bulky potato pig with toothpicks for legs, match-heads for eyes and a dry woodbine tendril for a tail.

"Who in the world made that?" she laughed, tears close to the surface, for she had expected nothing this Christmas day.

"Mr. Strong," gulped Peace, dancing with delight at her sister's evident surprise. "Look at his back! We put a saddle on the old porker. Isn't that cute? It's a spandy new dollar with this year's date on it. See?"

Gail turned the curious animal over, and sure enough, there was a bright, shining Goddess of Liberty, skilfully sunk in the pig's potato back.

Swallowing back the lump in her throat, which threatened to choke her, Gail whispered, "Where did you get it, dear? The money, I mean."

"We took up a c'lection," was the startling answer.

"A collection!" echoed Gail.

"Yes. You know last Sunday was Home Mission day, and the money was to be sent to poor ministers' families on the pioneer – "

"You mean frontier," corrected Hope.

"Well, whatever ear it was," continued Peace, serenely; "and that made me wonder why folks never took up c'lections for poor ministers' families right here among them. I asked Mr. Strong about it, and he said we would take up another c'lection straight away, and buy a Christmas present for a 'hero minister's hero mother-daughter.' He made me learn those words; and we got a dollar in ten cent pieces without half trying. I 'spect we could have raised a fortune if we'd had more time, but this was on our way home from school yesterday. We couldn't find anything pretty enough to buy here at the village, and it was too late to go to Martindale for it, so we changed the dimes into a dollar and put it in the potato pig. He said it ought to be a shining white angel, but I told him right away that we had angels enough in this family already, and he better make a horse. That is what he tried to do, but it looked so much like a pig when he got done that I pulled off the string tail and mane and put on a pig's tail, and he said it did look better. You are to use the money for your very own self and – "

The clock began to strike. One – two – That was all.

"Mercy me!" ejaculated Peace, staring at the accusing faces of her sisters. "I truly did hear that clock strike as much as five a long time ago."

"No doubt you did," laughed sunny Hope. "It struck midnight and you woke up in the middle of the count."

"Let's go back to bed," suggested Gail, anxious to be alone with her tumultuous thoughts; and to her surprise no dissenting voice was raised, although as she crept once more beneath the covers of her cot, she heard Peace say decidedly, "I sha'n't take off my clothes again. Once a day is enough for any huming being to dress. Do you s'pose Santa will come again while we sleep?"

It was daylight before they woke from their second nap, and as Peace flew out of bed once more, she cried in delight, "Oh, it's snowing again!

Now it will seem like Christmas sure! Let's clean off the walks before breakfast. Gail won't let us eat our candy yet."

She made short work of her toilette, threw on her wraps and was out of doors almost before Cherry had opened her eyes; but the next moment she came stumbling back into the house with the wild yell "Girls, girls, Santa Claus did come again, and left a tre-men-jus big mince pie on the porch – I picked a teenty hole in the top to see for sure if 'twas mincemeat – and a bundle of something else. Hurry up, I can't wait to open it! Oh, the paper fell off, and it's shoes – tennis slippers in the winter! Think of it! That is worse than Mrs. Grinnell's hair-ribbon, ain't it?"

"Peace!" cried Gail in shocked tones, entering the kitchen with the rest of the family at her heels. "You should be grateful for the presents people give you and not poke fun at them."

"I am grateful, Gail, truly. I ain't poking fun at them, honest, though they are funny presents for this time of the year. I s'pose, maybe, my hair will get long enough for a ribbon sometime, though Mrs. Strong says it is too curly to grow fast. And when summer comes, we can wear these slippers, if they aren't too small. They look awful little already. These are marked for Allee, and here are mine, and those are Cherry's. There aren't any for the rest of you. I s'pose the pie is for you. You're lucky. I would rather have the pie than the shoes."

"Oh, Peace!"

"Well, wouldn't you? There is someone at the front door."

Gail disappeared through the hall to answer the knock, and Peace, with her new shoes in her hand, slipped out of the kitchen door. "Just as I thought," she muttered to herself. "Mr. Hardman brought them over. He thinks they will make up for that money he never paid us last summer, but they won't. He can just have his old shoes right back again!"

Out to the barn she marched, hunted up a scrap of paper and a pencil left there for just such emergencies, laboriously scribbled a note, which she tied to the slippers, and deposited the bundle on the Hartman steps, where he found it when he came out to sweep paths. "Well, I swan," he exclaimed, half in anger, half amused, as he picked tip the rejected shoes, "if she hasn't trotted them slippers back! Peace, of course. Let's see what she says." Carefully he untied the little slip and read:

> "Here are your shoes. Im greatful but this is the rong seesun for them. By summer they will be to small as they aint very big now. Ive got over wanting tenis shoes anyhow. The muny you owe us would have come in handier. Peace Greenfield."

He tucked the note in his pocket, dropped the shoes on the kitchen mantle, and went chuckling about his morning work. Hardly had he finished his numerous tasks, when he was surprised to see Peace coming slowly up the path, with eyes down-cast and face an uncomfortable red. She knocked lightly, as if hoping no one would hear, and looked disappointed when he opened the door.

"Merry Christmas, Peace. Come in, come right in," he said cordially, his eyes gleaming with, amusement. "What can I do for you this morning?"

"Give me back the shoes I left on your porch," she answered, in tones so low he could hardly hear. "Gail said I must come over and get them and ipologize for being so rude. She says it is very rude to return Christmas presents like that. If you meant them for a present, why, that's different; but I thought likely it was our pay for picking strawberries last summer. Now, which was it, a present or our pay?" The old, independent, confident spirit asserted itself once more in the little breast, and Peace raised her eyes to his with disconcerting frankness.

"Well, well," stammered the man, hardly knowing what to say. "Suppose they are a Christmas present, will you accept and wear 'em?"

"When it comes summer time, if I haven't outgrown them. My feet are getting big fast."

"But if they are in pay for the strawberry picking, you won't take them? Is that it?"

"I s'pose I will have to take them after Gail's lecture," Peace sighed dismally, "but I'll never put 'em on – never!"

Delighted with her candor and rebel spirit, he said, after a brief pause, "Well, now, I mean them for a Christmas present, Peace, and I'd like mighty well for you to wear them. If they are too small, come next summer, I will get them changed for you. Will you take them?"

"Y – e – s."

"And be friends?"

Peace hesitated. "Friends are square with each other, ain't they?"

"I reckon they are."

"Then I don't see how we can be friends," she said firmly.

"Why not?" His face was blank with surprise; and his wife, who had been a silent spectator of the scene, laughed outright.

"'Cause you owe us a dollar and a half for picking strawberries last summer, and if you don't pay it, you ain't square with us, are you?"

"Well, I swan!" he mumbled. Then he, too, laughed, and thrusting his hand into his pocket, drew out a handful of silver. "Here are six silver quarters, a dollar and fifty cents. That settles our account, doesn't it?"

"Yes."

"And I've treated you on the square?"

"Yes."

"And you will come sit on my lap?"

"I don't s'pose it will do any hurt," she answered grudgingly, for she had not yet adjusted herself to this new friendship with her one-time enemy, but she went to him slowly and permitted to lift her to his knee.

"There, now," he said, settling her comfortably. "That's more like it! Now that I have settled my account with you, tell me what you are going to do about the money you owe me?"

"Dave!" interposed little Mrs. Hartman, but he laughingly waved her aside.

"What money that I owe you?" gasped poor Peace, the rosy color dying from her face.

"Didn't you dump twenty boxes of my strawberries into the chicken yard last summer?"

"Y – e – s."

"Those berries sold for twenty cents a box. Twenty times twenty is four dollars. You spoiled four dollars' worth of berries, Peace Greenfield. Are you being square with me?"

The child sat dumb with despair, and seeing the tragedy in the great, brown eyes, Mrs. Hartman again said, remonstratingly, "Dave!"

"Hush, Myra Ann," he commanded. "This is between Peace and me. If we are to be friends, we must be square with each other, you know."

There was a desperate struggle, and then Peace laid the shining quarters back in his hand, saying bravely, "Here's my first payment. I haven't the rest now, but if you will wait until I earn it, I'll pay it all back. I will have Hope figure up just how much I owe you, so's I will know for sure. Can you wait? Maybe you will let me pick strawberries next summer until I get it paid up. Will you? 'Cause what money I get this winter I'd like to give to Gail for a coat. She has to wear Faith's jacket now whenever she goes anywhere, and, of course, two people can't wear one coat at the same time."

"No, they can't," he answered soberly, with a suspicion of a tremble in his voice. "Is that what you meant to do with this money?"

"Yes. Gail got a dollar for Christmas, and I thought this would 'most make enough to buy a good coat for her. She needs one dreadfully."

Mr. Hartman slipped the money into the grimy fist again, cleared his throat and then said, "Now, I've got a plan. You keep this dollar and fifty cents for your work last summer, and when the strawberries are ripe again, we'll see about your picking some more to pay for the spoiled ones. Is that all right?"

"Yes," cried Peace, giving a delighted little jump. "You aren't near bad, are you?"

"I hope not," he replied with a queer laugh. "Can you give me a kiss, do you suppose?"

"If you will skin me a rabbit," she answered promptly.

"If I'll what?" he yelled in amazement, almost dropping her from his lap.

"Skin me a rabbit. Winkum and Blinkum are starving to death – Faith says so – and they really don't seem as fat as when Bryan gave them to me; so if we can save them by eating them up, we better do it. Don't you think so?"

"Well, now, that might be a good idea," he answered slowly, for he regarded rabbits as a nuisance, and was not anxious to see any such pests in his neighborhood. "Stewed rabbit makes a pretty good dish, too."

"That's what I had heard. Will you skin them for me?"

"Yep, any time you say so."

"All right, I'll get them now and we will have them for dinner."

She was off like a flash before he could say another word, returning almost immediately with the squirming rabbits in her apron, and he dressed them carefully. By the time the long process was finished her face was very sober, and she offered no objections when he claimed two kisses instead of one as his reward, but gathering up the hapless bunnies, she departed for home.

"Here's our Christmas dinner, Gail," she announced, dumping her burden onto the cluttered kitchen table. "I wish it had been chicken, but Mr. Hartman says stewed rabbit is real good."

"Where did you get these?" demanded Gail, surmising the truth.

"They are Winkum and Blinkum. Mr. Hartman undressed them for me. I got my shoes back, and here's the strawberry money for your new coat, Gail." As clearly as possible she made her explanations, and went away to put up the tennis slippers, leaving dismayed Gail to face the unique situation.

"What can I do?" she cried, almost in tears.

"Get yourself a new coat, if you can find one for the price," answered Faith, listlessly scrubbing a panful of turnips for dinner.

"I don't mean the coat. I had scarcely thought of the money. I mean the rabbits."

"Cook them! People eat rabbits."

"But these were pets."

"They are dead now. You might as well use them as to throw them away. We have no turkey or chicken for dinner."

Gail shivered, but obediently cut up the rabbits and put them on the stove to cook, mentally resolving not to eat a bite of them herself.

The morning hours flew rapidly by, the dinner was done at last, and the hungry girls were scrambling into their chairs when Faith cried sharply, "Hope, you have set seven plates!"

Instinctively each heart thought of the absent member, gone from them since the last Christmas Day, and Gail reached over to remove the extra dishes, when Hope stopped her by saying, "Teacher read us a beautiful poem of how some people always set a place for the Christ Child on His birthday, hoping that He would come in person to celebrate the day with them, and I thought it was such a pretty idea that – I – I – "

"Yes, dear," said Gail gently. "We will leave the extra plate there."

"It does seem queer, doesn't it, that we have big dinners on Christmas Day 'cause it is Christ's birthday, and then we never give Him a dish," observed Peace, passing her plate for a helping.

"Did the Christ Child come?" asked Allee eagerly. "In the story, I mean."

"Not in the way they looked for Him," answered Hope. "But a little beggar child came. Some of the family were going to send it out into the kitchen to eat with the servants, but one little boy insisted that it should have the empty chair they had set for the Christ Child. So the ragged beggar was pushed up to the table and fed all he wanted. When the dinner was over, a great shining light filled the room and Christ appeared to tell them that in feeding the little beggar they had entertained Him. It was all written out in rhyme and was so pretty. What is the matter, Gail? You aren't eating anything."

The other sisters paused to look at the older girl's plate, and Gail's sensitive face flushed crimson, but before she could offer any explanation, Peace abruptly dropped her knife and fork, pushed her dishes from her, and burst into tears.

"Why, what ails you, child?" cried Faith, who herself had scarcely touched the dinner before her.

"I can't be a carnival and eat my bunnies," sobbed Peace. "I'd as soon have a slab of kitten."

"That's just the way I feel," said Cherry, and no one laughed at Peace's rendering of cannibal.

In the midst of this scene there was a knock at the kitchen door, but before anyone could answer, Mrs. Grinnell rustled in, bearing in her arms a huge platter of roast turkey, which she set down upon the table with the remark, "It was that lonesome at home I just couldn't eat my dinner all by myself, so I brought it over to see if you didn't want me for company."

"You aren't a ragged beggar," Peace spoke up through her tears, before the others had recovered from their surprise; "but I guess you'll do. You can have the chair we set for Jesus."

Gail explained, while the platter of stewed rabbit was being removed, and once more dinner was begun. The turkey was done to a turn, the dressing was flavored just right and filled with walnuts and oysters, the vegetables had never tasted better, the biscuits were as light as a feather, Mrs. Strong's cranberry sauce had jelled perfectly, and the Hartman mince-pie was a miracle of pastry. The seven diners did the meal full justice, and when at last the appetites were satisfied, the table looked as if a foraging party had descended upon it.

"That was quite a dinner," remarked Peace, as she pushed her chair back from the table. "If I had just known it was going to happen, Mr. Hartman needn't have skinned the rabbits. There is a whole platter full of Winkum and Blinkum left, and it's all wasted. Mercy me, what a shame!"

She went out into the kitchen and surveyed the rejected delicacy with mournful eyes. Then a new idea occurred to her, and, with no thought of irreverence, she murmured to herself, "I don't believe the Christ Child would have cared whether He had turkey or rabbit for dinner. I'm going over and get that passle of half-starved German kids to eat this up."

Throwing Gail's faded shawl over her head, she ran across the snowy fields to the old tumble-down house on the next road, where the new family lived. The children were at play in the yard – seven in all, and none of them larger than Hope – but at sight of her they came forward hand in hand, jabbering such queer gibberish that Peace could not understand a word.

"Come over to my house and have some dinner," she invited them, but not one of them moved a step. "We've got a whole platter of stewed rabbit," she urged, but they only stared uncomprehendingly. "Perhaps you have had your dinner. Are you hungry?"

"Hungry," suddenly said the oldest boy, putting one hand to his mouth and the other on his stomach. "Ja, sehr hungrig."

Peace was delighted with the pantomime method of making herself understood, and imitating his motions, she pointed to the little brown house and beckoned.

"Ja, ja," cried the chorus of seven, their faces beaming with pleasure, "wir kommen." And they quickly followed her across the snow to the kitchen door.

"Gail, I have brought the Christ Child," she announced, as she ushered the ragged, hungry brood into the house. "I thought it was a pity to waste all that salt and pepper you used in fixing up Winkum and Blinkum, so I invited these ragged beggars over to eat it up."

Mrs. Grinnell gasped her surprise and consternation. Faith exclaimed angrily, "Peace Greenfield!" But Gail, with never a chiding word, sprang to the table and began clearing away the soiled dishes, while Hope ran for clean plates; and in short order the seven little towheads were hovering around the platter of stewed rabbit and creamed potatoes, revelling in a feast such as they had never known before; nor did they stop eating until every scrap of food had vanished. Then they rose, bowing and smiling, and trying in their own tongue to thank their hostesses for the grand dinner.

Peace was captivated with their quaint manners and reverent attitude, and when they had backed out of the door, she went with them to the gate, kissing her hand to them as they disappeared down the road, still calling over their shoulders, "Du bist das Christkind!"

"I don't know what they are saying," she murmured, "but it makes me feel like flapping my wings and crowing." She leaped to her tall gatepost to give vent to her jubilant feelings, but tumbled quickly to the ground again without stopping to crow. "Abigail Greenfield!" she shouted, racing for the house. "See what was on the gatepost, – a nenvelope with money in it, and on the outside it says, 'Christmas greetings to the Six Sisters.' Now will you believe someone lost it? It ain't Mr. Strong's writing, though. Maybe the Christ Child brought it. Oh, Gail, do you s'pose He did?"

CHAPTER IX

Faith's Awakening

"Do you know where Faith is?" asked Gail one Saturday morning in early spring, finding Hope busy at making the beds, which was the older sister's work.

"She discovered a heap of old magazines somewhere about the place and is in the barn reading. Says her head aches too hard to work today," answered Hope, with an anxious pucker in her usually serene forehead.

"I don't know what to do with that girl," sighed Gail, as she adjusted her dustcap and picked up a broom. Her face looked so worried, and her voice sounded so discouraged that Hope paused in her task of plumping up the pillows to ask in alarm, "Do you think she is any worse than usual?"

"She gets worse every day," answered Gail, somewhat sharply, and two tears rolled slowly down her pale cheeks.

"Oh, dearie, don't cry," coaxed Hope, dropping her pillows and throwing her arms about the heaving shoulders. "It will be better pretty soon. I'll do all of Faith's work. I only wish I were older."

Peace waited to hear no more. She had gone upstairs for a clean apron before setting out for town with a basket of eggs and, unknown to the two sisters in the room across the hall, had heard all they said.

"I didn't s'pose Faith was sick," she whispered with white lips as she flew down the path to the gate, swinging the heavy basket dangerously near the ground in her heedlessness. "I thought she was just lazy. She never does anything but mope around the house and read or play the organ, but I thought it was 'cause she didn't want to. S'posing she should die! Then we'd have three angels. Oh, dear, I don't see why one family should have so many! I wonder if there isn't something that will cure her. Gail hasn't called the doctor yet. I am going to ask him myself!"

She slipped through the gate and sped up the road toward town, still musing over this new trouble, and so completely wrapped up in her thoughts that she did not even see her beloved Mr. Strong until he called to her, "Why, hello, Peace! Are you coming over to see our baby today! Elizabeth, will be glad to have you."

Her face lighted up at sight of her friend, but she shook her head at his invitation, and soberly replied, as she hurried on, "I'd like to, but I can't this time. I must take these eggs to the doctor's house. Some other day I'll come and play with Baby Glen."

Not to stop to discuss the welfare of the precious new baby at the parsonage was very strange for Peace, for she loved the beautiful boy as much as she did his parents, and was always eager to hear of his latest tricks, no matter how pressed for time she might be. But today she was too worried to think of even little Glen.

Breathlessly she climbed the steps to Dr. Bainbridge's big house, just as the busy physician appeared in the doorway ready for his round of calls, and in her eagerness to stop him before he should climb into the waiting carriage, she quickened her pace to a run, tripped on the door mat, and tumbled headlong, eggs and all, into a drift of half-melted snow in the corner of the porch, announcing in tragic tones, "Dr. Eggs, I have brought you some Bainbridge, and here they are all spilled in the snow. It's lucky you aren't a very neat man, for if you had cleared off your porches the way you ought to, these eggs would likely have been everyone smashed. As 'tis, there is only one broken, and one more cracked. I'll bring another – "

"Are you hurt?" the doctor managed to stutter in an almost inaudible voice, so overcome with surprise was he at the avalanche of eggs and explanation.

"No, and only two of the eggs are, either – Oh, don't go yet!" She scrambled hastily to her feet and laid a trembling, detaining hand on his coat sleeve, as she demanded in a shaky voice, "Is Faith real bad, do you think?"

"If people had more faith – " he began jestingly; then stopped, seeing the real anxiety in the serious brown eyes, and asked gently, "What is troubling you, child?"

"Faith, as usual. What is the matter with her? Gail cried about her this morning, and Hope said maybe she would get better pretty soon. They didn't know I heard. Is she real sick? I thought she didn't do any work 'cause she was lazy – I mean 'cause she didn't want to. I didn't know she was sick. What d'sease has she got?"

"Well, as near as I can make out," answered the doctor gravely, "she has a case of acute imagination. She thinks she is mourning, but she is too selfishly wrapped up in her own grief to see the sorrow of others. She has stepped out from under the burden of the home and let its full weight fall upon shoulders too slender to bear it. The sun doesn't shine for her any more, the birds don't sing, the flowers have lost their fragrance. What she needs is a good dose of common sense, but we don't seem to be able to administer it. If only we could put a cannon cracker under her chair, maybe it would rouse her. Oh, I was just speaking figuratively; I didn't mean the real article," he hastened to assure his small audience, as a gasp of horror escaped her.

The doctor had waxed eloquent in his diagnosis of the case, and though Peace failed to understand half that he said, the grave, almost harsh look about his mouth and eyes struck terror to her heart, and she faintly faltered, "Is – do you think Faith will be an angel soon?"

He looked at her in amazement. "No!" he thundered, and she shivered at his tone. "It will take ages to make an angel of Faith if she keeps on in the way she is going. Gail is the angel if ever there was one, and Hope's wings have sprouted, too – "

"Oh," moaned Peace, with wide, terrified eyes, "I don't want Gail and Hope to be angels! We need them here! We could spare Faith easier than them. Oh, Dr. Bainbridge, ain't two angels enough for one family?"

The kindly old doctor suddenly understood, and patting the little hood, covered with bits of eggshell and particles of ice, he said remorsefully, "There, there, honey, I didn't mean that kind of angels! I mean just dear, good, blessed girls, such as make the world better for having been in it. There is no danger of their flying away to the other land just yet, my child; though goodness only knows what will become of Gail if Faith isn't waked up soon. I must go call on my sick folks now, little girl. I'd drive you home if I were going that way, but I am due this very minute at the opposite end of town. Don't you fret, but be an awfully good girl yourself and help Gail all you can. When Faith comes to her senses and goes to work at something, she will be all right."

They parted, and Peace slowly wended her way home again, somewhat relieved, and yet considerably alarmed over the doctor's words. Down to the barn she wandered, and up the rickety ladder she climbed into the cobwebby loft. A figure moved impatiently at the far end of the loose boards, and as Peace's eyes became accustomed to the dim light, she saw it was Faith, curled up among a lot of ragged papers and coverless magazines, musty and yellow with age.

"What are you ba – crying about!" asked Peace in awed tones, as the other girl sniffed suspiciously and then wiped her eyes, already red with weeping. She expected to be told to mind her business, but contrary to her expectations, Faith answered:

"This is the saddest story, – all about a girl who loved one man and had to marry another."

Peace's nose curled scornfully, and she said, with great contempt, "I don't see any use in bawl – crying about that. Those story people never lived. Real folks have more sense."

But Faith had gone back to her magazine of sorrows, and never even heard this small sister's criticism. So Peace dropped down on a heap of sacking, propped her chin up with her elbows on her knees, and fell to studying the face opposite her, noting with alarm how thin it had grown, and how darkly circled were the brown eyes so like her own. Fear lest Dr. Bainbridge did not know how ill she really was gripped her heart, and she sighed heavily just as Faith finished her chapter and roused to search for the next number of the magazine.

"What is the matter?" she demanded, looking at the sober little face with surprise.

"Are you sick?" asked Peace in an awestruck whisper, ignoring her sister's question.

"No. Why? My head aches some, but that is all."

"I sh'd think it would ache," cried the child in sudden indignation. "Why did you poke up here where there ain't any window to read by? You'll be blind some day if you amuse your eyes like that. Teacher said so to all our class the day she found Tessie Hunt reading on the basement stairs. If you've got to read all the time, why don't you go out-doors or by a window? It's enough to make anyone's head ache the way you mope around reading all the time. Dr. Bainbridge says as soon as you get up and go to work you'll be all right."

Faith's face flushed angrily and she demanded, with some heat, "What do you know about what Dr. Bainbridge says?"

"I asked him a-purpose to see whether you were going to be an angel soon."

For a moment Faith was too startled for reply, and then she asked curiously, with a queer flutter in her heart, "What did he say!"

"He just howled, 'No – o!' as loud as he could shout, and after that he said, more quiet-like, that you'd never be an angel as long as you kept on the way you are going. He says you need a good, common dose of sense and a cannon under your chair. He said Gail and Hope are the angels, and when I cried and told him we could spare you easier'n we could them, he said that he didn't mean sure-enough angels which fly away and never come back, but good, sensitive blessings that make the world better. He says you've got a cute minagination, and when you wake up and help Gail bear the slender burden on your shoulders, everything will be all right."

Profound silence reigned in the barn for what seemed an eternity to Peace, and then Faith burst forth hotly, "I never saw such a meddlesome child in all my born days, Peace Greenfield! What did you tell the doctor? Why did you chase to him in the first place? Do you want to get the whole neighborhood to gossiping about our affairs? I suppose you gave him the whole family history, from the time of Adam."

"I never did!" Peace indignantly denied. "I don't know of any Adam 'mong our relations. I found Gail upstairs crying about you this morning, and Hope promised to do all your work. I couldn't see why Hope should do your work unless you were going to be an angel, so I went to the doctor about it, and that is why he told me. He said we must help Gail all we could – "

"Why don't you, then, instead of causing her trouble whenever you turn around? You are into something the whole time to fret and worry her. Don't talk about me until you are perfect yourself!"

"I ain't perfect, but I try to help, and you know it. Don't I help Cherry with the dishes every single day, and dust the parlor and bring in wood, and hasn't Hope turned over setting the table to me?"

"And don't you break half the dishes?"

"I've broken only one plate and three cups, and I bought new ones out of my snow money, so there! When summer comes I'm going to pick strawberries for Mr. Hartman, and when I've paid up for those I spoiled last year, I'm going to give the rest of the money I earn to Gail to help her all I can. 'F I could make the lovely cakes you do, I'd go 'round the streets peddling them."

"If you were I, you'd do wonders," Faith broke in bitterly.

"Well, Mrs. Abbott told me herself that if the village baker could cook like that she would get all her delicate things there instead of bothering the girl with them, 'cause, in a little subu'b like this, she can't get a cook and a second girl to stay at the same time, and a common hired girl doesn't know beans about cakes and nice cookery. Mrs. Lacy said she'd take a cake reg'lar every week if she could get such nice ones as yours; and the butcher – guess what the butcher asked me yesterday! I went in his shop on my way home from the minister's, and he asked me when we were going to break up housekeeping here."

"What did you say?" cried Faith, as the meaning of his question dawned upon her, though Peace evidently had not understood.

"I didn't know what he was driving at, so I asked him, and he said he had heard that we were going to leave this house and go to live with different people in town. He wanted to know if he could have Cherry, 'cause he thinks she is so pretty. I told him he needn't joke with me like that, but he just laughed and insured me that Mr. Strong was going to take Allee, and Dr. Bainbridge wanted Hope, and that you and Gail were to work in Martindale, and I was the broom of condemnation."

"The what?" cried Faith in amazement.

"The broom of con-dem-nation," repeated Peace slowly, seeing that she had made a blunder, but not understanding just wherein it lay. "It means when a lot of people want the same thing."

"Perhaps you are trying to say 'bone of contention,'" suggested Faith, somewhat sarcastically.

"Maybe 'twas. Anyway, he says Mr. Hardman wants me – but I don't want him, I can tell you that!"

"I thought you had signed a treaty of peace and were friends now," murmured the older girl, considerably amused at the child's belligerent attitude, in spite of her troubled thoughts.

"Oh, we are friends all right, but not bad enough so's I want to go live with him. Though I don't know as it would be any worse there than with Judge Abbott, and he's the other fellow who wants me. My, the way he glared at me Thanksgiving morning, when we shoveled the snow off his porch, scared me stiff! I thought he was going to make us shovel it back on again, but he didn't. And the time my snowball knocked Hector's teeth loose, I was sure he was going to 'rest me, but I couldn't help if Hec opened his mouth just in time to get that ball; and anyway, he deserved it, 'cause he was pulling Mamie Brady's red hair and calling her Carrots till she cried. I told the Judge that Hec needed to have more than just his teeth knocked loose, and he laughed and marched him home by the ear."

"Peace, have you told Gail this?"

"About Hec's teeth?"

"No, about what Mr. Jones said to you?"

"Not yet. I didn't think it was a very nice joke, so I never told anyone but you and the preacher. Mr. Strong said he'd see that the butcher didn't tease me any more."

"Well, if I were you, I would forget all about it, but don't ever tell Gail. She might take it in earnest and feel badly about it."

Peace eyed the older girl, as if trying to fathom her meaning, but Faith's face was like a mask, and after a brief pause, the child answered, "I don't mean to; but ain't I glad she can't guess all my thinks! Just s'posing everyone knew what everyone else was thinking, wouldn't some folks be scrapping all the time? Brains are queer things. I used to wish I could see one when it was doing its thinking, but I guess God knew his business when he put them inside our heads, where no one else can watch them."

"Peace, Peace! Where are you?" called an excited voice from below, and the brown-eyed philosopher jumped up from her burlap couch with the shout, "Coming, Allee! I hope you find your senses pretty soon, Faith, for the doctor says when that happens you will be all right and not have any more headache."

The faded red coat disappeared down the ladder, and Faith was left alone again. But she read no more. The sad story had lost its interest, and she cast aside the magazines without another glance. Was what

Mr. Jones had told Peace true? Was there a possibility that the home must be broken up? Was the doctor right in his verdict? Did all the sisters feel that she could be spared the easiest? That was a fierce battle Faith waged with herself in the barn, but when it was ended a determined-faced girl rose from the dusty floor, descended the old ladder, and hurried away toward the village. It was noon before she returned, and the five sisters, anxious over her unusual absence, were just sitting down to a frugal dinner of mush and milk when she entered the door, looking excited and queer, but with a happier light in her eyes than had been there for months.

The minute grace was said, Peace demanded suspiciously, "Where have you been all this time?"

"Drumming up trade," was the startling answer. "I've got six regular cake customers, and several who promised to buy of me when they needed anything in my line."

Faith was awake at last.

CHAPTER X

Company For Supper

"Cherry, do you know it's 'most night, and those girls aren't at home yet? They said they'd sure be here by four o'clock, and here 'tis five and they haven't come." Peace was plainly worried, and with a half-impatient sigh, Cherry closed her fascinating story book and joined her sister watching at the window for the belated girls who had gone in town with Mrs. Grinnell that morning.

"P'r'aps the horse run away," suggested Allee.

"They were coming back on the car, 'cause Mrs. Grinnell was to stay all night with her relations."

"Then maybe the car run off the track."

"That's just what I've been thinking. S'posing they don't come home tonight! What will we do for supper?"

"Hope will get some when she comes home from Edwards'."

"This is the day she stays so late. She won't get home until Mr. Edwards brings her, at almost bedtime."

"Can't we help ourselves?"

"'Course, if we wanted to, but that won't be supper for Gail and Faith when they get home all tired out."

"Well, then, can't we cook a supper?"

"What?"

"Why – potatoes and – "

"Eggs, I s'pose you'll say. I'm tired of eggs. If we don't stop having them so often, we will all turn into Humpty-Dumpties. S'posing we were eggs and had to walk and act so careful or else get smashed. 'Twouldn't take long to finish me, would it? I don't want eggs for supper. Let's have rice."

"Is there any?"

"A whole sackful."

"Do you know how to cook it?"

"Why, in water, of course, just like mush or oatmeal, only it takes longer to get soft."

"Then maybe we better put it on to boil now. How much shall we cook?"

"I don't know as I ever saw Gail measure it She just guesses at it; but I think we could each eat a big cupful, don't you?"

"I'm hungry enough to eat two cupsful," said Allee.

"P'r'aps 'twould be better to cook two for each of us. It's good cold, s'posing we shouldn't eat it all tonight."

"Maybe that would be best," conceded Cherry; and the three embryo cooks repaired to the kitchen to get supper ready.

"There is the rice and here is a cup. Hold the pan, Cherry, while I measure it out. One – two – three – four – five – six – seven – eight – nine – that makes a big hole in that bagful, doesn't it? Maybe nine will be enough. Do you think so?"

"Yes," hesitated Cherry; "and besides, Hope won't be here for supper."

"That's right! Then nine will be enough. Now we'll pour in the water, – lots, 'cause it boils away in cooking."

"If Gail doesn't get here soon, how will we get any milk for our rice?" asked Allee, watching them. "Bossy hasn't been milked yet."

Peace paused on her way to the stove with the heavy saucepan. "Why didn't we think of that before? Rice isn't good without plenty of milk and sugar. I don't like molasses on it."

"Nor I," shivered Cherry.

"Let's milk the cow ourselves," suggested the daring spirit.

"We don't know how," protested the cautious one.

"Oh, that's easy! I've watched Gail lots of times, and all she does is pull hard like the janitor pulls the rope that rings the church bell. We've both of us rung that bell, Cherry. I'll do it if you are afraid."

"I'm not afraid," Cherry declared, "but I don't think I know how. I'll watch you and see how you do it first."

"Come on, then!"

Away to the barn they hurried, and the process of milking began, with Peace astride the stool. But somehow Bossy resented being pulled like a bell-rope and the milk didn't come.

"I don't see what is the matter," cried Peace impatiently, after a few moments' struggle. "Bossy never acts so with Gail. She has kicked me twice already, and here we are clear out of her stall. Allee, you hold her tail, she has slapped me in the face with it till I'm tired. Whoa, Boss, stand still! Maybe I don't jerk hard enough."

Peace settled herself once more on the stool, righted the pail and gave a tremendous pull at two of the teats. There was a surprised moo from Bossy, her heels flew into the air, Peace was thrown backward from her seat, the pail whirled across the floor, and Bossy rushed out of the barn door, dragging little, tenacious Allee after her. Cherry screamed, Peace scrambled to her feet and raced madly after the terrified beast, shouting at the top of her lungs, "Let go, Allee! Whoa, Bossy!"

Allee let go, but Bossy did not whoa until, with a wild plunge, she lurched against the stone watering trough, groaned and lay down with one leg doubled under her.

"Oh, she's broken her leg!" yelled Cherry, dancing up and down in fright. "What shall we do, what shall we do?"

"Go into the house and see that the rice doesn't burn while I'm gone," commanded Peace, after a hasty look at poor Bossy's leg, to make sure it was really broken; and away she flew up the street toward the village, muttering to herself, "Maybe he has closed his shop, though it isn't quite time, but I hope not. No, he hasn't, for there comes the doctor out of the door. Oh, Mr. Jones, what will you give for a cow, a broken-legged cow? I didn't stick her, 'cause I wasn't sure just how to do it, but her leg is just freshly broken, so she is good for meat. You bought Mr. Hartman's heifer when she broke her neck. Bossy's an awful nice cow, and we hate to lose her, but of course we'll have to kill her now.

Bring your butcher knife and run! I don't want her to feel bad any longer'n she has to."

"Hold your horses, Whirlwind, hold your horses a bit," cried the amazed butcher. "Now tell me what has happened."

"You grab that knife and come along!" she shouted, almost frantic with grief and fear. "That cow can't be left with a broken leg." And seizing him by the hand she dragged him toward the door. The sight of the child's great distress touched the big man, and pausing only long enough to close his shop, he followed her flying feet down the road to the little brown house where poor Bossy lay.

"There she is! Ain't her leg broken?"

"Yes, and a bad break, too. She will have to go, kidlet. It's a shame, for she's a mighty fine looking critter. I'll give you fifteen dollars for her. Where is your oldest sister?"

"In Martindale. Oh, don't wait for her to come back! I can't bear to have Bossy look at me like that! I broke her leg trying to milk her. She's worth a lot more'n fifteen dollars alive, but as meat I s'pose we'll have to let her go cheap. You can have her. Gail would say so too, if she was here. Give me the money and then stick her as soon as I get inside the house."

The butcher hesitated, then counted out fifteen dollars in bills and handed them to the trembling, grief-stricken Peace, saying, "You couldn't get any more for her in the city, under the circumstances, I know. Butchers don't ordinarily buy milch cows for beef, and I shouldn't take her if she wasn't in first-class condition. If Gail ain't satisfied, send her up to the shop."

Peace snatched the bills with shaking hands and disappeared up the path, calling back over her shoulder, "Stick her easy, Mr. Jones, and quick! I'm going upstairs and cry."

But she didn't carry out her intention, for as she flung open the kitchen door, the pungent odor of something burning greeted her nostrils, and there stood Cherry beside the red-hot stove, dipping rice from one big saucepan into other kettles which Allee was bringing out of the pantry for her.

"Oh, Peace," she cried in relief, "I don't know what we will ever do with all this rice! It's sticking faster than I can scratch it up, it's boiled over the stove three times, and I've filled up four pans already. Give me another, Allee!"

"It needs some more water," said Peace, catching up a dipper of cold water and pouring it into one sizzling pot. "Mercy, how it has grown since we put it on to cook! That kettleful won't burn now."

"But it has turned yellow and smells dreadfully smoky," answered Cherry, sniffing at the discolored, unappetizing mess in the pan.

Peace examined it critically, tasted it, made a wry face, and finally announced, "It's spoiled, I guess. Never mind, there is plenty of good rice left – "

"Oh, Peace!" yelled Allee excitedly, dancing in the chair, where she stood trying to stir the heavy contents of another pan. "Something else is burning, sure! See the black smoke!"

There was a knock at the door, but Peace was frantically tugging at the big kettle stuck fast to the stove cover, and without pausing in her task, she called crossly, "You will have to wait till we can get this rice 'tended to before we can see what you want, whoever you are. We are all busy in here."

There was an audible chuckle from without, the knob turned, Cherry screamed, and a gray-haired, shabby, old man stood smiling at them from the steps. Peace scarcely looked at him as she succeeded in freeing the panful of smoking, blackened rice from the cover, but that quick glance had told her the visitor was a tramp, and she snapped sharply, "I s'pose you want a bite to eat. Well, I don't see how you are going to get it here! I've just killed the cow, and the rice has burned up. Cherry, stop stirring that mess and take it off! Can't you see it's smoking like a chimbly?"

The tramp strode across the room, grabbed the teakettle and poured the boiling water into the pan, over which Allee had mounted guard, and which fortunately was on the back of the stove so it had not yet arrived at the burning point. He caught up one other, dumped about half its contents into a clean saucepan on the hearth, saturated it with water, threw in some salt, and set it back on the stove, at the same time removing a third kettle of burning rice and carrying it out of doors.

"There!" he said, entering the kitchen again. "All the rice isn't spoiled.

Now we will open the windows and let out this smoke, and we are all right. How did you come to cook so much?"

"We were hungry, and thought we could eat a lot – "

"But rice swells – "

"We have found that out for ourselves," said Peace, blushing furiously at his quizzical grin. "It's the first time we ever cooked it alone."

"Where are the sisters?"

"Gail and Faith are in the city, and Hope hasn't come home from Edwards' house yet."

"And you are hungry? Well, now, that is too bad. I'll tell you what I will do. You show me where you keep things and I will get supper, if you will permit me to share it with you. Tramps have to work here, you know – "

"Oh, Mr. Tramp! You are my tramp that broke the raw egg all over your potato, aren't you?" cried Peace with undisguised joy. "And you never stole that cake, did you?"

"What cake, child?"

"The one Faith was baking the morning you ate breakfast here 'bout a year ago."

"I never stole a cake in my life, – or anything else."

"There, I knew it! I told them so at the time. Was it – have you lost any money around here?"

"Money?" he echoed, his face the picture of innocence, as he deftly set the table and beat up an omelette. "I should say not! Why?"

"'Cause we found some on the gatepost the night you were here, and I thought maybe you had lost it. No, I didn't think so, either. Gail thought you might have lost it." Into his ears she poured the whole story of the long, hard year.

"And so you thought, – or Gail thought I had lost the money you found on the gatepost! Well, don't you think it would be a funny tramp who would have all that money with him!"

Peace's face fell, and she slowly admitted, "Yes, I s'pose it would, but I thought maybe you might be a story-book prince. Those things always happen in books. But Gail won't use the money, 'cause she says someone might come along and claim it some day. When mamma was a little girl there was a queer old man lived in her town that people called crazy. He used to give pretty things to the children and then months later he'd go around and c'llect them and give them to someone else. Maybe that's the kind of a man who leaves the money on the gatepost. It has happened twice there, and once in the barn. Gail says we can't tell, and 'twould be terrible embracing" – she meant embarrassing – "if he should try to c'llect after we had spent the money."

"That's a fact," agreed the tramp, "but I think she could spend the money without any such fears, because I think the fairies brought it."

"Do you b'lieve in fairies?" cried Peace in shocked surprise.

"Oh, yes, and I always shall. I don't think the fairies fly around like butterflies, the way they are pictured in books. I believe they live in the hearts of men."

"Then how could they bring money and pin it to the gatepost and grain sacks? They use sure-enough, every-day pins."

"Oh, maybe they whisper to some good friend that a little extra money would make things easier at the brown house, or the green one, or the gray one, and this friend, who has lots of money to spare – "

"That's just the way I thought it all out," interrupted Peace eagerly. "But Mr. Strong hasn't lots of spare money. He is a minister, and they never have enough for themselves. Besides, he crossed his heart that he didn't know who put it there. The Dunbars aren't rich. Miss Truesdale can't afford it. Even Mrs. Grinnell couldn't do it. Judge Abbott has lots of money, but folks have to work for what they get out of him, and old Skinflint is so stingy that he borrows the city papers so's he won't have to buy them himself. Hec Abbott told me so. I can't think of a single soul who would give us the money."

"Maybe this is a friend whom you don't know."

"That's it, I guess. But I'd like awfully well to know them, and 'specially whether we can really use the money for ourselves. Now that Bossy is gone, I don't know what we are going to do for milk. Mr. Jones paid fifteen dollars for her, but that won't buy a whole new one."

"I think I know where you can get a fine cow for fifteen dollars. If you will give me the money I will call around by the place and have the man bring it to you the first thing in the morning. It is quite a piece from here, and maybe he wouldn't sell it to you for that price, but I know he would to me."

Peace sat lost in thought, a bit of bread poised half way to her mouth.

"Is it a good cow?" asked Allee, timidly.

"The very best."

"Gentle, like Bossy?" Cherry questioned.

"Gentle as a lamb."

"Does she give four gallons of milk a day?" Peace interrupted.

"More, sometimes."

"Is she pretty?"

"Handsome as a picture."

"Does she give good milk, with lots of cream? We make our own butter, you know."

"She's a splendid butter cow."

"Has she got brown eyes, like mine, and a curly tail, and two good horns – not too sharp? Will she eat sugar out of your hand and not drive folks out of the stall when they try to pet her?"

"She is the finest cow I ever saw – "

"Then it's funny the man will sell her for; fifteen dollars," declared Peace, with sudden suspicion, studying the old man opposite her, but seeing only a sandy, untrimmed beard, a strong, honest face, with square jaws, and a pair of the kindest eyes she had ever looked into.

"Not at all," said the man, chuckling to himself at the trap she had laid for him. "He wants to get rid of his herd, but doesn't need the money; though, of course, he wouldn't care to give the cows away."

"Well," hesitated the brown-eyed girl, "I guess – I will have you order the cow for us. Gail won't feel so bad about losing Bossy if we can get another just as good. Here is the money. Do you have to go so soon? I would like to have you stay until the girls get here. Now, don't you forget about the cow!"

"She will be here early tomorrow morning. Good-night, and many thanks for the supper." Out into the spring night walked the tramp, with the precious fifteen dollars in his pocket, and again the three children took up their vigil at the window, watching for the sisters from town.

When at last Gail and Faith reached home, expecting to be met by tears and reproaches from three hungry maids, they were surprised to find supper spread on the table awaiting their coming, and to hear a strange tale of mishap and adventure that would have done credit to the age of Mother Goose or Robinson Crusoe.

"Doesn't that sound like a fairy prince?" asked Peace, when the recital was ended. "But he says he isn't one."

"I should say it sounded like a plain robber story," said Faith bitterly, while Gail sat white-faced and silent with despair. "What did you give him that money for! It's the last we will ever see of it. You are worse than Jack and the Bean-Stalk. You haven't even a handful of bean blossoms to show."

"I've got a curl from Bossy's tail," said Peace indignantly, and then burst into tears, unable to bear the sight of Gail's drawn face any longer.

"Yes, and a robber on our trail. Supposing he comes tonight for the rest of the money you told him about. No, Cherry, I don't want any supper. Come and help me bolt the windows and fix things for the night. I wish Hope was here now."

The supper remained untouched, the dishes were cleared away in silence, and as soon as Hope arrived the unhappy little household climbed wearily, fearfully upstairs to bed, where Peace sobbed herself to sleep, with faithful Allee's arms about her neck. But no robber came to disturb the brown house and at length even Gail and Faith drifted away to slumberland, in spite of this added trouble.

In the dusk of early morning, while the world was still asleep, a heavy wagon drew up at the gate of the Greenfield cottage, unloaded its precious burden and drove rapidly away again; while Peace, in her restless tossing, dreamed that a gentle, brown-eyed cow stood in Bossy's stall, lowing for some breakfast. She awoke with a start, to hear a familiar, persistent mooing, and the tinkle of a bell in the barnyard, and, leaping out of bed, she rushed to the window with wildly beating heart. There in the yard, tied to the old watering-trough, stood a plump, pretty Jersey cow! Peace rubbed her eyes, pinched her arm to make sure she was not still dreaming, and then startled the whole house awake with a whoop of joy: "She has come, she has come! The cow has come! My tramp isn't a robber or a beanstalk at all!"

CHAPTER XI

Gardens and Gophers

"Have you got any more corn or potatoes to drop, or onion sets to cover, or radishes and beans and turnips to plant, or wheat or barley to scatter, or – or anything else to do?" Peace panted breathlessly one warm Saturday afternoon late in May.

"No," smiled Gail, looking tenderly down into the flushed, perspiring face. "You girls have worked faithfully all day, and now you can rest awhile. Mike is coming next week to finish the planting."

"Can – may we fix our own gardens, then? Mr. Kennedy gave me a whole lot of seed the gove'nment sent him to plant, but he can't, 'cause he's going to Alaska."

"Government seed! What kinds?"

"Cucumbers and beets, and parsley and carrots and – "

"But, child, we have all of those in our big garden now. I thought you wanted your little plot of ground for flowers?"

"I do. One of these packages is sweet peas."

"Oh, dearie, I guess you have made a mistake. Mr. Kennedy wouldn't have any use for sweet pea seed."

"Hope said that was the name on the package."

"Well, then I suppose they are, though I never heard tell of the Kennedys raising flowers before. Sweet peas ought to be planted along a fence. We will have Mike dig a little trench just inside the front yard fence, and plant the peas there."

Peace's face fell, but she offered no objections to the plan, and Gail straightway forgot all about it. Not so with the enthusiastic, youthful planter, however; and, while the older sister was bustling about the hot kitchen, the curly, brown head was bobbing energetically back and forth in the front yard, where she and Cherry were digging a trench as fast as they could turn the sod with an old broken spade and a discarded fire-shovel; while Allee followed in their wake, dropping the seed into the freshly-turned earth and carefully covering them again.

"Mercy, but this yard is big!" sighed weary Peace, as she began digging along the third and last side. "Have you got enough left to stick in here, Allee?"

"This is all," answered the blue-eyed toiler, displaying a handful of flat, black seed in her apron.

"Those don't look like peas," cried Cherry, pausing to examine the queer-looking things. "All I ever saw were round."

"Garden peas are round," answered Peace, with a knowing air, "but these are sweet peas, and they are flat."

"Did you ever see any before?" demanded Cherry suspiciously, nettled by her sister's manner.

"No – o, but doesn't the sack they were in say 'sweet peas?'"

It certainly did, there was no disputing that fact, so Cherry discreetly remained silent, and began her vigorous shoveling once more.

When the supper hour was announced the shallow, uneven trench was completed, the seeds all covered, and three dirty gardeners perched in a row on the fence, planning out the list of customers who would buy the sweet blossoms when the vines had matured.

"There's the horn for supper," said Cherry.

"And I know Mrs. Lacy will be glad to get them sometimes, 'cause she hasn't any flowers at all," continued Peace, ignoring the interruption. "That makes ten people."

"Well, hurry up! I am hungry, and we'll have to wash before Gail will give us anything to eat," cried the tallest girl impatiently. "I'll race you to the pump."

"You are late," Hope greeted them, when, after a noisy splashing and hasty wiping of faces, they entered the room. "Doesn't Allee's face look funny with that black streak around it where she didn't hit the dirt? What have you been doing to get so warm?"

"Planting sweet peas," answered Allee.

"Oh, Peace! After I said we would have Mike dig a trench by the fence!"

"You didn't say we couldn't plant them, Gail. We dug it so's to save Mike the trouble. Anyway, the seeds ought to be in the ground by this time if they are ever going to blossom this year, and Mike is so slow. We thought it was best not to wait. When do you s'pose they will come up?"

"Oh, in about two or three weeks, maybe," Gail answered. "You better rub your arms well with liniment before you go to bed tonight, or you will be so lame tomorrow you can't move."

The incident was closed, and the sweet peas forgotten until one day about three weeks later Hope called excitedly from the front yard, "Gail, Gail, come here! What ever are these plants coming up all along the fence? They are not sweet peas."

Gail came, examined the fat sprouts and looked at Hope in comical dismay. "They are pumpkins or cucumbers or melons, and the whole front fence is lined with them!"

"Poor Peace!" said Hope, when their laugh had ended. "She will be heartbroken. She made her fortune a dozen times over on the blossoms those vines are to bear."

"Yes," sighed Gail. "She has the happy faculty of trying to do one thing and getting some unexpected, unheard-of result. Poor little blunderbus! But what shall we do with these plants? There are enough to stock a ranch. We can't leave them here, and I don't think they will bear transplanting."

"And so they ain't sweet peas at all!" exclaimed a disappointed voice behind them, and there stood Peace herself, contemplating her treasures with solemn eyes.

"No, dear, they are pumpkins, I guess. What kind of seed did you plant?"

"I planted sweet pea seed," came the mournful reply. "Leastways the sack said so. Hope read it herself."

"Yes, the sack was labelled plainly, but I never thought to examine the seed. What did they look like?"

"They were black and flat."

"Melons," said Gail. "Well, I would rather have melons than pumpkins, for we already have planted a lot of them. Still, it will spoil these to transplant them, so they might just as well have been pumpkins. It is a shame to have to throw them all away, though."

Peace said nothing, but in bitterness of heart helped pull up all the green sprouts and throw them over the fence. Then she sat down beside the heap to mourn over her fallen aircastles.

"Seems 's if I can't do anything like other folks," she sighed dismally. "I plant sweet peas and get melons. I wonder if melons wouldn't sell better than peas. Gail says these won't grow, but I am going to try them anyway."

She filled her apron with the hapless plants and carried them away to her small garden plot behind the shed, where she patiently set out every one, regardless of the flower seeds already hid beneath the soil. And, strange to say, they grew, – at least many of them did, choking out the poppies and marigolds and balsams which finally climbed through the three inches of ground the zealous gardener had hid them under, and formed a thick tangle of promising vines.

Then the gophers began their destructive work, tunnelling the little farm into a perfect labyrinth of underground passages, much to the dismay of the little household, so dependent upon the success of their crops. Traps were set, the holes were flooded, cats by the score were let loose in the fields, but still the little pests continued to dig, as if laughing at the futile attempts made to get rid of them. At length Gail sighed, "I am afraid we will have to resort to poisoned grain. I hate to, because I am so afraid the children will get into it, or something dreadful happen on account of it."

"I don't see how either the youngsters or even the hens could get at it if it was put down the holes," said Faith. "Say nothing about it but fix up a mess and Hope and I will drop it some day when the children are away and the hens in their yard."

So Gail mixed up a huge bucket full of poisoned grain, and while the younger trio were gathering flowers in the woods one afternoon, the other sisters sallied forth with their deadly bait, bent on exterminating their small foes.

All might have gone well had not the smaller girls suddenly decided to play hare and hound, and it fell to Peace's lot to be the hare. With an apron full of gay dandelion blossoms for the trail, the active little body set out on a wide detour of the woods, across the bridge, up through the Hartman pasture land, reaching the barbed wire fence on their own little farm just in time to see Hope dropping a last handful of grain into a gopher hole before returning to the house with her empty pail.

"Now what has she been doing?" thought Peace, peering out from a thicket of hazel bushes. "Oh, I know! I bet she is trying to poison the gophers, like Mr. Hartman did. I wonder if they will come up after the corn right away. I am going to watch. I'd like to see how it kills them."

She carefully wriggled her way under the lower wire, and sat down in front of the nearest gopher mound, forgetting all about her dandelions, sisters, and play, in the prospect of witnessing the death of one of the enemy. But either Mr. Gopher was not at home, or else he suspected the presence of an unwelcome caller, for he did not come up in sight for even a nibble of the tempting corn; and at last, weary of her fruitless vigil, Peace cried aloud, "He prob'ly can get all he wants without letting me see him. I'm going to dig it all out on top, so he will have to come out in sight."

She quickly scratched the poisoned bait out of the runway, scattered it liberally about, and settled back in her former position, with her eyes glued on the mouth of the tunnel; but still Mr. Gopher did not come.

"You tiresome old thing!" she exclaimed impatiently, after what seemed hours of waiting. "I shan't watch for you another minute. I'll find another hole and see if they will do any better there." So from mound to mound she scurried, digging the grain up into view, and then watching for the appearance of the tenant – with no result.

"Well, of all provoking people!" cried an indignant voice behind her, and there were Cherry and Allee crawling under the fence. "How long have you been sitting there like a bump on a log? You didn't drop enough dandelions, and we had an awful time following you. What on earth are you doing here? Let's go up to the pump for a drink. I am nearly burned up." Without giving the weary Peace a chance to answer her questions, she raced away through the pasture toward the house, dragging Allee with her; and the third girl, after one last, hopeless glance at the gopher hole, followed more slowly.

Some time later Hope came tearing across the field, with hair flying, and her eyes filled with alarm, calling shrilly, "Gail, Faith, the hens have broken out of the yard and are eating the poisoned grain! There are more than a dozen down there now!"

"Oh, dear," cried Peace, with guilty conscience, "I scratched the corn out of the holes so's I could watch the gophers die. And I let the hens out, too, 'cause they looked so hot shut up in that mite of a yard after they have been running loose for so long."

With despairing eyes, Gail looked down at the dying fowls, and not daring to trust herself to speak, she hurried away to the house to sob out her grief alone.

Faith paused long enough to count the hapless hens, clutched the wretched culprit and shook her vigorously, then silently followed her older sister, leaving the heartbroken child alone with the victims of her curiosity.

"Did you ever see my equal?" she said aloud, addressing herself. "You are the worst child that ever lived! You wash the labels off the spice boxes so Faith gets ginger instead of mustard in her salad dressing; you try to milk cows and break their legs instead; you spoil cakes and steal eggs and bother Gail and Faith till they are nearly crazy; and now you've taken to killing hens just to see how gophers die. Peace Greenfield, aren't you ashamed of yourself? Yes, I am, but there's no use in wasting those perfectly good hens – twenty of them – we had only forty in all. It's a wonder the rest of them didn't get a dose, too. Hope has got them locked up at last. There comes Cherry; I'll make her help. Oh, Cherry, here's a job for you!"

"What is it? And why are the girls crying? They wouldn't tell me."

"I've killed a lot of hens for them, playing hare and hound. That's the very last time I will ever be hare, Charity Greenfield! Help me undress these chickens. We'll have some for supper, and the rest we'll peddle to the town folks."

"Oh, Peace, I can't pull feathers! It makes me shiver every time a bunch comes out in my hands."

"You will have to. You don't expect me to pick them all, do you? I guess the girls never thought of selling the hens, and I can't ask them to help now. We will get the ax and chop off their heads and then hang them in the crab-apple tree while we strip them. You really must help, Cherry.

Gail says they pick better while they are warm."

She hunted up the ax, and one by one hacked off poor biddies' heads; but when it came to the picking process, they found it was slow work for small, inexperienced fingers, and gave up in despair when the third nude body lay in the grass at their feet.

"It is almost night, Peace, and we've picked three. What shall we do? 'Twill take us hours to finish that whole bunch."

"We'll sell them for as much as we can get, and see if the butcher won't take the rest with the feathers on. We can keep two or three for ourselves. Where is Allee's cart?"

All that remained of the poison victims were loaded into the small wagon, and their strange pilgrimage through the village streets began. The picked fowls were readily disposed of, and one neighbor bought the largest of the feathered birds, but no one else wanted to bother with them, and it was only after much persuasion that the butcher consented to take six, at the fancy price of twenty-five cents each.

"Well, that is better than nothing, though he wouldn't sell me one for that little last Christmas," sighed Peace, much disappointed at the result of their peddling. "Three dollars and fifty cents will buy quite a few chickens, and chickens make hens if you give them time. What do you s'pose Gail will say when we give her the money?"

They were not long in finding out. The two red-eyed girls were busy in the kitchen when the children returned with the unsold hens in the wagon; and with fear and trembling, Peace laid the coins on the table, saying humbly, "Mrs. Munson took one, and Mrs. Bainbridge, and Mrs. Edwards and Mrs. Lacy, and the butcher bought six. That's all the hens we could sell. We left three here for supper and – "

"Peace Greenfield!" shrieked the horrified sisters in unison. "Did you sell those poisoned hens? You march straight upstairs to bed – and Cherry, too!" Then Gail flew one way and Faith the other, to collect the birds before the buyers had a chance to dish up the delicacy to adored families.

When they had seen the last fowl safely disposed of, and were home once more, Gail said despairingly, "I don't know what in the world to do with that child!"

"She needs a good, sound thrashing," answered Faith sharply. "She gets into more mischief in a day than a monkey would in a month."

"She doesn't mean to," pleaded Gail. "Mother never believed in whipping. If it were mischief for mischief's sake, I could punish her, but her intentions are good – "

"Good intentions don't amount to much in her case. A good trouncing might make her think a little more."

"I can't whip her, Faith, but I'll go up and lecture her good. I believe that will be more effective than harshness."

So the perplexed mother-sister mounted the stairs to the chamber above, from which sounded a low murmur of voices, and she paused in the hallway to assemble her thoughts, when Peace's words, evidently in supplication, floated out through the open door: "And, O Lord, don't blame Gail for getting mad. It's the first time I can remember. She is usu'ly very good. S'posing she was a stepmother, like lame Jennie Munn's, wouldn't we have a time living with her, though? And I am truly sorry about the hens. Hope says we can't get many eggs now, 'cause half of the flock is gone, and if we keep all our customers we will have to do without eggs here at home. I don't mind that at all myself, 'cause I've eaten eggs and eggs till it makes me sick to hunt them now; but what will Faith do for her cakes? That's what is worrying me. It was so we could buy more live hens that Cherry and me sold the dead ones. We didn't know they would make people sick, and p'r'aps kill them, too. I am sorry the money had to go back and that the hens are just wasted now, but I 'xpect they'll make an elegant funeral tomorrow. So forgive Gail and keep her from getting mad any more, and forgive me and keep me from being bad any more, and make us 'happy children in a happy home.' Amen."

Softly, silently, Gail stole down the stairs again, with her lecture unsaid.

CHAPTER XII

The Raspberry Patch

One hot, dusty afternoon in midsummer Faith trudged wearily up the road from the village, climbed the steps to the vine-covered piazza where Gail sat shelling peas, and dropped a handful of silver into her sister's lap, saying, "Three dollars clear from my cakes this week! Wish I could make that much every time. Mrs. Dunbar was perfectly delighted with my jelly roll, and has ordered another for next Saturday."

"Isn't that fine!" smiled Gail. "You will have a bakery of your own some day if you keep on. I thought she would like the roll; it was the best I ever tasted."

"I think I could find quite a few customers for them if I only had the jelly, but it costs so much to buy it, and all we have is that little bit of apple jelly you made last summer."

"The crab-apple trees are loaded with mites of green apples," volunteered Cherry from the lower step, where she was making cats-cradles with Allee.

"Yes, but they won't be ripe for weeks yet; and, besides, a sour jelly is best for jelly rolls."

"Do blackberries make sour jelly?" asked Peace, pausing in her occupation of fitting paper sails to the empty pods Gail had dropped. "Cause the creek road is just lined with bushes."

"They are better than crab-apples, but it will be days before they are ripe enough for use. I had thought of them, and investigated the bushes only yesterday. Mrs. Grinnell says raspberries are best for the purpose."

"Lots of people around here have raspberries," said Peace.

"And they want money for them, too."

"Mr. Hardman doesn't pay any 'tention to his down in the pasture. I've helped myself there lots of times."

"But his wife does. I saw her there this morning."

Peace said no more, but, waiting until she saw their neighbor bring up his cows to be milked, she slipped through the fence onto his land and accosted him with the abrupt question, "How much will you take for the rest of your raspberries?"

"What?"

She repeated her inquiry, and after scratching his head meditatively, he exclaimed, as if to himself, "Another money-making scheme! If she don't beat the Dutch!"

"This is a jelly-making scheme," returned Peace, with comical dignity. "There is no money in it."

"Oh! Well, don't you know that raspberries are expensive?"

"Most people's are, but you never paid any 'tention to yours, so I thought you would be glad to get rid of them for little or nothing."

"Oho!" he teased. "Begging again!"

"I'm not!" Peace denied hotly. "I'll pay for them if you don't charge too high."

"How much will you pay?"

"I haven't any money, but I'll pick on shares."

"Share and share alike?"

"Yes; I'll keep half for my trouble, and you will get half for no trouble."

Her method of figuring always amused him, and now he laughed outright, "Seems to me I am entitled to them all. They are my berries, you know."

"Well," stormed Peace, "if that's the way you look at it, you can pick 'em, too!"

"Aw, don't get mad," he said soothingly. "I was just teasing. Of course you can pick all the raspberries you want. My wife said just this morning that the bushes were loaded, and she couldn't begin to handle them all herself. But – say – that reminds me – I've rented the pasture to old Skinner, and he's put his bull in there. You will have to watch your chance when the old critter is out, to pick your berries."

"All right," cried Peace, expressing her elation by hopping about on one foot. "It's awfully nice of you to give us the berries you don't care to pick yourself, and we will see that the bull doesn't bother."

She was half way across the field by the time she had finished speaking, eager to tell the good news to the girls; and before the dew was dry on the grass the next morning, three sunbonneted figures scampered down the road to Mr. Hartman's lower pasture, armed with big pails and Allee's red wagon, intent on picking all the berries they could for Faith's jelly.

"We'll have to leave Allee's cart outside the fence," said Peace, climbing the high rails with astonishing agility and dropping nimbly down on the other side. "Do you see the Skinflint's bull anywhere?"

"No," answered Cherry, taking a careful survey of the field from her perch on the top rail. "There isn't a thing stirring."

"Then maybe we can pick all we want before the deacon brings him down. Hurry, and keep a sharp lookout for the old beast. My, but these bushes are stickery!"

"I should say they are," Cherry agreed, ruefully eyeing her bleeding hands. "I don't believe it is going to be any fun picking raspberries. They are lots worse than blackberries."

"S'posing we had been the prince who crawled through the hedge to wake Sleeping Beauty. I bet he got good and scratched up, but he kept right on and fin'ly kissed the princess awake."

"There ain't any princess in these bushes," grumbled Cherry, pausing to suck a wounded thumb.

"No, but there are berries, and they are more important than princesses. We couldn't make jelly out of a princess, but we can out – Mercy, what was that noise?"

"It's the bull! Run, run! There it comes down the hill!" shrieked Cherry, standing as if rooted to the spot, and staring with horror at the angry animal tearing across the pasture toward them.

"Run yourself, you ninny!" screamed Peace, giving the older girl a push, and then scrambling for the fence with Allee dragging by one arm behind her.

There was no time to climb over, and the lower rail was too close to the ground for them to crawl under, but Peace did not linger to discuss the question. Grabbing the frightened baby by the heels, she thrust her between the slats, and gave her a shove that pitched her head first into a stagnant mudhole just outside the fence. Then pausing only long enough to see that Cherry was safely through, she followed, still clutching her now empty pail, and landing beside Allee in the mud.

"Whew! What a smell!" she spluttered, righting herself and trying to dig her sister out of the pool. "And all on account of that miserable, cowardly bull! Why don't you take someone your own size to fight?" She shook her fist defiantly at the pawing, bellowing brute by the fence, and not satisfied with that method of expressing her anger, she flung the empty bucket at his head, crying in frenzy, "Take that, you old sinner! It b'longs to the berries you've already got."

Her aim was truer than she had anticipated, and the pail fell with a rattling clatter over the beast's ugly-looking horns, frightening him so that for a brief moment he stood perfectly still. Then, with a snort of fear and fury, he set off across the field at a mad gallop, with the bucket still tossing on his head.

Peace glared angrily after the retreating enemy, too indignant over her loss to think of their peril until Cherry quavered, "Hadn't we better run while we have a chance? Suppose he should batter the fence down."

"No danger," Peace muttered shortly; but she picked herself up from the ground, where she was trying to scrape the ill-smelling mud off her shoes, and marched majestically up the road, trundling the cart behind her.

"Where are you going?" cried Cherry, when they reached the first cross street. "Here's where we turn."

"Turn, then! I'm going on to old Skinflint's house and tell him to keep that ugly bull out of Hartman's pasture until we get those raspberries picked."

"With that nasty mud all over you?"

"Mud and all," was the stubborn answer, and from force of habit,

Cherry fell into step beside her again, tramping along in silence until the Skinner place was reached.

It just happened that the old man himself was hurrying up the path from the barn as they approached, and Peace stopped him with an imperious wave of her hand, speaking straight to the point before he could even ask her what she wanted.

"Your bull won't let us pick raspberries in the lower pasture. Mr. Hartman said we might, but just when we got our pails 'most full, that old thing had to come along and bunt at us. We skipped, but he made us lose all our berries. We'd like to have you tie him up or take him out until we can get those berries picked."

The grouchy old fellow stood with open mouth, glaring at the mud-bespattered figures, as if he doubted his senses, and as Peace finished her speech, he laughed mirthlessly, screeching in his harsh, cracked, rasping voice, "I put that bull in pasture myself, and there he stays! I don't do any tying up, either. I rented that field and it's the same as mine for as long as I hire it. You can't have them berries at all. They are mine."

"Mr. Hartman said we could have them," Peace insisted; "and I guess he wouldn't give away what didn't b'long to him. He may have rented the pasture to you, but he never rented the berries."

Suddenly the old man changed tactics. "You can have all the berries you can get," he taunted, shaking a warning finger in their faces, "but that bull stays right there in that field!"

"All right, old Skinflint!" roared Peace, forgetting everything else in her furious passion, and shaking an emphatic finger back at him. "Just 'member that, will you? We'll get the berries in spite of your old animule!"

She stamped out of the yard and down the road toward home once more, nursing her wrath and trying to think of some way whereby she might get the disputed fruit, for she well knew that the deacon would do all he could to prevent her now.

Early the next morning she was at the pasture again, only to find the vicious enemy grazing close by, watching with wicked eyes every flirt of her dress, as if defying her to gather the luscious red berries hanging so temptingly near.

The second day it was the same, and the third. It looked as if the enemy had conquered; but Peace was not to be easily defeated. She had set her heart on picking that fruit, and she meant to have it at any cost.

The fourth morning, after reconnoitering and finding the bull still in undisputed possession of the field, an uncertain but daring thought dawned upon her busy brain, and when she returned home she casually asked Hope, "Didn't folks one time have bull fights in Africa?"

"In Spain, you mean," answered the other, always ready to share her small store of knowledge. "Yes, they still have them, though it is very wicked."

"How do they fight?"

"Oh, I don't know exactly, but I think a man rides around a big ring on horseback, flying a red flag until the bull is terribly mad, and then he has to kill it with his dagger or get killed himself. It is terribly cruel, teacher says."

"Why does the bull get mad at the flag?"

"Because it is red, and they can't stand that color. Neither can turkey gobblers. Don't you remember you had on a red coat when Mr. Hartman's gobbler chased you?"

"Oh," said Peace, much enlightened. She had received the information she sought, and was content.

"So the flag has to be red, does it?" she mused, as she stealthily climbed the stairs to the tiny, hot, cobwebby attic, where all the cast-off clothing was stored against a rainy day. "I thought it was something like that, but I didn't know for sure. There's an old red dress that b'longed to me, and here is my old flannel petticoat. I don't b'lieve we will ever use this mess of cheesecloth again, either; it is so dreadfully streaked. But there is enough red in it yet."

Gathering up an armful of worn-out garments, she crept down the stairway once more and slipped away to the lower pasture with her burden, where for the next half hour she might have been seen tying the scarlet strips to the fence rails in the corner farthest from the raspberry patch. When the last rag was fastened securely, she stepped back and viewed the result of her labor, sighing in deep satisfaction, "There are twenty-one hunks in all. It ought to take him a good long time to tear them all to pieces, and maybe if we work fast we can get most of the bushes stripped while he is banging his head down here."

Hurrying home, she quietly summoned Cherry and Allee, and the trio set out once more on their berry-picking excursion, finding their enemy too busy in the far end of the field to interfere with them, just as Peace had hoped.

"But he may come back here at any minute," argued Cherry, loth to enter the field. "I thought you said he was gone from the pasture."

"I said from the berries. Don't stop to talk. As long as he doesn't hear us, we are all right. We will pick close to the fence, so we can get out quick. There must be tons of berries right here in this clump. Mercy, what a racket he makes!"

Then how the nimble fingers flew, and how fast the deep-tinted fruit fell into the shining pails! But all the while the three pickers kept their eyes fastened on the grove of trees which hid the animal from sight, and three hearts pounded fearfully at every snort of the enraged brute.

"Are you sure he is tied?" whispered cautious Cherry, after an unusually loud bellow had made her jump almost out of her shoes.

"I didn't say he was tied. I said he wasn't apt to bother us this morning. Keep still and pick with all your might. One of the big pails in the wagon is full already."

"But how do you know he will stay there if he isn't tied?" persisted Cherry, glancing apprehensively toward the trees again.

"He is too busy to think of coming over here now," Peace assured her confidently, and that was all the satisfaction she could get, so she lapsed into silence, and worked like a beaver until the second big bucket was brimming over. Then the small taskmaster drew a deep breath of relief and said graciously, "Now we will go home. These ought to make quite a little jelly. We must have as much as twenty quarts. They don't take as long as strawberries."

Thankfully the sisters crawled through the fence and triumphantly bore their precious burden homeward, still hearing in the distance the angry mutterings of Deacon Skinner's bull.

"Just see the loads of berries we picked!" chorused three happy voices, as the rattling cart came to a standstill before the kitchen door.

"Faith can have all the jelly she wants, and you can make the leftover seeds up in jam, can't you?"

"Children!" cried Gail, white to the lips. "Have you been in that pasture with Mr. Skinner's ugly bull?"

"Yes," they confessed, "but he never came near us."

"I guess he didn't want to leave the grove," added Peace, marching complacently away to wash her berry-stained hands.

"Don't you ever go there again," commanded the oldest sister, still trembling with fright at what might have happened to the daring berry pickers, but she never thought to question them any further, and Peace's prank remained a secret for a short time longer.

The next day Deacon Skinner was early at the Hartman place, stalking angrily up to the low, green house, and, striding into the kitchen without the formality of knocking, demanded fiercely, "What do you mean by plastering your fence all over with red rags? Your pasture fence? I'll sue you for damages! My bull has lost one horn and is all battered to pieces, the rails are splintered, and it's a wonder he didn't get loose. Is that what you aimed at doing?"

Mr. Hartman faced his accuser unflinchingly, saying, with quiet emphasis, "I don't know anything about the matter. The fence was all right yesterday morning, for I was down there myself to see, before I left for town. You don't know what you are saying when you threaten to sue."

"But the fence is all tied up with red rags," blustered the angry fellow. "How comes that? You rented me the – "

"I rented you the pasture, but I didn't rent you watch dogs and dragons to guard it. That is your own lookout. I had nothing to do with it, and it's no affair of mine if the village boys are up to their pranks."

Mr. Hartman's air was convincing, and the deacon's wrath toward his neighbor cooled somewhat when he saw how groundless were his accusations. Nevertheless, his ire was thoroughly aroused, and he promised all sorts of punishment to the offenders when they were caught. "If 'twas the village boys, I'll warrant the Judge's youngster was at the head of it. I'll tan him till he can't stand when I get my hands on him," he muttered.

"You better make sure of the guilty one before you thrash him," suggested Mr. Hartman, dryly.

"That Abbott boy and the Greenfield girl are the ringleaders in all the mischief – by George, she's the one that did it! She vowed she'd get those berries, bull or no bull. If she has touched those bushes, I'll – "

"No, you won't," interrupted the other man, rising to his feet with an angry light in his eyes. "If that child went to you and asked about those bushes, you don't lay hands on her in any way."

"She didn't ask. She came and told me to tie up the animal so she could pick raspberries."

"And you refused."

"I rented that field, and you had no business to promise her the berries."

"If you wanted them, why didn't you say so? They were going to waste on the vines. You merely asked permission to put your animal in there for a month while you were repairing your corral."

"I didn't want the berries, but – "

"That is all I care to know. You can take your property out of my pasture at once. I won't rent to such a man as you. Sue if you like, and see what you will get in court."

"Very well, Hartman," fumed the fiery-tempered old fellow. "But I will settle even with you yet. Just remember that note of Lowe's, will you? It's apt to be called to your attention pretty soon in a way you won't like, I reckon, and you won't get a second's more time on it, either. You will find it ain't so funny to set up against me in this neighborhood!"

The irate man stormed out of the house, still shaking his fist threateningly, and Mr. Hartman, in a very disturbed state of mind, returned to his breakfast.

CHAPTER XIII

Peace Gets Even

"Peace, come here, I want to talk with you," called Mr. Hartman, leaning over the fence and beckoning to the child at work in her melon patch, measuring the mottled green fruit thickly dotted through the vines.

"It's grown two inches since I measured it last," said the brown-eyed gardener to herself, leaving her task to see what the man wanted. "Here I am."

"Do you know what kind of a mess you have got me into now?"

Peace looked her surprise, and answered saucily, "You don't fool me any more, my friend. You've teased me so often that it is an old story now. I know just what to 'xpect when I meet you."

At any other time he would have been delighted with this reply, but under the circumstances – for he was really much disturbed over her latest prank – her jaunty, don't-care air nettled him, and he said sharply, "This is no joking matter, Miss Greenfield, I can tell you that! Why did you tie red rags all over my pasture fence?"

"So's to keep the deacon's bull busy. We couldn't get those berries any other way."

"Well, I guess you succeeded. He broke one horn off and pretty near skinned himself, I judge. The only wonder is that he didn't tear the fence down and get loose."

"As long as he didn't, I shouldn't care about his horns," answered Peace with provoking indifference. "The deacon said I could have all the berries I could get, and he didn't say how I was to get them, either. I thought and thought, and I couldn't see any way out but the red flags. It worked beau – ti – fully. We got two buckets chock-full!"

"Yes," groaned Mr. Hartman; "and got old Skinner red hot at me! I signed a note a year or two ago for a friend of mine, expecting by this time that he would be on his feet and able to take care of it, but he isn't, and I've got to settle. Where the money is coming from is more than I can tell. It took all my ready cash to build that new barn, and old Skinner is so blamed mad that he won't give me any more time. And all this fuss on account of those berries. Plague take the old bushes, and you, too, you little rascal!"

Peace drew herself up haughtily and with eyes flashing fire, demanded, "Do you mean that?"

"Every word. I'd just like the chance to give you a good trouncing."

He was not in earnest, but he looked so harsh and stern that Peace for a moment trembled in her shoes. Then all her natural childish passion was aroused, and stamping her foot, she declared wrathfully, "I'll not be friends with you any longer. You said I could have the berries, and the deacon said I could have all I could get. You aren't being square with me, and I won't have anything more to do with you." She turned on her heel and flung herself indignantly across the garden to the road, leaving Mr. Hartman still leaning against the fence, lost in thought.

The forest was her favorite retreat in times of trouble, but today the cool shadows and whispering trees did not soothe her, and after wandering about until the afternoon began to wane, she started for home, still wrathful and passionate, for she felt that Mr. Hartman had been very unfair in his treatment of her.

While she was still some distance from the little brown house, a carriage drove up to their gate, and stopped, but she did not recognize the rig, nor could she make out who had alighted; and for the time being, her rage was lost in her greater curiosity. "Wonder who it can be," she said to herself. "It isn't the doctor's horse, nor the Judge's buggy, and that woman is too little for Mrs. Lacy or Mrs. Edwards. She's got a big bundle. Maybe it's the Salvation Army bringing us some old duds like they did the German family last week. But s'posing it was some rich aunt or grandmother we didn't know we had. It's awfully hard not to have any relations like other folks. I am going through old Cross-Patch's cornfield, 'stead of running clear around by the road."

She crawled between the strands of barbed wire and ran swiftly down the rows of rustling, whispering, silken corn, thinking only of the unexpected visitors at home, until a big barn loomed up before her, shining in its newness. Then she stopped abruptly, having suddenly remembered her grievance.

"He isn't square!" she cried. "I'd like to fight him good. I'll get even with you some day, Mr. Hardman! Bet he's going to paint his old barn. Here is a whole ocean of red paint in this pail, and there is a stack of brushes. I – I'm going – to tell – him what I think of him in red paint. Yes, sir, I'm going to do it this very minute!"

All thought of the mysterious visitor at home had vanished, all thought of the consequences were stifled, and choosing the smallest brush in the heap beside the pail, she began daubing scrawly, tipsy letters across the new, white boards: Mister Hardman isnt square.

"There!" she breathed, as the last straggling "r" was finished. "I'll bet that makes him mad, but maybe next time he won't blame me for his old fusses. He said I could have those raspberries."

She dipped the brush into the paint once more, made a few little red spots below the printed letters, and labelled them raspberries for fear they might not otherwise be recognized. Then dropping the brush back where she had found it, she skipped off home, feeling an uncomfortable sense of guilt and shame in her heart for having wreaked her revenge in such a manner.

At the gate Allee met her, shouting, "Mrs. Strong is here with the baby, and she's going to stay for supper. Elva Munson brought her in their new buggy. Come see Glen. We've hunted all over for you, and even blew the horn."

The excited child danced up the path, and Peace followed, forgetting her mean prank in her pleasure at seeing her beloved friends. Nor did she remember any more about it until the next morning, when, seated on the shed-roof, under the overhanging boughs of a great elm, she saw Mr. Hartman striding angrily up the path to the kitchen door. Then her heart gave a great thump and seemed to sink clear to her toes, as she thought of her miserable method of getting even. Her passion had subsided during the night, and try as she would, she could now think of no justifiable excuse for her mean act.

Gail answered the imperative knock, and Peace heard him demand wrathfully, "Where is Peace?"

"Somewhere around the place. She was under the maple there at the corner a few moments ago. Is something wrong? Has she been annoying you again?"

"Annoying me? She has daubed letters all over the back of my new barn. I shall have to paint the whole building now, and it isn't very funny business. If I had got hold of her when I first saw her work, I'd have given her a thrashing she wouldn't have forgotten in one while. You will whip that child like she deserves, or pay for the damage she has done, – one or the other, and I mean it, too!" Without waiting for her reply, he started down the path again, leaving Gail white-faced and distressed in the kitchen door.

As soon as he was out of sight Peace slid from her perch to the ground below, deserting the corncob doll she had been dressing, and scurried away to the barn loft to face the new and undreamed-of situation. A licking or pay for the damage done! Why had she been so thoughtless and mean? She might have known that Gail would be the one to suffer. She hated herself, as she always did after her mischievous pranks, but that didn't help matters any. She must take her medicine. There was no money to settle for her wanton mischief; it would have to be the licking.

"I wonder whether she'll use a shingle or her shoe," she thought nervously, making ready to descend and brave Gail's displeasure, when Cherry's head appeared on the ladder, and the older girl announced excitedly, "Now you've done it, Peace Greenfield! Mr. Hartman is as mad as a hornet about your painting his barn, and he says Gail must either whip you hard, or pay for it. There isn't any money to pay – "

"Then I s'pose I'll have to take the licking," answered Peace with a great show of indifference, though the pounding of her heart nearly stifled her.

"But Gail says she can't lick you, and even Faith has backed out, though at first she said she would give it to you good."

Here was an unlooked-for state of affairs – no money, and no one willing to use the rod, though she undoubtedly deserved it.

"What are you going to do about it?" asked Cherry curiously.

"Lick myself likely," retorted Peace sarcastically. "You better lug those eggs up to the doctor's. I've d'livered my bunch."

Cherry vanished as quickly as she had come, and as the sound of her footsteps died away in the distance, Peace slid down the ladder. But instead of going to the house for an interview with Gail, she slipped through the garden, crawled under the fence, and presented herself at the door of the new barn where Mr. Hartman, still in a blaze of anger, was at work.

"What do you want here, you tormented rascal?" he yelled in fury, shaking a hazel switch threateningly at her.

"I came to get licked," she answered steadily, though quaking inwardly.

"Wh-at?" he gasped in unbelieving amazement.

"I heard what you said to Gail about paying or licking me, and she hasn't got any money to pay for my meanness, and she says – she says she can't whip me; so I've come to you for it."

She really did not expect him to punish her in that manner, for ordinarily he was not a hard-hearted man; but in view of Peace's misdemeanor, Gail's hesitation angered him only the more, and catching the child by her shoulder, he gave her a dozen sharp, stinging lashes with his switch, then released her, thoroughly ashamed of himself.

He expected her to cry and scream, but she bit her lips, blinked her brown eyes rapidly to keep the tears back, and stood like a statue until he dropped his stick. Then choking back the sobs in her throat, she faced him with the curt demand, "Give me a receipt, please."

"A – a what?"

"A receipt. Gail says we should never settle a bill without getting a receipt."

"What do you want of a receipt?"

"So's I can show Gail that this bill is settled."

"Aha!" he mocked. "You are afraid Gail will repent and give you another thrashing, are you?"

"No, I'm not! But I want to be sure you don't try to c'llect twice."

He stared at her open-mouthed, too hurt for words; and she, unaware that she had deeply offended him, urged impatiently, as she rubbed her smarting shoulders, "Hurry up! Write it on a piece of paper, so's I can have it to keep always. Haven't you got any in your pocket?"

Mechanically he searched his pockets, drew forth a scrap of an envelope, wrote the receipt she demanded, and handed it to her gravely. She accepted it as gravely, spelled it through, and turned to go, saying piously, "Thank you, Mr. Hardman. I hope you will get your reward in heaven." She meant this in all reverence, thinking only of the receipt he had given her, but he thought she was sarcastically referring to the whipping she had suffered at his hands; and with a queer tightening of his throat, he returned to his work, while she hurried homeward with her precious bit of paper.

"Here is Mr. Hardman's receipt, Gail," she announced, briefly, entering the kitchen where the two older girls were still discussing the new problem.

"Where did you get the money!" asked Faith severely.

"I took the licking," was the short answer.

"Took the licking! From whom!"

"Mr. Hardman."

"Do you mean to say that Mr. Hardman whipped you!"

"Yes, I do. I went over and told him to."

"Did it hurt?" whispered Allee, with eyes brimming full of sympathy.

"It might have been worse, s'posing he had used a piece of iron instead of a stick."

Profound silence reigned in the little room. Then Gail said abruptly, "Come upstairs with me. I want to see you alone."

Peace glanced apprehensively at the pale face, which looked unusually stern and severe, and said, "That is a sure-enough receipt, but if you don't b'lieve it, you can ask Mr. Hardman about it."

"I am not doubting your story in the least," answered the big sister, smiling in spite of herself, "but I want to talk to you, dear."

When Gail said "dear," she was never angry, so, without further hesitation, Peace followed her to the small room under the eaves, wondering what was coming next. Gail seated herself in the rickety chair by the window, and drawing the small girl down into her lap, she asked, "Now what is all this trouble about? Tell sister everything."

So Peace related the story of the raspberries and her anger at their neighbor, which had led to the painting of the barn.

"What did you write on the building?" questioned Gail when Peace paused at this point in her recital.

"Just the truth. I said, 'Mr. Hardman isn't square.' Then, so's he would know what he wasn't square about, I made a lot of raspberries under the printing."

"Peace! After Mr. Hartman has been so kind to us! What do you think of a little girl who will do a thing like that!"

"At first I thought she was all right," answered the candid maiden. "But now I've changed my mind, and I guess she was pretty bad when she did it. Though he needn't have said what he did to me. He told me we could have the berries."

"At the same time he warned you about Mr. Skinner's bull."

"Yes, and I warned Mr. Skinflint – I mean Mr. Skinner."

"Mr. Skinner is a hot-tempered man, and I am afraid if the Hartmans owe him money, as you say, he will make it very uncomfortable for them."

"Maybe I better go see old Skinflint – I mean Mr. Skinner – and tell him – "

"No, indeed!" cried Gail in alarm. "You have done damage enough already. Promise me that you won't say anything to him about it, Peace."

"I promise. I ain't anxious to see him anyway, only I thought if it would do any good I would go and tell him how it happened. I am awfully sorry now."

"Then don't you think you better apologize to Mr. Hartman?"

"Wasn't the licking a napology enough?"

"The whipping only settled your account. It didn't say you were sorry. And it was wrong to tell him that you hoped he would get his reward in heaven."

"Why?" cried Peace in genuine astonishment. "That's what the lame peddler woman always tells you when you buy a paper of needles or pins."

"That is different. She means what she says. The words are no idle mockery to her. Every penny she can earn, helps her that much, and she is truly grateful – "

"And I am truly grateful for my receipt, too! It isn't every man that would give me one. Old Skinner now – "

"Oh, Peace!"

"But, Gail, dear, I wasn't mocking him. I wanted him to know that I knew how much that receipt was worth. S'posing he hadn't written it, how would you have known that I had settled that fuss?"

Gail gave up in despair. She never could argue with this small sister, who so sadly needed a mother's wisdom to keep her sweet and good; so she abruptly ended her lecture by gently insisting, "Mr. Hartman deserves your apology. What if he had made us pay for the damage you did, or had had you arrested? He was good to let you off with just a licking, Peace, even if you do think it was hard punishment. If you are going to be a bad girl, you must expect whippings."

"I don't think he likes me any more. He may chase me home before I can apologize," suggested the unhappy culprit, with hanging head.

"I guess not," smiled Gail behind her hand. "Try it and see."

"Well," sighed miserable Peace, "I s'pose I must, then."

She reluctantly descended the stairs again, and disappeared down the path toward the Hartman house, wishing with all her heart that the ground would swallow her up before she had to meet the enemy. Suddenly a way out of the dilemma presented itself. She searched hastily through her pockets for paper and pencil, and folding both among the clutter, she wrote her apology on a ragged, dirty scrap, and carried it to the green house, intending to leave it on the doorstep and hurry away, but as she peered cautiously around the corner of the shed she saw Mrs. Hartman sitting on the porch, and retreated, murmuring, "Oh, dear, I s'pose I'll have to say it to him after all. I might pin it to the barn door, or – maybe 'twould be better if I fastened it beside the painting. That's what I'll do!"

She stole away to the barn, tacked the paper to the new boards, and was about to depart when her eyes chanced to fall upon her sprawling decorations of the previous day; and she halted, horrified at the glaring scarlet letters. "Mercy! How they look! No wonder Mr. Hartman gave me such a tre – men – jous switching. The paint is still here. I will cover it all up."

The big brush did the work this time, and in a brief period a wide, brilliant stripe of red hid the uneven letters from sight. But somehow Mr. Hartman did not think the barn had been improved very much when he found it, and was wrathfully; setting out in search of the artist when the fluttering paper caught his eye.

"She's a great one for notes," he muttered, jerking the scrawl down, half impatiently, half amused. "What does she say this time? Whew!" Involuntarily he whistled a long-drawn-out whistle, for this is what Peace had written:

> "I ipolijize for painting your barn cause Gale says I otto and anyway I didn't know it was going to look so bad so Ive erased the letters with some more paint but I still feel the same way about the raspberries. Also I hope you don't get your reward in Heaven.
>
> Peace Greenfield.
>
> "P.s. Gale said I should come myself and say this but I thot it was safest to rite as long as youre still mad."

CHAPTER XIV

Peace, the Good Samaritan

Down the sloping hillside browned with the summer sun strolled Peace one afternoon late in August, gathering the purple foxgloves which waved invitingly in the breeze. It was one of those rare days of waning summer, clear, beautiful and cool, with just a hint of autumn haze in the air; and it cast its magic spell over the bare-headed, flower-laden maid, wandering dreamily through the crisp, crackling grass, with no particular destination in view, no particular thought in mind. She had set out an hour before with Cherry and Allee as her companions, but had wandered away from them without being aware of it, and was now some distance from home, still busy pulling the gorgeous stems of bloom, still unconscious of her loneness, still lost in her own realms of fancy.

This Peace was one few people knew. Allee was most familiar with the brown-eyed dream-child, the little family at the parsonage were quite well acquainted with her, and occasionally Gail caught a fleeting glimpse of that hidden spirit, but to the rest of the little world in which she lived she was a bright-eyed, gay-hearted little romp, whose efforts to lend assistance to others were always leading her into mischief, oftentimes with unhappy results.

So it is no wonder that busy Dr. Bainbridge was surprised when he discovered her in this strange mood as he came puffing and panting up the hill toward town, for she was so completely lost amid her dreams that she did not see him nor hear his brusque greeting until he stepped directly in her path and clutched her arm. Then she started as if suddenly awakened from a sleep, and exclaimed, "Why, Dr. Bainbridge, what do you mean by making me jump so? I nearly lost my skin! I never saw you at all. Where did you come from – the clouds?"

"No, miss. If I had been there you would have seen me before this, for if ever anyone was walking in the clouds, it was you just this minute. Come along, I want you, dreamer. Can you do me a favor, a big one?"

"'Pends upon what it is," answered Peace, thoroughly awake now.

He laughed at the judicious tone of voice and the familiar cant of the curly brown head, and answered promptly, "I want you to play Good

Samaritan for a little while, be nurse for one of my patients – "

"Nurse?" She looked at him with wide-open eyes, secretly wondering whether he knew what he was talking about.

"Yes, ma'am, nurse!" he thundered. "Annette Fisher is sick, very sick, and I have told her mother time after time that she must not be left alone, yet in spite of all my cautions, that red-headed ignoramus has taken the rest of the caboodle and gone off to town, leaving Annette all alone in the house until the father gets home tonight. The child's fever has been soaring sky-high for days, and I was just beginning to think I had it in control and could pull her through when that old termagant-gossip of a mother, who doesn't deserve to have chick or child, hikes off to spend the afternoon with relatives in the city for a chance to look up bargains at The Martindale. What are embroideries and dress goods compared with the life of a child? Won't she get a piece of my mind the next time I lay eyes on her?" So angry and indignant was the old doctor that he had wholly forgotten himself, and spoke as he would never have thought of doing under different circumstances.

Peace brought him to the earth by agreeing heartily, "Well, I would 'f I was you, and I'd give her a good big piece, too. I'll nurse Annette if you want me to. Shall I give her a bath and dose her with medicine every few minutes, like we did mother? Does she need to be wrapped up in wet rags or painted with irondye? Or do you want me to feed her grool and broth?"

"You don't have to do a single thing but stay with her and keep her from fretting until I can get someone from the village to go down there. I gave her a bath just now myself, and she has taken her medicine – all I want her to have for the present. She isn't to eat a thing, but she can drink all the milk she wants, and occasionally have a little water if she asks for it. Now remember, Peace. She is too sick to pay attention to much of anything, but sometimes she is fretful and talks a good deal. Try to be as quiet as possible yourself, – don't say things to excite her – don't speak at all unless she wants you to. Do you understand?"

"Yes."

"I'll send someone down to relieve you the minute I can get anyone. Hurry along now, and don't forget what I have said."

"All right," was the cheery response; and Peace, with a curious thrill of awe in her heart, sped down the hill as fast as her nimble feet could carry her.

The door of the Fisher house stood open, so, without knocking to make her presence known, she stepped softly inside the hall, and crept up the stairs to the little, hot chamber, where thin-faced Annette lay burning with fever. The invalid was awake, tossing fretfully among her pillows, but the instant she saw Peace in the doorway her eyes brightened, and she called in a shrill, weak voice, "Is it really you, Peace, or has my head turned 'round again?"

"It's really me. Dr. Bainbridge sent me up."

"That's funny. He wouldn't let you or any of the other girls come when I asked for you before. Did you bring all those flowers for me?"

"Yes," Peace answered readily, glancing down at the huge bouquet in her arms, which she had entirely forgotten. "Where shall I put them? No, don't try to tell me; I'll find a dish myself."

"Would you please bring me a drink, too?" Annette asked hesitatingly.

"Sure!"

"Fresh from the well?"

"Yes."

Peace disappeared down the creaking stairs again, returning quickly with a dripping dipper full of sparkling, ice-cold water from the well, and the sick child drank feverishly, sighing as she relinquished the cup, "That's awful good. If only it would stay cold all the time! But the next time I want a drink it is warm and horrid, and ma says she can't be always chasing to the well just to get me some water. Harry won't, either. Pa ain't here but a little while night and morning, and Isabel is too little to fetch it. Set the flowers here on the chair where I can see them good. When ma comes home she'll likely throw them out. She says she can't see the good of cluttering up the house with dishes of weeds like that."

"Your mother is an old turnacrank, – Doctor says so," muttered Peace indignantly, as she tugged at the heavy jar of foxgloves she had arranged with artistic care.

"What did you say?" asked Annette, querulously.

Peace suddenly remembered the doctor's instructions. "I say I know how to keep water cold. Gail used to do it for mother on hot days. I'll wet a rag and wrap the dipper in that and set it in the window where the wind will blow on it."

"Will that make it keep cool?"

"Yes, as long as the rag is wet. There is quite a little wind today, too, and that helps."

"Is it cool out-doors?"

"Yes."

"Oh, dear! I wish I could go out under the trees. It is so hot in here cooped up like I am."

Peace bit her tongue. How easy it was to forget the doctor's directions! Twice already she had said things which excited the poor, sick prisoner, whom she had been told to keep quiet. A happy inspiration leaped into her thought, and moving the jar of delicate blossoms closer to the bed, she slipped a spray into Annette's hand, saying, "S'pose we minagine these flowers are trees. They would make a lovely forest, wouldn't they? I often wish the trees had pretty flowers."

"Apple trees have," said Annette thoughtfully.

"That's so!" was the surprised ejaculation. "I forgot all about the fruit trees. All of them have flowers, but I like the apple-blossoms best, don't you?"

"Yes, they are so cool looking and so sweet and smelly."

"That's what I like about them most. When I go to the moon I wear a dress made of apple-blossoms and – "

"When you go to the moon?" repeated Annette, looking bewildered and wondering if the queer thoughts which the doctor called delirium were coming back to haunt her again.

"Oh, of course, I really don't go, but I like to s'pose what it would be like if I could go there. After Allee and me go to bed at night, sometimes the moon comes and shines in at our window and we talk to it. I don't care about the man-in-the-moon very much, though Allee likes him. She says he must be so lonely up there by himself all the time that she doesn't see how he can keep on smiling so. But I love the lady in the moon."

"The lady in the moon?"

"Well, we call her the moon lady. We like to think she is a beautiful, beau-ti-ful lady, with long, pale yellow hair that pretty nearly drags when she walks. It would drag if she didn't wear such big tails on her skirts. That's the kind of hair I wish I had instead of kinky, woolly curls. Hers isn't a bit curly, but just falls back from her face like Jennie Munn's after she has had it braided for a long time. And it trails out behind her like a – a cloud. Her dress is white stuff, and she never has it starched; it's just soft and shiny and swishy, and seems to b'long just to her. Oh, she is the prettiest lady, Annette!"

"What color are her eyes?" asked the invalid, much interested in the picture Peace was drawing.

"Blue, just like Hope's, only you don't think of them being blue when you look at the moon lady – they 'mind you of stars. I think they are stars, and she wears a star in her hair."

"Does she have a house to live in?"

"Not a house, but a palace, made of soft-looking, sparkly stones that flash like diamond dust, and inside it is white and still, – the kind of a still that makes you feel dreamy and nice. And there are fountains everywhere, with cool water splashing out of the top of them. They are made of white marble – the fountains are, I mean – and so are the pillows of the palace on the outside, where the moon lady walks in her garden."

"Is there a garden in the moon?"

"In my moon there is, and – "

"Ma says the moon is made of green cheese, and is full of maggots."

"I heard that story, too, and I look for them first thing every time I go there, but I haven't found any yet. Big, white Easter lilies grow along the paths, and lilies-of-the-valley blossom the whole year round, and water lilies make the lake almost white sometimes."

"Oh, a lake, too! How nice!"

"The moon lady's lake is the prettiest I ever saw. The water is always silv'ry, just like our lakes look when the moon shines down on them. You know, Annette, don't you?"

"Yes, the moon was shining one time when I went to Lake Marion with pa to hear the band, and we rowed around in a little boat and listened to the music."

"That's just what the moon lady does when we go to see her, only her boats are green-pea pods, and the sails are apple-blossom petals. We don't have to row; the boats just float of themselves, and we pick water lilies or listen to the music – "

"What kind of music?"

"Oh, sometimes the moon lady sings by-low songs, and sometimes it's just the frogs singing in the bottom of the lake."

"Oh, do you like frogs' croaking?"

"If I have been good I like it awfully well, but if I've made Gail or anyone sorry, I don't want to listen to the frogs, for they keep saying, 'Don't do it again, don't do it again,' till it makes me mis'rable. The frogs in the moon never say such things, though, and I like to listen to them. Sometimes we call across the water to hear the echoes answer; and sometimes we let the moonbeams light on our hands and hair and dresses, and talk to them."

"Talk to the moonbeams? How funny!"

"Why, our moonbeams are lovely little fairies, with wings like dragon-flies, and shiny, silv'ry gowns; and whenever they get tired of flying about they settle down and glow like fireflies. They b'long to the moon lady and are nice fairies. They make sugar stars and moon-ice for us to eat."

Peace clapped her hand abruptly over her mouth. Suppose Annette should ask for something to eat! But the sick child merely held the spray of foxgloves nearer her face and inquired, "What is that? Ice-cream?"

"No; it's shaped like icicles and has kind of a sourish taste, either lemon or strawberry, and it doesn't melt until you get tired of it. Then it's all gone. And it's the same way with moonbeamade. Allee made up that name from lemonade. It is just a heap of foam that tastes like the northwest wind and is cool and nice."

"S'posing things is a queer game, ain't it?" murmured Annette, drowsily.

"It's lots of fun, and sometimes when we go to sleep we dream about them, – the places we visit in the moon and the – "

"The water and lilies and fountains and cool things?"

"Yes, or the mountains, where the fairies and goblins live, or the forests, which belong to the brownies and elves, or the valleys, where the sunbeams play, or the caves, where the wind-voices hide, or – I do b'lieve she's asleep. Yes, sir! Both eyes are tight shut, and she has dropped the foxglove she was holding so hard."

Softly Peace dropped back into her former position upon the floor, hardly daring to breathe for fear of waking the little slumberer, for had not the doctor said she was a very sick child, and that she must be kept as quiet as possible?

At thought of the doctor she began to wonder why he had not sent the woman from the village as he had promised to do. Already the sun was sinking low in the west, and no one had come to watch over the invalid. Perhaps he had forgotten, perhaps someone was dreadfully sick and he had been called away before he could find a nurse for Annette. Perhaps – the brown head nodded gently, the long, dark lashes fluttered slowly over the somber brown eyes, and Peace, too, was fast asleep, curled up against the narrow bed, where the sick child lay in a dreamless, refreshing slumber. The sunset faded from the sky, twilight deepened into dusk, and the stars came out in their pale glory, but both the Good Samaritan and her patient were unconscious of it all.

In the little brown house among the maple trees great anxiety brooded. Peace had not come home with her sisters from their flower-gathering expedition, and no one in town had seen her. The whole neighborhood was aroused, and a search party was just being organized when the doctor's carriage drove up to the gate, and the physician, angry, dismayed and alarmed, hurried up the path as fast as his avoirdupois would permit, flung open the screen and called imperiously, "Miss Gail, girls, any of you! It's all my fault! Peace is down at the Fisher house watching over Annette. I sent her there this afternoon while I went after a woman to stay with the child, and have just this minute heard that Grandma Cole sprained her ankle on the way there and had to crawl back home again. Mrs. Fisher, the big idiot, is moseying up the road now, well satisfied with her bargains. I passed her and her tribe a piece back and stopped long enough to tell her what I thought of her. Now pile in and I'll take you back with me for that little sister of yours."

He had caught up a little shawl from the hat-rack as he talked, and throwing this over Gail's shoulders, he bundled her out of the house and into his buggy before she had recovered from her astonishment at his outburst; and after a moment of furious riding behind the lively bay horse, she found herself stumbling up the dark stairs in the unlighted Fisher house, at the heels of the panting, puffing, wrathy doctor. From somewhere he produced a lamp, and soon the dim rays of light dispelled the gloom of the place, and she stood beside him, looking down into the pale face of Annette asleep among her pillows, and the rosy one of smiling Peace, huddled in an uncomfortable bunch on the floor.

"What a picture!" murmured the doctor huskily, leaning over to touch the damp forehead and feel the pulse of his little patient. "This is the first natural sleep she has had for days. Bully for Peace! I confess I was worried about leaving her here in the first place. I was afraid she would fret Annette into a worse fever than she already had. I'd have gone crazy if I'd had any notion that the child must stay here all the afternoon, with only Peace to look after her. Excuse me if I seem more concerned about Annette's welfare than over Peace's long absence and your fright, Gail. I've had a big battle to pull her through, and I was wild when I found that fool mother had gone off and left her alone. Didn't expect to be gone long, and here it is hours! There, I won't storm any more, but we'll wake Peace up and take her home."

He shook the child gently by the shoulder, and as the sleepy eyes fluttered open they saw only Gail bending over her. "It's all right, Gail," the child said softly, still remembering her charge. "Dr. Bainbridge asked me to be a good sanatarium over Annette while that negrogrampus of a mother was hunting bargains of embroid'ries and he was hunting a sure-enough nurse. Oh, there is the doctor himself! Is Annette all right? She talked a lot at first, but I told her about my moon lady, and pretty soon she went fast asleep."

"Annette is doing splendidly, Dr. Peace, and I am tickled to death at the good work you've done. Run along with Gail now. I'll be down in a minute to drive you home."

CHAPTER XV

Peace Collects Damages

The hot summer was drawing to a close. Two weeks more and September would be ushered in, bringing with it the State Fair, always an event in the lives of the busy farmers of the State, and particularly of those around Martindale and Pendennis, as the fairgrounds were located midway between the two big cities.

Peace had never attended a State Fair in all her short life, but she had heard it talked about so much by the residents of Parker that she was wildly excited when Faith decided to enter a cake in the cooking exhibit, and immediately she determined to visit the Fair in person and see her sister's handiwork fitly rewarded. However, when she made known this decision to the rest of the family Gail said quietly, "I am afraid you can't, dear. It costs fifty cents to enter the grounds, and even if they admit children at half price, that would mean twenty-five cents for each of you three youngest, and Hope would have to pay the full amount, as she is now in her 'teens. We can't afford to go this year."

This was an item that Peace had not considered. Of course, if she went, the rest of the family were entitled to the same pleasure, and that would mean three half dollars and three quarters. She found her slate and laboriously added up the column of figures. "Two dollars and twenty-five cents! Mercy, that is a lot to spend just to go to the Fair for one day, isn't it? Oh, dear, why is it we always have to stop and think about the money? I wish dollars grew on trees, and all we had to do when we wanted any would be to go out and pick them. What fun we'd have! I do want to go to the Fair so much, though. If only there was some way to earn the money!"

She wandered down to the melon patch, the pride of her childish heart, and sat down on one of the green balls to meditate on the subject.

"I never saw the beat how your melons do grow," exclaimed a voice behind her, as Mrs. Grinnell, on her way to the brown house, paused to admire the tempting fruit. "If there was just some way of getting them into the city, you might make a pretty penny off them. Now, mine don't begin to be as big as yours, and there aren't half so many on the vines. That's a whopper you are sitting on. You ought to take it to the Fair – "

"Why, Mrs. Grinnell, do folks take melons to the Fair?"

"Yes, indeed, every year. Why, I've seen lots there that weren't as big as yours. Of course it's the biggest that win the ribbons, and you might not stand a show, but there would be no harm trying. I am intending to enter my two mammoth pumpkins and that Hubbard squash, along with my corn."

"Do you s'pose Gail would let me?"

"Yes, I think so. I'll take it in with mine if you like. I am to lug Faith's cake."

"Oh, then I'll do it! These two whollipers. That one is almost as big as the one I play is my armchair. The rest are too little to have a chance, aren't they? Maybe they will be big enough by Fair time, though. They have two weeks more to grow in."

"No telling what they will do in that time," laughed Mrs. Grinnell, moving briskly away up the path, leaving Peace still perched on top of the largest melon busily making her fortune from her small garden patch.

"If only we hadn't sold Black Prince," she mourned, "we could just cart these melons into Martindale and make a whole lot on them. There, why didn't I think of that before? Mike peddles garden truck in the city, 'most every day. I'll just have him tote these along. I've got – let me see – twelve, sixteen, seventeen, twenty-one good ones, besides my big fellows. I wonder if that will be enough. I'm going right over and see Mike now. He is at home today; I saw him."

She skipped away through the garden to the O'Hara place, some distance below them, and finding the red-haired boy grinding an ax in the dooryard, she startled him by her breathless demand, "How much do watermelons sell for in the city?"

"Shure an' it depinds on the size."

"Mine are great big ones. Mrs. Grinnell says they ought to bring a pretty penny in Martindale."

"Well, thin, I think maybe they'd be bringing a quarter."

"Each one?"

"Shure!"

"And how much would that make if twenty-one were sold?"

"Five dollars and a quarter," promptly answered Mike, who was quick at figures and proud of the accomplishment.

"That would be enough," cried Peace in great glee. "All I need is two dollars and a quarter. Come on over to my house and pick them right away."

"What?" yelled Mike, wondering if the child had gone crazy.

"Oh, I forgot! I haven't told you yet, have I? You can sell my melons in the city for me if you like and save me the trouble."

The boy stared at her, transfixed by her complacent self-assurance.

"Has the cat got your tongue?" Peace asked, when he did not speak.

"No, but you have your nerve," he stuttered. "What d'ye take me for, – a dray horse?"

"You've got a mule team, haven't you?" flared Peace, seeing no occasion for his anger. "And you peddle truck nearly every day. Then I don't see why you can't take my melons and sell them. Black Prince is gone, and we can't drive about any more ourselves."

"Well, where do I come in? Melons take up a sight of wagon room, nothing said of the time it will take to sell them. And then you expict me to do it all for nothing!"

"I – I hadn't thought about that," faltered Peace; and, sitting down on the windmill platform, she pulled a pencil stub from her pocket and began to do some figuring on the sole of her shoe.

Mike watched her serious face in amusement, and grinned broadly when, after five minutes of vigorous scratching and hard thinking, she released her foot and said in her most business-like tones, "I'll tell you what I will do. If you can sell all those twenty-one melons at twenty-five cents each, you can have half the money for your trouble. That will still leave me enough to get our family inside the Fair. Will you do it?"

Mike scratched his head thoughtfully and then replied, "I'll take a look at thim melons first."

So she led him to the small patch and proudly displayed her treasures. "You see there are more than twenty-one melons on the vines. Those two big ones Mrs. Grinnell is going to tote along with her pumpkins to the Fair, and the little ones and the crooked fellers we'll eat at home; but there are twenty-one nice ones to sell."

Mike expressed his admiration by the boyish exclamation, "Gee, ain't them bouncers? How 'd ye do it? Our'n don't amount to shucks this year."

"That's what Mrs. Grinnell said about hers. I guess it's 'cause I know how to grow watermelons," answered Peace, with charming frankness. "Mr. Strong says that must be the reason. You see, I planted sweet-peas and these came up. Maybe it's a sweet-pea melon. Do you s'pose it is?"

"I niver heard tell of such a thing," Mike soberly replied, "but maybe that's what's the matter."

"Will you sell them for me?"

Mike was busy thumping the green balls with his knuckles, and feeling of the stems, and when he had tested each in turn, he answered, "Yis, I'll sell thim for you, but ye'd better wait a week or two. They aren't ripe enough yit."

"Oh, dear," mourned the child, plainly disappointed. "The Fair begins in two weeks, and that is what I wanted the money for. Don't you think they will be ripe enough before that?"

"Don't look as if they would," Mike replied firmly. "And green melons won't sell well. Besides, the longer they grow, the bigger they will be."

"Then I suppose I must wait; but don't you tell the girls. I want to s'prise them if we can go, for they don't think we can."

So, with many promises of secrecy, Mike departed, and Peace from that moment became a devoted slave of the melon patch.

As soon as she was out of bed in the morning she flew down to the garden to exult over her treasures, and with the last gleam of the dying day she might be seen bending over the mottled fruit whispering encouraging messages to them, coaxing them to grow. Bucket after bucket of water she tugged from the well to pour on their thirsty roots, and load after load of fertilizer she dragged in Allee's little cart to spread over the ground in her eager desire to increase their size. But when Gail found her with soap and scrub-brush polishing off each precious ball, she was forced to curb her zealous gardening. However, the vines throve through all this heroic treatment, and it seemed to Peace that she could almost see the fruit grow in circumference. Each night she consulted Mike, convinced that they had ripened sufficiently during the day to be picked, but the boy steadfastly shook his head.

At length, as the second week of anxious waiting was drawing to a close, Peace could endure the suspense no longer, and one warm afternoon, while her sisters were occupied with their various duties, she snatched the sharp bread-knife from the pantry shelf, and with Allee in tow, stole down to her garden plot.

"What are you going to do?" whispered the blue-eyed tot, as if still fearful that she might be overheard at the house.

"Try one of my melons and see if it isn't ripe. This feller will do, I guess. It is big, but not too big." She plunged the shining blade deep into the green rind, and as the two halves fell apart, disclosing the bright red heart thickly dotted with black and white seeds, she cried triumphantly, "There, I knew I was right! Just taste it, Allee. Ain't it sweet and nice? Let's lug it down to the hedge and eat it up."

"That's a piggy," answered the smaller girl, smacking her lips over the delicious morsel.

"We can 'ford to be pigs this once, I guess," Peace retorted. "If we take it up to the house they will want to know why we cut it, and we'll have to tell them about Mike and the Fair. You don't want them to know that, do you?"

"No, but we are too little to eat it all ourselves."

"Half a melon each ain't much. Why, Len Abbott must have eaten two whole ones at the church sociable the other night. Can you carry your half?"

"Yes," panted the younger lass, bravely tugging at her heavy load.

So, with much puffing, and many stops for breath, they dragged the fruit through the cornfield to the creek road, scrambled in behind the dense brush and blackberry vines, and began to dispose of the sweet, juicy center.

"Let's eat one-half all up 'fore we begin the other," proposed Allee, who seemed to have some doubts as to the capacity of her stomach.

"All right," Peace agreed. "The melon does look pretty big, and maybe we can't hold it all at one sitting. I'll push the other half under the bushes and cover my handkerchief over it to keep off the flies. What a lot of seed this one has! Let's save some for planting next year. S'posing each of these seeds was a ticket to the State Fairgrounds, we could all of us go every day and invite everyone else in town, pretty near. Hush! There's a team coming up the road. Let's peek and see if it's anyone we know."

She drew aside the branches as she spoke, and two inquisitive, fruit-stained faces peered out of the opening just as a two-seated carryall drew up by the roadside, and a woman's voice said imperatively, "There is a cluster, Henry, – lovely berries. I thought they were all gone by this time."

Henry leaped over the wheel to the ground, gathered a handful of dust-covered blackberries, and passed them up to the other three occupants of the rig, remarking, "It's a shame we can't find watermelons growing wild along the roadside. I am afraid if we have a melon social at the church tomorrow night we must patronize the groceryman for the fruit."

"I am sorry to have caused you this wild-goose chase," said a meek voice from the back seat. "But last year we drove through this town when watermelon vines were the only things in sight."

"That is everything in sight today," laughed Henry teasingly. "The trouble is, they don't bear any decent fruit. I'd give five dollars if anyone would show me twenty good, fair-sized watermelons – "

"All right, sir!" exclaimed an eager voice at his feet. "Give me the five dollars, and I'll show you twenty-two!"

The man jumped as if shot, the three ladies screamed, and even the horses started at the unexpected sound, or perhaps it was at sight of a tousled brown head wriggling excitedly through the thicket, followed by an equally tousled golden head.

"Well, who are you?" stammered the startled young man, as the children gained their feet and stood shyly eyeing the city folks.

"Two of the Greenfield kids," answered Peace. "We were just trying one of my melons when we heard what you said. We've got some fine ones in our garden, and I'll sell them cheap. They b'long to me. I planted sweet-pea seeds and they came up."

The man roared, the young ladies giggled, and then one of them said sweetly, "Have you some of your melon left so we can see what it is like?"

"Yes," responded Peace, diving into the brush and dragging forth the untouched half, covered with her dirty handkerchief. "Here it is. You can eat it. Allee and me are 'most full now. Oh, it's black with ants! Never mind, just brush them off; they won't change the taste any."

But though the ladies admired the ripe red fruit, they seemed to have no appetite for it, and Henry was the only one of the party who sampled it.

"It's lickum good," he announced, after the first mouthful. "Better have some, girls. No? Well, I shall lug this piece back with us for refreshments. Say, Curly-locks, are all your melons as big as that?"

"Bigger – that is, most of them are. Mrs. Grinnell is going to take two in to the Fair, but there are twenty-one big ones besides. I mean twenty. This is the twenty-oneth."

They laughed again, and Henry proposed, "Let's go over and see them anyway. If we can't find the melons, we can have a good time today at least."

"Just as you say," chorused the girls; and bundling the soiled, sticky children into the carriage with them, they drove on to the little brown house.

As the team drew up in front of the gate the group of workers on the porch started to their feet in surprise, but Peace called, "Go on with your sewing! This is my company! They are going to look at my twenty watermelons to see if they are any good; and then I am going to charge them five dollars for them."

The laughing young people came up the walk to meet the embarrassed mistress of the house, and the situation was briefly explained. "Our League is planning for a lawn social tomorrow night," said one young lady.

"Ice-cream and cake," added the second.

"With watermelons for a side-dish," the young man put in.

"And we thought we could get better melons if we came out here in the country to buy them," said the fourth member of the party.

"The melon patch belongs to Peace," Gail told them. "We think she has some pretty good fruit. Come this way and see for yourself."

"Oh, what big ones!" cried the visiting quartette. "Surely you won't sell all these for five dollars?"

"No, only twenty," answered Peace gravely. "You can't have the two biggest ones, and of course you don't want the crooked fellers. Mike says they will sell for twenty-five cents each in Martindale."

So the twenty splendid melons were cut and loaded into the wagon, Peace was paid a spandy new five-dollar bill, and the visitors departed merrily. The child watched them out of sight, still holding fast to her money, and then turned to Gail, sighing contentedly, "Now we can go to the Fair! I've had an awful job getting rid of those things, but they are gone at last, and here is the money. I 'xpect Mike will be mad as hops, but he didn't know beans when he said they weren't ripe. I've raised melons enough so I know."

"But, dearie," interrupted the oldest sister, "you mustn't spend your money so recklessly for our pleasure. It will take almost half of that five dollars just to pay our way into the grounds, and another dollar for carfare."

"Then it's lucky Mike didn't sell the melons for me," said Peace, "or I 'xpect we'd have had to walk. I sold those watermelons just so's we all could go to the Fair, Gail, and now you mustn't say no."

"Then I won't," suddenly whispered the tired mother-sister, seeing the longing in the somber brown eyes, and realizing the child's unselfish love. "When is Mrs. Grinnell to take your big melons away?"

"Tomorrow," she said. "The Fair begins Monday, you know."

"Then you better go say good-bye to them now," teased Faith. "It is nearly supper time, and you will hardly have a chance in the morning."

But Peace shook her head, declaring seriously, "There will be time enough. And if the melons don't win a prize, we'll bring them back home, Mrs. Grinnell says."

When the morning dawned, however, and Peace ran eagerly down to visit her garden, she stopped in dismay at the sight which greeted her eyes. On the ground, strewn all over the patch, were broken, battered melon-rinds; and the two mammoth balls were gone.

"Oh, my darlings! my precious melons!" she cried in grief. "Someone has eaten them all up!" Throwing herself flat amid the wreck, she sobbed as if her heart would break, so overwhelmed by her loss that it never occurred to her to report the disaster to the rest of the family. It was too cruel!

When the hot tears had relieved the little heart somewhat, she sat up and looked about her once more, saying, with quivering lips, "I don't s'pose they would have won a prize anyway, but it was hatefully mean of whoever took them. I'll bet Mike O'Hara did it to get even with me for selling the others to the city folks and keeping all the money myself! I'm going straight over and tell him what a nice kind of a gentleman he is."

She bounced to her feet, started swiftly across the patch, caught her toe in a tough vine and fell sprawling on the ground again, rapping her head smartly on a small, unripe melon at the edge of the field. "Mercy! you're a hard-shelled old sinner!" she exclaimed, rubbing her bruised forehead and glaring at the offending fruit. "Well, no wonder! I hit a knife, as sure as you're alive! It ain't Mike's either. It's – Hector Abbott's! Why didn't I think of him before? Of course he is the culvert; but I'll bet he will wish he hadn't seen those melons when I get through with him."

Burning with indignation, she sped away to the village, never pausing until the Judge's house was reached. As she approached the place she could see the family gathered around the breakfast table, set on the wide, screened porch; and forgetting to knock, she threw open the door and rushed in as if on the wings of the wind. Straight to Hector's chair she stalked, and before the surprised family could recover their breath, she clutched the unhappy youth by the hair and jerked him out of his seat, crying accusingly, "Hec Abbott, you disgraceful son of a judge! You stole my melons, my State Fair melons! You can't say you didn't, 'cause

I've found your knife in the garden! I s'pose it walked there, didn't it? Well, maybe it did, but you walked it! You can just settle for damages this very minute!"

By this time the Judge had found his tongue, and loosening the angry fingers from his youngest son's luxuriant topknot, he demanded of Peace, "What do you mean by such actions? Where are your manners? Why didn't you knock? Who brought you up?"

"Why didn't Hec knock when he came for my melons last night? Where are his manners? What did he mean by such actions? You brung him up!"

Len Abbott choked over his coffee, Cecile hid her face in her napkin, and even the anxious mother smiled, but the Judge looked more ruffled than abashed, and he fairly thundered, "How do you know the knife is Hector's?"

"Don't you s'pose I have seen it enough to know whose it is? Didn't I grab it from him the day he pretended to cut off Lola Hunt's ears? I cut his hand, too, but he deserved it! He's the meanest boy at school next to Jimmy Jones. Teacher took the knife away one time when he was skinning a frog, and I saw it then. Anyway, it's got his name on it, – not just his 'nitials, but his whole name. And there it is!"

She held out the article for the Judge's inspection, and that worthy gentleman, seeing the look of guilt in his small son's face, pocketed it, saying whimsically to the wrathful accuser, "That is merely circumstantial evidence. He might yet be innocent of the charge."

"He might," Peace retorted grimly; "but he ain't! Ask him!"

The Judge turned gravely to the crimson-cheeked lad and asked severely, "Son, are you guilty or not guilty?"

"Guilty," muttered the miserable culprit.

"Didn't I tell you?" triumphed the girl.

"What would you recommend as his sentence?" asked the Judge.

"Sentence?" repeated Peace, with the uncomfortable feeling that she was being laughed at.

"Punishment, I mean."

"A good, sound thrashing that ain't all show and no hurt," was the harsh verdict.

"Very well! I will administer it now. Len, hand me that strap. Hector, come here!"

Leonard passed the strap to his father, the younger son shuffled across the porch to receive his sentence, and Peace stood breathlessly by, watching with frightened eyes. The Judge raised the strip of leather and brought it down with a resounding thwack across the boy's legs. He squirmed, let out a wild yell, and began to blubber. The strap rose and fell the second time, there was a second yell, and Peace, with blazing eyes and blanched face, flew in between man and boy, snatched the upraised strap and flung it clear across the room, screaming in fierce indignation, "Don't you touch him again! You're a pretty kind of a judge! Aren't you ashamed of yourself?"

"You sentenced him yourself," stammered the surprised man.

"Well, I'll let him off this time," she replied slowly, "but he will have to pay for those melons."

"How much?"

"A dollar each."

"Whew! They are pretty expensive fruit, aren't they?"

"I've put more'n a dollar's worth of trouble into getting them ready for the Fair, and now he's et up my blue ribbon."

"Your blue ribbon?"

"Yes, maybe those melons would have won a blue ribbon. Now I'll never know."

"Well, well, that's too bad," sympathized the amused Judge. "Hector will have to pay for them, surely. Son, go get the money out of your bank."

"I didn't eat all of them. Jimmy Jones and Ted Fenton and the Beldon boys helped," said Hector, wiping his eyes sullenly.

"You can c'lect from them later," retorted Peace. "You were at the head of it, I know."

"Get the money, son," repeated the father sternly, and the unhappy boy thought it wise to obey without further demur.

When the two silver dollars were laid in her hand Peace smiled her relief, and with a curt "Thank you," turned to go, when to the utter amazement of the whole family, she whirled suddenly about and confronted Hector again, saying calmly, "While I am here, I might as well c'lect for that cake you stole more'n a year ago."

"Cake?" echoed the group, while the boy's face grew scarlet with guilt once more.

"Yes, cake! We thought my tramp took it at first. Faith made it for the minister's reception and put it on the wash-bench under a dishpan to cool. 'Twas gone when she went to get it again. Hec stole it."

"Hector, did you?"

The boy nodded, too miserable to speak.

"How much was that worth, Peace?"

"It was bigger'n a fifty-cent one. I guess it will be seventy-five cents."

"Get your bank and settle your account, Hector."

And once more the boy was forced to obey.

"There!" breathed Peace, closing her fingers over the added coins. "I guess we are square now. I just happened to think of the cake. Isn't it lucky I did? I wasn't quite sure he took it, but seeing that my tramp didn't do it, I knew it must be someone in town, and I couldn't think of anyone else mean enough. Good-bye!"

She ran lightly down the steps and away toward home, chanting to herself, "He had to pay up, he had to pay up!" Suddenly she halted by the roadside and listened. "Yes, sir! That's Hec a-howling! I guess the Judge got hold of that strap again. Well, he deserves a good licking, but I'm glad I'm not there to see him dance."

CHAPTER XVI

The State Fair Cake

"What are you doing with all that torn-up paper, Peace?" asked Allee, finding her sister busy stripping old papers into tiny shreds up in the barn loft, after she had searched all over the place for her.

"I want to make a map like Hope's class had to," answered Peace, pouring an apronful of scraps into a bucket of scalding water. "I asked her how she did it, and she said they drew the maps first, and then mixed up a lot of blotters in boiling water. I hunted all over the place for blotters, and couldn't find but four, so I'm trying these newspapers. They make an awful looking mess, but I guess they will work. You can tear paper if you want to."

Allee took the hint, and accepting the magazine Peace offered her, she fell to pulling it to pieces, adding her mite to the mixture in the pail. "How many must you have?" she ventured to ask, after an hour at this monotonous occupation.

"I guess this will be enough," answered the older girl, critically examining the nasty mess, and stirring it so energetically that a goodly portion of it flew out of the bucket into her lap.

"Have you drawn a map?" Allee inquired, looking around the dingy loft in quest of such an article.

"No – o, I can't seem to get a good one. The first time I tried, it looked like an elephant with two trunks, and the second time the Mississippi River came out of the middle of Florida. In this last picture, the land is so fat there isn't any room for the ocean. But I found two old g'ographies in that heap of trash, and Gail said I could have them. So I've pulled out all the maps of the United States that I could find, and now I'm ready to cut them out. Then we'll paste them onto that board and stick the paper mush on top."

"Why do you want so many all alike?" asked the inquisitive little sister, watching the shining scissors snip in and out around capes and peninsulas with painstaking care. "I should think you would make a c'lection of different maps like Hope has in her book."

Peace paused to consider the suggestion, and then answered, "Well, that's something I hadn't thought about. It would be better to have them all different, wouldn't it? I'll just hunt up some others that aren't alike. This United States one is too small, then; but maybe we can use it for something else. I'll finish cutting it out anyway, though we'll want the biggest we can get for our paper mush."

She finished snipping it out as carefully as she could in view of the many ragged coasts of our country, and laid it aside, while she chose another larger one to be honored with the "paper mush" covering. It took a long time to complete all the maps selected – Europe, Asia, Africa, the Americas, and Australia – but at last they were finished; and Allee, the patient, joined in the sigh of satisfaction which escaped Peace's lips as she dropped the scissors from her cramped, tired hands.

"Now we'll stick on the mush. Hold this map, Allee, so's it won't wiggle." She daubed on a great handful of the dirty gray pulp and tried to smooth it over the colored map surface, but evidently the paper had not soaked long enough, for it still held its own shape, and refused utterly to form the paste Peace had watched Hope handle with such ease and success.

"It doesn't stay very well, does it?" remarked Allee.

"No, it doesn't!" snapped Peace in exasperation. "I shall not bother with it any more. I'm tired of fooling with it when it acts like that. I'll throw it out and play with my corncob doll this morning."

"Are you going to throw away all these nice maps that you have cut out, too?" asked Allee, as the angry girl flung down the wet newspaper scraps and started for the house.

Peace paused, surveyed the gorgeously colored heap which she had spent so long a time in preparing, and answered, "Well, I'll keep them awhile, for maybe some day we may want them again." Gathering them up, she descended the ladder and marched off toward the kitchen, thoroughly out of patience with the whole world and with herself in particular.

Through the open windows and door came savory smells of something cooking, and she quickened her steps, sniffing the air and saying, "Faith has been baking; maybe there are some dishes to lick. I wonder if she made any frosting. Mrs. Lacy always wants caramel, and I just love that."

"Faith's cross like you are," warned Allee, following in her sister's steps, nevertheless.

"Cakes always make her cross," answered Peace, ignoring her share of the compliment. "Gail says it makes her nervous thinking p'r'aps the oven will be too hot or too cool, or the dough not just right, or something. But Faith hardly ever gets so cross that she won't let us clean out the pans."

They entered the room in search of the cooking dishes it was so often their privilege to scrape, but the warm kitchen was in spick and span order, with nothing of the kind in sight; and Allee suggested hopefully, "Maybe they are in the pantry."

"And maybe Faith is, too," whispered Peace, cautiously opening the door and peeping within. "No, she ain't, but she has made four big cakes. My! Don't they look fine? One choc'late loaf, two caramel layers, and one white square one. Looks like a graveyard with them all set even in a row, doesn't it? There ought to be three frosting pans to lick."

"I don't see a single any," remarked Allee, poking into every nook and cranny in hope of finding their treat. "I guess she licked them all herself."

"That's too mean of her," cried Peace, joining in the hunt with no better success. "She could have saved those dishes for us as well as not. What have you found?"

Allee at that moment had unearthed two mysterious little packages, and in trying to investigate one of them, she dropped it, and the bag's contents were scattered all over the floor.

"Candies!" gasped Peace. "Sh! Don't cry! I'll help you pick them up. They must be for Minnie Eastman's birthday cake. I s'pose that is the white frosted one. The candies aren't hurt a mite, Allee. Stop snivelling. Let's see what is in that other sack. Sugar, green sugar! Looks poison, doesn't it? But it tastes all right. Oh, see what I've done! My little United States map fell right on top of the white cake."

"It fits, too," gulped tearful Allee. "Looks as if it b'longed there."

"It's going to b'long!" cried Peace with sudden decision. "I shall trace around it with this pointed knife and then fix it up like Hope does her paper mush maps. See, the frosting is soft enough to work easy."

"You better not," Allen protested. "Faith might not like it."

"Faith's tickled to death when she can find some new way of dec'rating her cakes, and as this is Minnie's birthday cake she'll be awfully pleased, 'cause she got the highest mark in geography of anyone in their room, Hope says."

As she talked, she wielded the sharp knife with surprisingly good results in tracing the ragged outlines of the map in the soft icing, and even critical Allee was charmed when the paper was lifted, disclosing the knife marks. "You have to put all those blue lines in, too, don't you?" she asked. "How can you do that?"

Peace pondered. "Those are rivers and these brown smudges are mountains. I asked Hope once. They all ought to go in, but I'm afraid I can't draw straight enough. Oh, I know what I'll do. Mrs. Strong uses pin-pricked patterns for stamping Glen's dresses. I'll try that." Carefully, laboriously, she pricked in the rivers, mountains and state boundaries, mistaking the latter for railroads; and then drew back to survey her work.

"The pin marks don't show much, do they?" ventured Allee.

"No, but I shan't leave them there anyway – not alone. We'll cover the railroads with these colored candies, and the rivers we'll make of green sugar. They are blue on the map, but green and blue ain't much different, anyway. We'll jam down the ocean and cover that with green, too. These curly choc'late candies will make good mountains, and by heaping up the frosting we dug out of the ocean we'll have islands and lighthouses. Now, ain't that elegant?"

"Oh, my precious State Fair cake!" cried a dismayed voice behind them, and before either guilty decorator could face the angry sister, they were seized firmly by the shoulders, jerked through the doorway, vigorously shaken, each dealt a smart blow across their ears, and left dazed and tearful in the middle of the kitchen, while the avenger rushed sobbing upstairs.

Neither culprit had recovered her breath when Gail was upon them, not the gentle sister they were accustomed to seeing, but a stern, indignant, justice-dealing judge.

"Peace Greenfield," she said severely, "what have you done? Ruined the cake Faith has taken such pains with for the Fair!"

"I – I thought it was Minnie's birthday cake. I – I just dec'rated it."

"Just decorated it! What for? What business had you to touch it? That was pure mischief and nothing else. She intended making a spray of roses and green leaves on that cake and now you've spoiled it. Go sit down in your little chairs and stay there until noon. For fear you will forget about staying there, I shall tie you in."

"Oh, Gail, as if we were little kids!"

"That is what you are when you meddle with things that don't belong to you. I have talked until I am tired. You don't pay a bit of attention, so I must punish you some other way. Next time I shall send you to bed. Perhaps I better do that today."

"Oh, Gail," sobbed miserable Peace, "I didn't mean to be bad, truly! I thought Faith would like some new way to dec'rate her cakes. I – please don't send us to bed! I'm awful sorry! Allee isn't to blame! She tried to make me leave it alone, didn't you, Babe?"

"Yes," hiccoughed the equally penitent, but loyal young sinner, "and then I helped dig up the rivers and pile on the mountains!"

Gail's face relaxed a little; a great tenderness for these little orphan sisters swept through her heart, and she felt herself relenting. Then Faith's tragic despair rose before her inner vision again, and she hardened her heart, drew out some stout cord from the cupboard drawer, and tied the humiliated duet into their rickety, worn-out old rockers, leaving them to their unhappy thoughts while she went back to her work upstairs.

For a long time, it seemed to them, they sat jogging back and forth in the warm kitchen, mournfully dabbing their eyes and sniffing tearfully. Then Peace sat up, drew a deep, quivering breath, and said decisively, "I'm going to take that cake over to Mrs. Grinnell's – "

"Gail said we had to stay here until noon," quavered Allee.

"She said we had to sit in these chairs till then," Peace corrected.

"Well, that's the same thing. How can you go over to Mrs. Grinnell's and stay in your chair?"

"Easy enough. I'll take it along. Gail didn't tie our hands."

Allee gasped. "But you can't carry the cake, too!"

"I'll put the cake in the big egg basket and you'll take hold on one handle and I the other. That will leave us each a free hand to hold onto our chairs with."

"Oh!"

"Will you do it?"

"Course."

With some difficulty they rose to their feet, made their way into the pantry once more and found the market basket; but it was another task to get the heavy cake into it, and they were almost in despair, when Peace's fertile mind found a solution to the problem.

"It's 'cause my chair keeps slipping that I can't do it," she said, after several vain attempts to lift the cake. "I have only one hand to pick this heavy thing up with. Stick this piece of string through the back of my chair, Allee, and I'll tie it to the arms in front. There, that makes straps and holds the chair better. It cuts into your shoulders, though, doesn't it? Never mind, it won't be so bad when we get started and can hold onto the chairs. Are you ready? Don't make any noise, for Gail mustn't hear us."

Slowly, cautiously, they tiptoed across the kitchen floor, let themselves out, and with wildly beating hearts hurried, as fast as the bumping chairs tied to their backs would permit, toward the tiny red cottage where Mrs. Grinnell lived all alone. Owing to their burdens, they made slow progress, and both conspirators expected any moment to hear Gail in pursuit. But it chanced that the busy housekeeper was too much occupied in the front chambers to discover their absence, and they reached the red house all out of breath, but without a mishap.

"For the land sakes!" cried the plump, motherly woman, upsetting a pan of apples in her surprise. "What are you young ones playing now?"

"This isn't exactly a play," Peace answered. "We've spoiled Faith's State Fair cake and now she ain't going to send it. I thought maybe you could tell us some way to fix it up." She set down the basket, lifted the paper covering and disclosed the queer, geographical decorations to the woman's astonished gaze.

"Well, now, if that ain't the cutest!" exclaimed the worthy lady in genuine admiration. "Who'd ever have thought of putting the United States on a cake top but you, Peace Greenfield!"

"I never thought of it," answered the child honestly. "The map fell there, it fitted and I scratched it in. Now it is spoiled for the Fair and Faith is bawling her eyes out."

Mrs. Grinnell looked keenly at the two sober, tear-stained faces before her, guessed the rest of the story, and rubbed her chin thoughtfully. Then she laughed in childish delight. "Why, I've got the finest scheme, you ducklings! We will just do a little juggling, and I think Faith will stand a better chance for the blue ribbon than she would with this white cake."

"What do you mean?" faltered puzzled Peace.

"Just this: I ordered a caramel layer of Faith for a little supper some of my people in the city are intending to give a niece of mine and her beau. They are to be married next week. She is a school teacher, and this cake will tickle her immensely. I'll just trot this in for the supper, and we'll take the caramel layer to the Fair. According to my notion of thinking, Faith's caramel cakes beat her others all hollow."

"But – but – the caramel cakes haven't any red candy roses and green leaves on them," stammered Peace.

"They don't need them," said Mrs. Grinnell, scornfully. "Goodness knows they are pretty enough plain, and as for taste – they are the finest I ever ate, and I used to be a pretty good cake-maker myself when the children were at home and my husband living. Now, not a word to Faith about this. Don't even tell Gail unless you have to. You better scamper for home now before you are missed."

So they shambled back to the close kitchen, with the chairs still bumping and rubbing at every step, and were safely settled in their corner once more before Gail had finished her Saturday sweeping and dusting above. When she came downstairs to prepare their simple lunch and found the geographical cake missing from the pantry shelf, she thought Faith had disposed of it in some way, and consequently asked no questions, but released the sorry little sinners from their chairs, gave them their dinner and sent them off to play.

When red-eyed Faith put in appearance late that afternoon, ready to deliver the other three cakes to her customers, she looked stealthily about for the ruined white mound, and not finding it, decided that Gail had hid it until her heavy disappointment should have eased somewhat; and she, too, asked no questions.

At first she refused to accompany the sisters on their visit to the fairgrounds, but Peace's bitter misery softened her heart, and she went, though still too sorely grieved to enjoy much of the gay scenes and beautiful exhibits. However, all day long she studiously avoided the building where the cooked food was on exhibition, though Peace was wild to investigate its mysteries, and even Gail tried to persuade her to enter. Late in the afternoon, just as the oldest sister was proposing that they start for home, Cherry caught sight of a familiar figure entering the Horticultural Building, and raced after her with a yell of recognition, "Mrs. Grinnell, Mrs. Grinnell, we are all here!"

"Well, well," exclaimed the woman, smiling into the flushed face at her elbow, "this is great luck. Come, all of you! I have found something I want you to see. You, most of all, Faith."

She led them down one street and up another, into a white doorway before any of them had a chance to discover the name of the building, through a maze of aisles and a surging throng of weary sightseers, and paused in the cake department, pointed toward a blue-ribbon cake in one case, and said triumphantly, "Peace's geography cake was the hit of the evening last Saturday, but it took the caramel layer to win the prize, Faith!"

CHAPTER XVII

The Circus and the Missionary

"Oh, look, Allee! See the elephants and lions and giraffes and zebras on that poster. It's the cirkis as sure as I'm alive! Do you know I've always wanted to see the cirkis, and this is the first time I ever knew one to stop at Parker."

"How do you know it will stop here?" asked skeptical Allee, who was just beginning to read, and found the long words on the billboard too much for her to master.

"'Cause it says so. Parker, the eighteenth, Allee. Just think, that's only next Saturday! Just a week from today! Isn't it lucky it's on Saturday? Do you s'pose we can go?"

"I 'xpect it will take money for that just like it does for everything else," answered the blue-eyed baby with a comically philosophical air; "and you know Gail never has any for such things as that."

"Well, this is cheaper than most things, 'cause it says 'a-dults twenty-five cents, and children fifteen cents.' The Fair cost half a dollar for a-dults and twenty-five cents for children. If there is a chance to go to anything cheap, we better try hard to go, Allee, for that doesn't happen often."

"Maybe Gail might not like to have us go even if we could get the money."

"She does have some queer notions about places, doesn't she? At first she didn't want us to see that moving picture show at the church, but when Brother Strong went and took us, she thought it was all right. We'll ask about the cirkis before we tell her that it's coming, and maybe we can find out that way whether she would let us go."

"I don't think we would have to ask much, 'cause she thinks cirkises are bad, and I don't b'lieve she would like to have us there."

"What makes you so sure? I never have heard her say a thing about them."

"She told Hope so the time Hope wanted to see 'Julio and Romiet' when they studied it in school."

"That wasn't a cirkis, that was a theatre, Allee. That's different. It takes painted people to play out the words in the theatre, but at the cirkis only real animals act, and do tricks that take brains to learn. Why, this picture shows a nelephant beating a drum. Now, elephants live in the jumbles of Africa, Hope says, and they don't have drums to beat there. Hunters go to their houses and catch them and teach them how to drum, 'cause they have brains enough to learn. Look at that lion with its mouth open and that woman with her head chucked clear inside. She must like to be licked better'n I do. It makes me shiver when Towzer sticks his big, hot tongue on my face. Ugh! S'posing the lion should shut his mouth and bite her head off, what do you guess she'd do?"

"I guess they'd have to get another woman for the lion," answered Allee. "I don't b'lieve those animals really do those things, do you, Peace?"

"Yes, I do. Why, that book of natural history that Hector lent us after he got licked for stealing the melons tells about the way hunters train them to act in cirkises. I'd like to see them awfully much myself."

"Then let's ask Gail. She might have a little spare money."

"No, I don't think she would. We'll have to earn the money ourselves, but I'm afraid she won't want us to go. That's what is bothering me. I tell you what let's do. We'll earn the money first and buy our tickets, and then I'm sure she will let us go. Shall we?"

"Maybe that would be the best way. But how'll we earn the money? It's only a week from now, you said yourself, and that won't leave us much time to do anything, 'specially as school keeps 'most all day long. There ain't any strawberries to pick or blackberries to sell or snow to sweep or – "

"Let's give a nentertaimnent in our barn like Hec and the boys did last week in their carriage-shed. They charged a cent apiece, and earned more'n a quarter, Hec told me. And I know we could give a better entertainment than they did. You could sing and Cherry could speak. Perhaps we could coax Hope to read to us. She does it splendidly, though usu'ly she thinks she's too big to play with us any longer. I am pretty sure Hec would turn summersets for us. He has been quite respectable since that last licking the Judge gave him. Jimmy Jones would likely play the bones for us, too, if Hec asked him to. They don't make a pretty noise, but it's a sight to see his hands fly. Tessie is learning the fiddle and I know she'd be glad to show off, and so would Effie, if we could get our organ out into the barn."

"And you can whistle," put in Allee, all excitement as Peace unfolded her brilliant plan. "You sound just like the birds, and Gail said only the other night that you did better than lots of people who have taken lessons. But do you s'pose she will let us have the organ? Do you s'pose she'll even let us have the barn? It is in an awful clutter, and I don't see where we could put the people who come."

"I was wondering about that myself, but it won't do any harm to ask. There is Hec. We can find out from him right away if he will be one of our show."

"Shall you tell him about the cirkis?"

"No, not a word. We'll have that as just a secret among our two selves until we see how much money we can earn. See?"

"Yes."

"Don't you tell a soul!"

"Of course I won't!"

"Hector, wait a minute! We want to see you. Say, will you be in a nentertainment me and Allee are getting up in our barn?"

The boy looked somewhat surprised at this request, for Peace had been very slow in accepting his friendly advances, though he had showered her with every possible attention ever since the day of the double tragedy in their breakfast room, owing to certain forceful remarks made by his irate parent. Here was an opportunity not to be disregarded, but with a great show of indifference, he leisurely faced the two conspirators, and lazily drawled out, "What kind of an entertainment?"

"One to make a little money," Peace answered briefly.

"What for?"

"'Cause I need it," was the very satisfactory reply.

"How much do you expect to make?"

"You said you got more'n a quarter, didn't you?"

"Yep. Twenty-eight cents."

"Then I think we ought to get more'n fifty cents, 'cause we mean to have a good program."

Hector felt as if a dash of cold water had suddenly struck his face, but he was quite accustomed to Peace's characteristics by this time, so did not resent her implied doubtful compliment, but asked, with somewhat more of interest in his manner, "Who's going to be in it?"

"Tessie and Effie and Cherry and Allee – "

"And Peace is to whistle," put in the small cherub with sisterly loyalty.

"Aw, a girls' crowd! There ain't any boys in it."

"You'll make one if you will turn summersets. And we thought you might get Jimmie to play the bones for us, and p'r'aps Lute Dunbar might bring over his accordian. I b'lieve Mike O'Hara would speak that Irish piece of his that makes folks laugh so much, and maybe we could get the minister to stand on his head. He does that elegant. Whenever I visit there, that's the first thing I ask him for, and he nearly always does it, too."

"Whoop-ee!" shouted Hector, turning a handspring. "I know a boy that stands on his head, and he will do it any time I ask him to. Mr. Strong prob'ly wouldn't in front of a big crowd like you'd have in your barn. The Sherrars are coming down from Martindale Monday to stay a whole week with us, and Victor plays the cornet to beat the band. He's a little bigger'n us, but he will do anything for Cecile, and I'll get her to ask him. What'll you do for chairs at your place?"

"I don't know," Peace confessed. "Maybe Gail won't even let us have the barn, but I think she will. We must give it this week, before next Saturday, I mean, 'cause that's the time we have to have the money – " She stopped abruptly, fearing that he would guess her secret, but he showed no trace of suspicion, so with freer breath she continued, "I'm going home now and see Gail. I think Wednesday or Thursday after school would be the best time, don't you? Then if it should rain, we would still have another day left before Saturday. It won't take us long to get ready, seeing we each do our part all alone."

"Yes," agreed Hector, with unusual readiness, "I think Wednesday will be all right, and I'll get up the tickets for you."

"Goody! You might get them ready while I go see Gail. I'll be right back."

She and Allee disappeared up the road in a cloud of dust and Hector repaired to his home to manufacture the bits of cardboard necessary for admission to the wonderful entertainment. It was an hour later that Peace appeared at the Judge's door and asked to see the young gentleman of the house, but it required no words from her to tell him that her errand had been fruitless.

"She won't let you give the entertainment!" he said, the instant he saw her woe-begone face.

"She doesn't care about the entertainment at all, but she won't let us have the barn, and here I've been and asked Effie and Tessie and Mike, and they all promised to take part. Oh, dear! I did want that money so bad!"

"Are you sure Gail won't care if you give the entertainment?" Hector stood in considerable awe of the big girls at the little brown house, and he wanted to run no risks in the daring plan his own brain had suddenly evolved.

"No, she doesn't care a single speck. She said we could give it in the orchard, but then anyone could come and look on without having to pay a cent, and I can't get my money at all."

"Yes, you can. We will give the entertainment in our carriage-shed if you'll divide the money with me, Peace. Course if I furnish the building I've a right to part of the money."

"But half is quite a lot," demanded the girl with some hesitation. "See, I've got to make at least thirty cents for Allee and me, and I wanted fifteen cents more for Cherry."

"We could have Cecile's old organ in the shed," said Hector, ignoring her objections for the moment; "and there is a big lantern hanging from the roof, so we could light it if it got dark before we were through. We had better light it anyway, I guess, and draw the curtains so no one outside can see. Then everyone who wants to hear the program will have to buy a ticket. If we get up such a swell entertainment, Peace, it is worth more'n a cent. Let's charge two for a nickel; then if we can get fifty people to come it will give us each quite a neat little pile out of it. What do you say?"

"I – don't – think – many folks would buy at such a high price," said Peace, doubtfully, though the picture he drew was very alluring.

"Why, of course they will for such a bang-up program as we'll give them. Mamma and Cecile and Mrs. Sherrar and Frances will go; and Nancy and Marie, the girls. That makes six right there. Of course we can't charge Victor anything if he takes part. I bet Miss Truesdale would buy a ticket, too. You ask her, or get Allee to. Allee is in her room now. The minister and his family are coming over some night for dinner while the Sherrars are here, and I'll get mamma to invite them Wednesday, and you tell them to come early enough for the program. They'll be glad to. Mr. Strong was here the day we boys had our time in the carriage shed, and he clapped and stamped the loudest of anyone."

"Have you written the tickets yet?"

"No, just cut them."

"Well, that's good. We'll charge a nickel for two tickets, and give it in your shed next Wednesday. Get to work now. I've just thought of Montie Fry and his trick dog, and Dick Sullivan and his mouth-organ. I am going right over and see if they will take part."

She was as good as her word, and when the following Wednesday afternoon arrived it would have been hard to tell which was the largest, the audience in the carriage shed, or the company of participants arranged on the platform which Leonard had built for just such gatherings; but every one of the fifty tickets had been sold, and late arrivals had to present cash, at the door, where Hector presided.

The program, was certainly original and varied, if somewhat lengthy, and the audience was kept in a thrill of expectation from one number to the next, for Peace was a master hand at arranging her numbers, and instinctively had saved the best for the last. Just as she herself had taken her place in front of the motley gathering to give an exhibition of her whistling, the big door swung noiselessly, and the company from the great house arrived in a body, – the Judge's wife and daughter, their guests, the Sherrars, and the minister and his small family. They looked very much surprised to find the place crowded to its utmost capacity, but were even more astonished when, after a preliminary bar or so on the mouth-organ, Dick Sullivan began softly to play The Blue-bells of Scotland, and Peace's red lips took up the melody, whistling with beautiful accuracy and clearness, trilling through measure after measure with bird-like notes, following all of Dick's variations, and adding a few of her own under the inspiration lent by the presence of her beloved friends.

"Cecile," exclaimed her friend Frances, "why didn't you tell me you had such a genius in your midst? I'd have been out here the first one to hear the whole program. Why, she looks like an angel, and her whistling is divine. Who is she?"

"Peace Greenfield," answered Cecile, almost too amazed for speech, for this was the first time she herself had ever heard the young whistler. "Father calls her the dearest little nuisance in town. She is one of the most original pieces I ever saw in my life – always into mischief, and always trying to help someone. But truly, I had no idea she could whistle like that. Mr. Strong, what do you think of it?"

"She is doing splendidly!" he whispered enthusiastically. "She is a regular genius at it. Why, a year ago she came to me and begged me to teach her."

"So she is a pupil of yours?" asked Mrs. Sherrar, as much enchanted with the musician as were her young people.

"Not exactly. I helped her what I could, but I think most of the credit belongs to Mike O'Hara and the birds in the woods. He set her to imitating them; and she is an apt mimic, you will find. Clap with all your might."

The very rafters rang with the applause of the enthusiastic audience, as the small whistler took her seat among her mates on the platform, and she was forced to give another selection, and a third. Allee came to her aid in the fourth, and sang to a whistled accompaniment, but the applause was more tremendous and insistent than before; and poor, weary Peace rose to her feet for the fifth time, but instead of pouring forth the torrent of melody they expected, she faced the audience belligerently, and cried in exasperation, "My pucker is tired out and my throat aches. Do you 'xpect me to stand here all night? Victor Sherrar will play on his cornet now and then you can go home."

"Mamma," whispered Frances, while her brother was rendering the closing number of the program, "I simply must have those two tots at my party next week. They will be a novelty and everyone is sure to like them. Cecile thinks I can borrow them all right, seeing that it is to be Saturday night."

"Well, we'll see," smiled the mother indulgently, as the crowd broke up and departed, while Peace and Hector divided the spoils in the corner. "She surely is an interesting specimen, and it was worth ten times the money just to hear her squelch her audience. Where is Brother Strong?"

He was interviewing the brown-eyed girl, who, with her money in hand, was about ready to follow her companions for home; and they clustered around the little group by Hector's table just in time to hear Peace's dismayed voice cry, "You're fooling! I didn't believe that of you. Why, Mr. Strong, I read it myself on the poster!"

"Where? What poster?"

"That big one up on the corner back of this house. Allee and me were picking gentians when we saw it. Didn't we, Allee?"

"But, Peace, that was last year's sign. There hasn't been a circus in town this summer, and there isn't going to be. It is past circus time."

"Are you sure?" she faltered, opening her fist and looking tragically at the pile of nickels and dimes she held.

"Perfectly sure! They were to have been here last year just about this time, but it rained pitchforks, as you children say, and they didn't stop. That poster is ragged and faded with time. If you don't believe me, just come up to the corner and I'll show you the date."

"Oh, I b'lieve you! Ministers don't often tell lies; but I was just thinking of this heap of money I've earned all for nothing. Eighty cents was my share, and I thought that would take most of our family – s'posing Gail would let us go."

The amused grown-ups smiled behind her back, but the preacher understood how disappointed she was, and taking her hand sympathetically in his, he drew her aside and whispered a few words in her ear which brought back the sparkle to her eyes and the happy glow to her face, as she exclaimed enthusiastically, "I'll do it! Sure! No, I won't tell a soul. Course Gail will let me. All right! Good-bye!"

She was off like a shot down the road, and the pastor joined his hostess on the way to the house, with the irrelevant remark, "Dr. David Peak, a missionary to Africa, is to speak at our Sunday morning service. I hope we have a large attendance, as this will be a rare treat. It isn't often a little country church can secure so notable a speaker. Spread the good news all you can."

Something in his voice made the Judge's wife say suggestively, "He is not to be the only unusual attraction, is he?"

"The only one to be advertised," smiled the parson, and she understood.

The following Sabbath day was glorious, bright, warm, and with the smell of fall in the air. The church was packed; pastor and people were at their best; and an expectant hush fell over the little audience when Mr. Strong took his seat after reading the weekly announcements. The organ began to play softly, necks were craned to catch a glimpse of the singer, and then a buzz of surprise filled the room. Peace, dressed all in white, and looking like a rosy cherub, had mounted to the organ loft where Faith was playing, and at the proper moment, she began to whistle a beautiful bird melody which surprised even those who had heard her the previous Wednesday. The whole audience sat spellbound. It seemed incredible that Peace, – little, blundering Peace, riotous, rebellious, happy-go-lucky Peace – had such a soul of melody bottled up within her. It was as if the songsters from the forest were suddenly let loose, and even her own sisters were amazed at her song.

Mr. Strong had been wise when he chose that moment for Peace's music, for the whole congregation was in tune for the grand missionary plea which followed, when Dr. Peak rose to address them; and so inspired, and uplifted was the speaker himself that he preached as he never had done before, bringing his cause so close to the people that they were thrilled and fired with his enthusiasm.

Parker was a well-to-do little village, built originally for the express purpose of permitting wealthy business men of the city to find peaceful retreat from the noisy metropolis, where, week in and week out, they spent the long days of labor. It had now somewhat outgrown this reputation, but still numbered many rich men among its inhabitants, and boasted of an unusually fine church for such a small place, although it was not noted for its spiritual zeal, and particularly was it lacking in its missionary spirit. These were difficulties which the ardent young preacher, Mr. Strong, had sought for many long months to overcome, and while the earnest missionary from Africa was pleading the cause of the heathen, the pastor praying with all his might for his own congregation.

When the wonderful sermon was finished, and Mr. Strong saw the unusual interest in the faces before him, he determined to strike while the iron was hot, and though that Sunday was not scheduled for a missionary collection, he sprang to his feet and made an urgent plea for more funds for the grand and glorious cause.

"Give from the depths of your heart," he urged. "Think of these millions of people needing the Gospel. Brother Peak has come direct from the field, he knows conditions better than anyone else can know them. He tells us they need more missionaries. How are they to get them? Through us in our civilized countries. We can't all go in person, but I don't think there is a soul here this morning but can give something to help a little. The ushers will now wait upon you. Who will be the first to give, and what shall it be, – yourself, time, m – "

"My cirkis money!" cried a shrill voice from the organ loft, and there stood Peace, fishing coin after coin from the depths of her pocket and dropping them over the pulpit into the missionary's outstretched hand. "I earned it so's me and Allee and Cherry could go to the cirkis – that is, if Gail would let us – and then, come to find out, it was last summer, and on 'count of the rain it never stopped at all. Next best to seeing the cirkis is hearing what that man said about the little black babies in Africa, – that's where the cirkis animals come from, too, – and I couldn't help wondering how I'd feel s'posing I had to live there and be black and eat such horrible things and be boiled in a kettle to take the dirt off, and buy my wife for a junk of cloth and wear strings of beads for clo'es. Here's my eighty cents, Dr. Missionary, to buy them a little more Gospel, and when I'm grown up if there are still heathen living in that country, I b'lieve I'll come down and help."

Whether it was the missionary's sermon, Mr. Strong's plea, or Peace's postscript that did the work, perhaps no one will ever know, but when the ushers brought their loaded baskets to the pulpit and the extraordinary collection was counted, it was found that over one hundred dollars had been raised for the missionary cause that morning in the Parker Church.

CHAPTER XVIII

The Hand-Organ Man

Hardly had the four younger girls disappeared across the fields on the way to school the next morning, when the Abbott carriage drew up in front of the little brown house, and Cecile and Frances hurried up the path to the door. Gail answered the imperative knock, and looked so surprised and pleased at the unexpected call that the Judge's daughter's face crimsoned with contrition and shame to think she had neglected this old-time friend so long.

"Why, Cecile!" stammered Gail, glancing involuntarily from the girls' fresh, white suits to her own shabby print frock and rolled-up sleeves. "This is a great treat. Come right in! We are so glad to have you call. Don't apologize; you are more than welcome. But please excuse my appearance. It is Monday morning and Faith and I are washing."

"Then don't you apologize, either," said Cecile, trying to laugh easily and failing utterly. "We should not have called at this outrageous hour, but Frances is to return to the city this afternoon, and she insisted upon coming to see about the children before she left."

"Oh!" The bright light died from Gail's eyes, and the girls looked uncomfortable. So it was an errand after all and not a friendly call which brought them. "What is the matter with the children? Has Peace – "

"No, oh, no, nothing has happened," Cecile began hastily, when Frances interrupted, "It was on my account. Your little whistler has captivated me completely – and mamma, too. We wanted to know if we might borrow them next Saturday, Peace and Allee, to help out in the program at a party I am giving that night. Oh, don't say no! I have set my heart on it. We will take the best care of them and bring them home early Sunday morning. We are coming out here for dinner at Mr. Strong's house that day, and of course must arrive in time for church service. Please say we can borrow them. I do want them so much!"

"Dear me," exclaimed Cecile in mortification. "I haven't even introduced you two girls. No wonder you think I am crazy, Gail. This is my chum from Martindale, Miss Sherrar, Miss Greenfield – "

"I'm Frances," again the radiant-faced stranger interrupted.

"And I am Gail," smiled the other. "I have heard the Strongs speak of you often."

"No oftener than we have heard them speak about you," Frances assured her. "We have known both of them for years, and ever since they took charge here in Parker we have heard lots about you."

"No doubt. Mr. Strong is quite a champion of Peace's, and she certainly needs one. I am afraid I don't make much of a success in bringing up the little ones."

"I think Peace is a perfect cherub – in looks."

The trio laughed merrily, and Cecile added, "She means to be in actions, but nothing she ever does comes out the way she intended it to, and she keeps everyone guessing as to what she will do next. You ought to hear Daddy rave about her. He thinks she is the smartest child he ever saw."

"I think she is the sweetest," said Frances, "she and Allee. They are both too cunning for anything. I simply must have them at my party. Won't you say they can come?"

"They have nothing to wear for such a grand occasion," Gail hesitated, anxious to please, and yet not quite willing to trust two of the precious sisters with strangers for even a twenty-four hours.

"That is easily remedied. I have some little cousins who are sure to have dresses that will fit. It is to be rather a dress-parade, I must admit, but you needn't worry on that account. Mamma knows how to fix them up in Sara's and Marion's clothes. We must have them. Mr. Strong will give us a good recommend, I know."

Gail laughed. "There is no need of that at all. I am willing that they should go, only you can hardly blame me for hesitating a little, as this will be the first time either one has been away from home over night; and besides, Peace is such a blunderbus, I rather dread to let her go anywhere for fear she will get into trouble."

"Now you oughtn't to feel that way at all," cried Frances gaily. "I was just such a child as she is, and see what a well-behaved young lady I have grown to be! But really, she has such a sweet disposition and great, tender heart, she will come out all right, I know. Mr. Strong says so, and he is a splendid character reader. Oh, of course, I suppose she has her bad days. We all do, but she is too much of a darling to stay bad long. You should hear your preacher sermonize about her. He says just as sure as she gets into mischief of any kind she comes to him and tells him all about it, cries over it, and goes away promising to be a better girl. Oh, I have lost my heart to her completely! We won't let her get into mischief of any kind, I promise. And I know she will enjoy herself."

"Well," answered Gail, slowly, "they may go, if you wish them so badly. How – "

"Cecile will bring them when she comes Saturday morning, if you are willing. That will give us plenty of time to get everything fixed up properly. I thank you so much for your permission; and, Gail, though we must hurry away this morning, the next time I come out here for a visit, I shall run in to see you for a nice long chat. May I?"

"Oh, if you just would!" cried gentle Gail impulsively, longing to take the bright face between her hands and kiss it. "We are too busy here to get out very much ourselves, but we do like company 'awfully bad,' as Peace used to say. I hope you come soon. The children will be ready for Cecile Saturday when she gets here. Good-bye, I am sorry you must go so soon. Come again, Cecile." The girls were gone, and Gail went back to her wash-tubs in a daze.

Needless to say, the little girls were wild with excitement when told of the coming gala day, and Cherry was green-eyed with envy, though, like the well-behaved child she was, she never said a word to mar the beautiful time in store for the two more fortunate sisters. Long before Cecile arrived Saturday morning, the stiffly-starched duet stood on the steps, waiting in a fever of impatience; and by the time the Sherrar house in the great city was reached, both little girls were almost transported with joy. They nearly talked Cecile's head off, so eager were they to find out all about the grand party, and everything else of interest they could think of; so she was more than relieved to turn her lively charges over to Frances the minute that young lady put in appearance.

"You little darlings!" the hostess exclaimed at sight of them. "Take them right upstairs, Sophy; mamma wants them at once. Cecile, you look tired out. Oh, yes, I can understand just how you feel for Sara and Marion were here all day yesterday, and what do you think? They haven't a thing suitable for us to borrow. Mamma says we'll have to go downtown and buy something ready-made for Peace and Allee. She is dressing now, and if you aren't too tired, I'm going to drag you along."

"Oh, I'm never too tired for gadding," replied Cecile with animation. "But I can't answer half the questions those chatterboxes ask, and this morning Allee was as bad as Peace. She wants to know if a chandelier crows and is just an ordinary rooster. Peace thinks those green-houses we pass on the car ought to be called 'white-houses,' because they are painted white. Just before we got off at our avenue she suddenly demanded to know for whom 'Vandrevort Street' was named. I couldn't think for the life of me what she meant until I remembered we cross Twenty-fourth Street, and the conductor was a foreigner who doesn't pronounce his words distinctly. She is possessed to know why, if the world is round, the houses on the other side don't fall off; and why, when we lift our feet to step, they always come down to the earth again instead of staying in the air. Why is it we can't pick ourselves up in our own arms; why don't women's shoes hook up like men's; what is the reason policemen's clothes are always blue and the grass is never anything but green; why don't mules look like horses and what makes them kick?"

Cecile stopped for breath, and Frances screamed with delight. "Maybe we better stop and consult the doctor while we are in town," she suggested.

"No, I guess that won't be necessary now, for I have resigned them to your tender mercies, and you must answer their questions after this. If you don't get enough of it, Frances Sherrar, before tomorrow morning – "

"Don't prophesy, Cecile! If they can hold a candle to Marion and Sara, I'll give you my opal ring."

"I stand a pretty good chance of getting the ring, then," answered Cecile, half-laughing, half-serious; but at that moment Mrs. Sherrar hustled down the stairway, with the two children in her wake, and the merry group set out for town.

"This is the corner, mamma," said Frances, as the car came to a standstill at one of the busiest streets; "and, oh, if there aren't Mrs. Tate and Lucy! I haven't seen them for an age. Hurry, mamma, you know you are as anxious to see them as I am."

Peace and Allee found themselves bundled hurriedly down the steps, jerked through the surging crowd of people, teams and automobiles in street, and landed on the opposite corner breathless, but game.

"Stay right here," they heard Mrs. Sherrar say; and the next instant the older members of the party were wholly absorbed with those unexpectedly-met friends. The children listened impatiently for a few moments, but finding the conversation very uninteresting, looked about them for other more congenial amusement.

Just then a wheezy old hand-organ behind them began a familiar melody, and Peace beheld the player, a bent, white-haired, blind man, sitting in the shadow of a lamp-post on the edge of the curbing, slowly, patiently turning the crank of the little machine. She was at his side in an instant, staring into the sightless face with her great, brown, pitying eyes. His clothes were very shabby, his cheeks were pinched and pale; his cup, she noticed, stood empty on the top of the organ; his hands were terribly thin, and trembled as he played, so that he had to stop frequently between songs and rest.

"Are you sick, Mr. Blind-man?" she asked before she was aware she had spoken her thoughts aloud.

The white, unseeing eyes of the organist turned in the direction of the voice, and he answered with a show of cheerfulness, "Not now, little lady."

"Then you have been?"

"Yes, this is my first day out for two weeks."

"Oh, you poor man! It must tire you dreadfully to have to grind that box all day. Won't you let me try it awhile? I know I can do it all right. You can count your money while I play."

"There ain't been any to count so far this morning," he murmured, unconsciously dropping his hand from the organ as the quaint, old-fashioned song was finished; and before he had a chance to remonstrate, Peace had seized the crank with both hands, and was grinding away with all her might. But, though the crank seemed to turn easily enough, the music came in jerks, and the blind player took possession of his organ the minute she had completed the last bar, saying gently, "I am afraid you don't know how to make the music, little one. But I thank you a thousand times for your great good-will. I shall soon be strong enough to play as well as I always have. The first day is a little hard. Tomorrow it will be better. We'll change the roll now, and give them another tune." He fumbled about the organ for a moment or two, and then the strains of Annie Laurie filled the air.

"Oh, I know that!" cried Peace, with animation. "Allee, you come and sing, while I whistle. We can do it lovely. Now begin again."

Nothing loath to humor his strange, sympathetic little guests, he began the second time to grind out the wheezy notes of the beautiful, time-honored song, and Peace's red lips took up the accompaniment, while Allee's sweet, childish voice warbled the words:

> "Maxwellton braes are bonnie,
> Where early fa's the dew,
> And it's there that Annie Laurie
> Gied me her promise true –
> Gied me her promise true,
> Which ne'er forgot will be;
> And for bonnie Annie Laurie
> I'd lay me doon and dee."

Mrs. Sherrar wheeled in amazement at the sound; the girls broke off their animated conversation to stare at the quaint group on the corner; a crowd gathered quickly; and with sudden, characteristic impulsiveness, Peace caught up the battered tin cup from the old hand-organ, and held it out invitingly. Hand after hand plunged deep into scores of pockets; coin after coin rattled into the little dipper; the old man played eagerly, breathlessly; and the children sang again and again in response to the applause from the street.

How long the impromptu concert might have continued no one knows, but through a break in the sea of faces surrounding them, Peace caught a glimpse of Mrs. Sherrar's portly form, and it reminded her suddenly of where she was and how she came to be there. Breaking off in the midst of her song, she thrust the heavy cup back into the owner's hands, bowed to the astonished throng, and cried shrilly, "He's been sick and can't play as much as he used to could, until he gets strong again; so he needs all the money he can get. Don't forget him when you go by again."

Grabbing Allee by the arm, she whisked away to where her friends were waiting, fearful lest they might not approve of her impulsive action; so before they had a chance to speak a word either of blame or praise, she began, excusingly, "Just s'posing we all had our eyes punched out so's we couldn't see, and had to sit on street corners and grind out music all day long. Wouldn't it be terrible? I – I – thought – maybe it might help a little if we joined in the music, and it did. He's got a whole cupful of money, and now maybe he'll go home and rest a bit. He's been sick."

Tears filled the eyes of the little company of grown-ups, and Frances, with an understanding heart, drew the childish figures close, saying tenderly, "For these bonnie little lassies I'd lay me doon and dee."

CHAPTER XIX

Heartbreak

It was a wild, stormy, October night. The rain fell fitfully, and the howling wind raced madly through forest and over farmland, shrieking down chimneys, rattling windows and doors, whistling through every conceivable crack and crevice, and rudely buffeting any traveler who chanced to be abroad. In the brown house three rosy-cheeked little maids lay fast asleep in their beds in the tiny back chamber, blissfully unconscious of wind and rain; but in the room below Faith and Hope kept anxious vigil, awaiting Gail's return from the darkness and the storm.

"I should have gone, too," croaked Faith, in a voice so hoarse she could scarcely speak above a whisper.

"No, indeed," Hope declared. "You have a dreadful cold now; but I think she might have let me go. Towzer isn't enough company on such a night, and like as not he will get tired of waiting and come home without her. What was that? Oh, only the clock. Eleven! I had no idea it was so late."

She rose from her chair and paced restlessly back and forth across the room, pausing at every turn to look first out of one window and then out of the other, as if trying to penetrate the inky blackness of the stormy night. The unlatched gate creaked dismally on its hinges; somewhere a door banged shut; and then an old bucket blew off the back porch and down the steps with a rattlety-clatter which made the two watchers within start and shiver.

Peace heard it, too, and sat bolt upright in bed, not knowing what had awakened her, but trembling like a leaf with nervous fear. A terrific gust of wind roared around the corner, shaking the little brown house from rafter to foundation; the great elm trees tossed and groaned in sympathy, and the leafless vines over the porch beat a mournful tattoo against the walls.

> "Have you ever heard the wind go 'Yoooooo?'
> 'Tis a pitiful sound to hear!
> It seems to chill you through and through
> With a strange and speechless fear,"

chattered Peace, hardly conscious of what she was saying. The gate shut with a clang. "What's that? Sounded 's if – it was the gate banging and someone is coming up the steps! I wonder who it can be this time of night and in all this storm?"

She listened intently for the visitor to knock. None came, but the front door was opened unceremoniously, a blast of wind tore through the house, and she heard two excited, relieved voices exclaim, "Oh, Gail! We thought you would never come. Take off your coat this minute! You are drenched!"

"What on earth is Gail doing out of doors in this rain?" said Peace to herself. "She was sewing when I came up to bed. I'm going to find out." Tumbling out of her warm nest, she crept softly down the stairs, and slipped behind the faded drapery which served as door to the tiny hall closet, from which position she could watch the girls in the living-room, and hear much of what they were saying.

The first words which greeted her ears as the curtain fell back in position with her behind it, were Faith's: "Oh, Gail, not Mr. Skinner!"

"Yes," answered the oldest sister in a strained, unnatural voice that struck terror to the little spy's heart, "Mr. Skinner!"

"But I thought Mr. Hartman held the mortgage," Hope began in bewildered tones.

"He did, dear," Gail answered. "I supposed he still held it; we paid the last interest money to him."

"Then how – "

"Two years ago Mr. Hartman signed a note for old Mr. Lowe on the Liberty Road. The Lowes have always been considered wealthy people, and the two families have been close friends for years, so he thought there would be no trouble about the note; but when it fell due in July Mr. Lowe couldn't pay, and Mr. Hartman had to. He owns quite a little property, I guess, but all his ready money had gone into fixing up his buildings and putting up a new barn. Mr. Skinner wouldn't give an extension of time on the note, and said he would take nothing but cash payment or the mortgage on our farm. He has always wanted this place, it seems, and had expected to get it when papa bought it – you know the first owner was a great friend of our family – and there was some bad feeling over it. He never liked us, and Peace's prank with his bull settled everything. He was fairly insulting – "

"Did you go to see him?" chorused the sisters.

"Surely. I thought there might be a chance of his extending the time on the mortgage, but – he wouldn't listen to me."

"Then we must lose the farm?"

"We have a month more before the mortgage is due, but I don't know where the money to pay is coming from. I am afraid – the farm – must go." She gasped out the words in such misery and despair that Peace found herself crying with the older sister across the hall.

"What will become of us?" choked Hope after a long pause.

"I – I don't know," murmured Gail, "unless you go to live with the neighbors until I can find something to do so I can get you all together again. It seems the village people have already talked this over among themselves."

"Did Peace tell you after all?" demanded Faith.

"No, I didn't! I never said a word!" cried Peace in great indignation, and the startled sisters beheld a frowzy head thrust from behind the closet drapery, and a pair of angry eyes glaring at them. "I won't go to live with the Judge nor Mr. Hardman, either. Len and Cecile tease me dreadfully, Hector I predominate with all my heart and I can't abide Mr. Hardman. He isn't square. He shouldn't have given old Skinflint the mordige. It b'longs to us. Oh, dear, I'll never pick raspberries again! That bull has made more fuss than any other person I know."

Gail caught the shivering, sobbing child in her arms, wrapped a shawl around her, and sought to soothe her grief by saying gently, "There, there, honey, don't cry like that! You are shaking with cold. How long have you been in the closet, and why were you hiding there?"

"I heard you come in and I had to see what was the matter. Oh, do say I won't have to go to the Judge or Mr. Hardman! I hate them both – "

"Peace," reproved Gail, "you mustn't speak so. I am sorry you have overheard anything about the matter. Mr. Hartman had a perfect right to sell the mortgage to Mr. Skinner, and under the circumstances we can't blame him. He wouldn't have done it if he could have helped it."

"What I can't understand," interposed Faith, with a deep frown disfiguring her forehead, "is why he waited this long before telling us."

"I guess he didn't relish breaking such news to us anyway, but he has been hoping right along that Mr. Lowe would be able to pay him for the note. Then he could buy back the mortgage, or loan us the money so we could meet it, which amounts to the same thing. Of course, it is barely possible that he will yet get the money in time, but we can't count on it at all. He was so broken up over the matter that he actually cried while he was talking to me."

"I sh'd think he would!" stormed Peace, who could not yet understand how their neighbor had any excuse for selling the mortgage; neither did she understand just what sort of a thing a mortgage is, but that it had something to do with money and their farm was perfectly clear.

"Isn't there someone we know who could loan us the money?" asked Hope, the hopeful, unwilling to accept the dark situation as it was presented.

"I can't think of a soul. Most of father's close friends were ministers, and they wouldn't be able to help us. We have no relatives living. We haven't anybody – "

"We have each other," whispered Hope; and Gail's clasp on the little form in her lap tightened convulsively as she wondered vaguely how much longer they could say those words.

"We have Mr. Strong, too," reminded Peace. "Maybe he knows how the money could be paid."

"I had thought of asking his advice, but of course it was too stormy tonight. We must wait until day."

"If he can't help us, ask him if he won't take me," said Peace, in her most wheedlesome tones. "I would rather live with him than with anyone else in the world if we have to break up our house. I thought he would like to have me, too, but Mr. Jones said he wanted Allee."

"Mr. Jones doesn't know anything about it. Don't fret, dearie! There may be lots of ways out of our trouble without our having to separate. I hope so. We have a month to think and plan; but if we must scatter for a time among our kind friends, I trust we will all go bravely and do our best to please."

"But I can't go to the Judge's, Gail! He's a perfect fury, gets mad at nothing, and chaws his mustache and glares so ugly I always listen to see whether he's going to growl like Towzer."

"He has the finest house in town," said Faith consolingly, "and a piano and a horse and buggy. He is going to have an automobile next summer."

"I'd rather live with nice folks than with pianos and nautomobiles," Peace interrupted. "I don't know what he wants of another girl, unless it is for Len and Hector to tease."

"I thought you liked Len?"

"He used to be nice, but since he's began going to scollege, he's horrid. He saw me yesterday morning in Cherry's dress, 'cause I tore my last clean one; and he bugged his two eyes out like he was awfully s'prised, and said, 'Mah deah child, yoah dress is too long! I don't like the looks of it.'" She mimicked the college dude's affected airs so perfectly that the three sisters shouted with laughter, forgetting for the moment their heavy burden of care.

"What did you say?" asked Faith curiously, although in her heart she knew that Len must have met his match.

"I looped my fingers up in circles like make-b'lieve eye-glasses, and said, 'Mah deah man, yoah hat is too tall and yoah pants ah too wide. I don't like the looks of them, but I am too p'lite to say so.'"

Another shout of mirth made the rafters ring, and the trio laughed till they cried, much to Peace's surprise, for the scene she had just depicted had caused her much indignation, and she could see nothing funny about it. "If you don't be stiller you'll wake the children," she warned them in her most grandmotherly tones, and they sobered quickly, remembering the ghost of trouble hovering over the little house.

For a long time they sat there in silence, each one busy with her own disturbed thoughts, unaware that the fire in the stove had died out, or that the chimes had long since struck midnight.

Suddenly Gail lifted her eyes from the hole in the carpet, at which she had been staring unseeingly, glanced at the old clock on the wall, and exclaimed, "Girls, it's a quarter to one! Fly into bed, every one of you! School keeps tomorrow just the same. Try to lay aside this trouble at least for tonight and get a little sleep. In the morning I will speak to Mr. Strong about it – "

"And remember to speak to God about it, too," murmured drowsy Peace, stumbling upstairs in front of the weary mother-sister.

CHAPTER XX

At the Broker's Office

"This is Saturday morning, Gail, and Mrs. Grinnell says I can go to Martindale with her if you will let me," said Peace, a few days after their midnight conference. She might have added that she herself had asked for the invitation, but for reasons of her own she made no mention of this fact.

Gail looked up from the pan of yeast she was "setting," and hesitatingly began, "Well – "

"I've wiped the dishes and fed the hens and dusted the parlor – "

"But I haven't swept the parlor yet," Gail protested.

"I can't help that. I have dusted," Peace answered, firmly. "If I had waited until you got ready to sweep, Mrs. Grinnell would have been gone."

Gail giggled in spite of her efforts to check the smile on her lips, and then soberly said, "But what about the eggs?"

"I have delivered my bunch already."

"Why, Peace, those baskets weren't full! What will Mrs. Abbott think?"

"Oh, I fixed that all right. There wasn't time to do much hunting for our own eggs, so I borrowed the rest of Mrs. Hartman."

"Peace Greenfield! What shall I do with you?" cried the older sister in utter discouragement, dropping her hands from her pan of mixing in a gesture of despair which scattered a cloud of flour over herself and the impatient pleader.

"Let me go with Mrs. Grinnell," was the prompt reply. "I won't be in your way all day, then; and while I am gone, the hens will have laid enough eggs to pay back Mrs. Hartman. I borrowed only five. Twenty-eight hens ought to be able to lay that many before I get back. The eight biddies I bought with the rest of my melon money could do better than that, Gail. Please say I can go!"

Perhaps it was the sight of the wistful little face, perhaps it was visions of a quiet day in which to attend to housework that won the desired permission; but at any rate Gail consented reluctantly, and Peace danced away to find the kind neighbor and report the sister's decision.

"My, but I'm glad," she hummed to herself as she scrambled into her best dress and flew out of the door into the warm autumn sunshine. "I thought she wouldn't let me go, and then I couldn't get the money. Oh, I am so glad, so glad!"

"Where are you going?" demanded a grieved voice, as Allee came through the barn door and caught a glimpse of her sister's best skirts under the flying coat.

Peace stopped short in the path and thoughtfully sucked her finger as she eyed the dirty pinafore and wistful face of this pet of the family.

"To Martindale," she said, briefly. "Come along! There isn't time to clean up. We'll hide you under the lap robe. Mrs. Grinnell won't care. Cherry, Oh, Cherry, tell Gail I have taken Allee with me! She ain't very dirty, and I'll keep her covered up out of sight. And now, Allee, don't you say a word to anyone about it, but I begged Mrs. Grinnell to take me. I want to get some money to buy back that mordige of ours from old Skinflint. Mind you keep it secret!"

"I will," promised Allee readily, for with her Peace's very wish was law.

"There is Mrs. Grinnell all harnessed and waiting. Hurry up! I had to bring Allee, Mrs. Grinnell, 'cause I wouldn't be at home to amuse her, and she might get into mischief," she explained as they arrived panting and breathless beside the big, roomy carriage, and she saw the questioning glance of the woman's eyes.

"Oh, I see," answered Mrs. Grinnell, smiling grimly. "But how about Gail? Does she know?"

"Oh, yes, she knows by this time. I sent Cherry to tell her. There wasn't time to change her dress, so we will have to keep her covered up pretty well, 'specially as she's wearing her old play coat. Say, Mrs. Grinnell, do you know some people named Swift and Smart who live in Martindale?"

"There is a firm of brokers by that name on Sixth Street. Why?" she demanded suspiciously, for when Peace asked such a question, it usually meant mischief brewing.

"Oh, I just wanted to know if there were really people called that or if Mr. Hardman was only teasing. He told me when I killed the hens that I better go there and borrow money to buy new ones with."

"He was just tormenting you," the woman replied, severely. "I hope you weren't thinking of doing such a thing?"

"Oh, no!" Peace exclaimed, the hopeful light in her eyes fading quickly. "Haven't I already bought eight good hens of O'Hara with my melon money? They lay better than our others do, too. That makes twenty-eight in all now. But I don't see why Mr. Hardman told me Swift & Smart would give me the money."

"He was playing smart himself, I guess. That firm is one of the biggest of its kind in the city. They buy mortgages and such things; they haven't time to spend on little loans."

"Oh," said Peace, but the glad light came back to the somber brown eyes once more, and she bounced happily up and down on the leather cushion. "That name seemed such a funny one to me, I couldn't forget it. Swift & Smart – I wonder if it fits?"

"If it fits?" echoed her companion.

"Yes. S'posing Mr. Swift was slower'n molasses in January and Mr. Smart was stupid as a stump, they would be as big misfits as I am, wouldn't they? Now if grandpa could just have known the kind of a girl I was going to be, I bet he never would have named me Peace. Faith says it would have been more 'propriate if he had called me Pieces. I was just thinking what if those breakers were the same way."

"Brokers, my dear, not breakers. Well, I can't say how well the names fit, for I don't know them except by hearsay; but I judge they must be pretty smart whether they are slow or swift."

Peace giggled gleefully as if she appreciated the pun, and said musingly, "I'd like to see for myself how well they fitted. The names sound so funny. Do you go near their store today?"

"Why, yes, we are just across the street from it when we stop at Darnell's Dry Goods Store, but they have an office and not a store, child, and no one goes there unless they want to borrow money or something of that kind. Here we are at Peterson's. Will you come in while I do my trading?"

"Well, no," stammered Peace, her face flushing crimson under her friend's searching gaze. "Allee is pretty dirty and we best sit right here, don't you think?"

Mrs. Grinnell hesitated, puzzled at this unusual resolve on the part of the children who liked nothing better than to wander through the big department stores and admire the pretty things; then she replied grimly, "Very well, but don't either one of you stir out of that buggy while I am gone."

"No, we won't," they promised in angelic tones, and the woman left them, still perplexed and somewhat ill at ease. Fearing that some mischief was on foot she cut short her bargain-hunting tour in Peterson's store and hurried back to her charges, only to find them sitting silent and erect on the seat where she had left them, busy watching the bustling crowds in the streets.

"Why," cried Peace, almost in dismay, "you weren't gone at all hardly! You must be a quick shopper."

"Yes, in this case," laughed the relieved woman, climbing into the rig and clucking at the horse, "but it may take me some time at the Martindale Dry Goods Store, and probably longer yet at Darnell's. Do you think you can wait patiently out here in the wagon?"

"Oh, yes, it's lots of fun watching the people go by. There was one man back there so fat and pusy that we wondered what would happen s'posing he should stub his toe. I don't believe his head and feet could hit the sidewalk at the same time, and he'd just roll away like a ball, unless someone helped him up, wouldn't he?"

Again Mrs. Grinnell laughed grimly as she remarked with some sarcasm, "What great sights you do see! You will be a genius one of these days, I'll warrant. This is the Martindale. Now don't get out of the buggy."

"S'posing she says that at the next store," thought Peace to herself, but aloud she answered cheerily, "Don't you fret, Mrs. Grinnell." The busy woman was gone fully half an hour that time and Peace was jubilant, but she did not show her delight, and merely remarked, as Mrs. Grinnell gathered up the reins once more, "How little time it takes you to buy things! Gail and Faith tramp all day to find a pair of stockings, and then like as not get cheated. It is perfectly splendid watching the way folks crowd, better than seeing things in the store. I never knew before how much fun it is. You just ought to have seen that lady in the purple hat fool two men. One man was coming towards her and the other was just behind her when they got jammed in the doorway there. The front man jumped one way and the woman jumped the same way so he couldn't get by. He hopped back in his first place, and she hopped back in hers, and all the while the long feather on her hat was spearing the hind man in the eye, but he kept hopping the same way the others did. I thought I should screech before the woman got enough jumping and stood still so the men could get past, and didn't they look mad and scowly! Mercy, is this Darnell's? Well, you needn't worry about us one mite, but take all the time you want. The horse is as good as gold, and I'm keeping Allee's dirty dress out of sight."

"I'll be back as soon as I can," promised Mrs. Grinnell when she could get in a word, and forgetting her usual parting admonition, she hurried sway through the crowd into the store.

"Now," exclaimed Peace, all a-flutter the minute the broad back had disappeared, "let's see where Swift & Smart live. There it is just across the street, but we'll have to hurry, 'cause there is no telling how soon she will be back. Here, wrap this lap robe around you to keep your clothes out of sight, and give me your hand. Mercy! I should think the p'lice would have certain streets for the nautomobiles and cars to go on instead of letting 'em all jumble up that way. We didn't get hit that time; don't wait for the next one to come, but run."

Dragging poor, frightened, stumbling Allee and the trailing robe through the turmoil of the street, Peace managed to land on the opposite walk without mishap, but how she ever did it was a marvel to the big, brawny policeman shouting warnings to them as he tried in vain to reach the little figures dodging so recklessly under horses' noses, in front of flying automobiles and across the path of clanging bicycles.

"Are we all here?" gasped the blue-eyed tot when Peace had set her on her feet once more and adjusted the dragging robe about her shoulders.

"Course! What did you think we left behind? I know how to get across crowded streets. Here is the door. I wonder which is Smart and which is Swift, – there are three men in the room."

She lifted the latch and boldly entered, then halted and took a careful survey of her surroundings.

There were several desks in the office, all dreadfully littered with papers and books, and at one of these sat a short, bald-headed man, talking rapidly to a pretty, smiley-faced young girl, who scribbled queer little scratches in a tablet. Beside another desk in the opposite corner of the room were two men, both tall and gray and pleasant appearing, but so much absorbed in their conversation that they did not notice the children's entrance. Through a nearby door came the fitful clicking of some machine, and Peace could see a second girl seated at a table pounding a typewriter, while another man hurried to and fro from a row of shelves to a big iron box against the wall. None of them, however, paid any attention to their anxious little visitors, and Peace, after waiting impatiently until she feared Mrs. Grinnell would be back looking for them, stepped across the polished floor to the gray men in the corner, shook the nearest one by the sleeve, and demanded, "Are you Swift or Smart, or; both – I mean neither?"

"Now, Mr. Campbell," the man was just saying, but at this interruption he broke off abruptly, glared at the small intruder and asked in quick, sharp tones, "What do you want?"

"Some money," stammered Peace, much startled by his nervous, half-irritated manner.

"Money! Well, I am afraid you have come to the wrong place," he said decisively, mistaking the children for beggars.

"Why, I thought – " began Peace, with quivering lips.

"Will a quarter be enough?" interrupted the other gray man, looking down into the troubled face with keen, kindly, gray eyes, which seemed strangely familiar to the child.

"Now, Campbell!" expostulated the tall, nervous man. "They come here in swarms some days. You wouldn't be so ready with your cash if you had to deal with the number we do."

Without reply, the man called Campbell drew a silver coin from his pocket and extended it toward trembling Peace, but she shook her head, gulping out, "It will take heaps more than that. Old Skinflint has got the mordige on our farm and won't give it up. I want money enough to buy it back, so's we can still go on living there."

"Oh!" shouted the sharp-voiced man, while Mr. Campbell pocketed his silver again. "So you thought you would come here to get the money, did you?"

"Mr. Hardman said you let people borrow money from you," whispered Peace miserably, wishing she had never left her seat in the carriage. "He told me that when I poisoned half our hens, but Mrs. Grinnell said you didn't bother with such little things; and anyway, I have bought eight new ones already, so we don't need hens so much as we do that mordige. Is your name Mr. Swift?"

"No, I am the other fellow – Smart."

"Hm, I thought it would be like that."

"Like what?"

"Why, that your names wouldn't fit. I told Mrs. Grinnell I bet Mr. Smart would be stupider than a stump and Mr. Swift would be slower than slow. Is that bald-headed man Mr. Swift?"

For an instant the two men in the corner stared at her in sheer amazement, and then both burst into a great roar of laughter, which brought the whole office force to their feet. "Say, Swift, come meet this young mortgage raiser," called the nervous partner. "If you ever get conceited, just interview a child."

The bald-headed man rose ponderously and joined the group, studying every feature of the children, as he demanded, in his most business-like tone, "What is your name?"

"Peace Greenfield."

"Where do you live?"

"Almost at Parker."

"Almost?"

"Well, we have a farm and Parker isn't big enough to hold farms. It's a nice place, though."

"How did you get here?"

"Mrs. Grinnell brought us in her wagon."

"Who is she?"

"The lady what lives on the farm right back of ours."

"Did she tell you to come and see us?"

"Oh, no! She said not to, but she doesn't know anything about our mordige, so while she was in the store we hustled over after the money."

"Who did send you?"

"Why, nobody. We came all by ourselves."

"Hm, I thought so. Is this mordige money to buy candy and dolls with?"

"No, it ain't!" snapped Peace, thinking he was trying to tease her. "It's to keep old Skinflint from taking our farm away, so that we will have to live around at different places."

"Where are your father and mother?"

"The angels have got 'em."

"Oh! Then you are orphans. Who takes care of you?"

"We all of us take care of ourselves, but Gail is the play mother."

"How many are there in your family?"

"Seven with Towzer. He's a dog."

They questioned her until the whole pitiful story was told, and then stood silently lost in thought, while Peace fidgeted impatiently, watching Old Gray across the street, expecting any minute to see Mrs. Grinnell put in appearance.

Finally Mr. Swift said, jestingly, "What security have you to offer?"

"Sickerity?" repeated Peace, wonderingly.

"Yes, when we loan money we have to have some security from the party. They must own some property or something of value to give us so if the money isn't paid back we won't lose anything."

Peace pondered deeply, then drew off a small, worn, gold ring which had lost its "set," and laid it in the man's hand, saying, "That's all the prop'ty I've got except eight hens which I gave Gail for those I poisoned. It had a ruby in it once, but the old rooster picked it out and et it. I used to have two bunnies, too, but last Christmas the German kids ate Winkum and Blinkum all up."

Mr. Swift smiled, but shook his head gravely, as he returned the ring. "I am afraid that won't be enough, Miss Greenfield," he began, when Mr. Smart cut him short, "What is the use of fooling any longer, Swift? She probably knows as much about such matters as your grandbaby. A kid her age knows a lot about business. Give her a nickel and send her packing."

The genial Mr. Swift led the disappointed duet to the door and dismissed them with the words, "I am sorry, but we deal only with grown-up men and women. Call again when you are twenty-one."

As the door closed behind them, however, the other tall, gray man, who had been a silent spectator of the scene, spoke reprovingly, "I think she has told you the truth, Smart. She is one of the youngsters I was just telling you about. I was afraid she would recognize me, but evidently she did not. I certainly shall investigate, for I am much interested. They have my wife and me by the heartstrings already and some of these days you may hear that a whole family has been adopted by the erratic Campbells. They are the children of that Pendennis minister who fought such a splendid fight in the Marble Avenue Church some years back, until he was forced to retire on account of his health. Well, I must be going. Good-day!" He stepped outside the office, and looked up and down the street for a glimpse of the children, but they were nowhere in sight; so he hailed a passing car, and was whirled rapidly away through the busy city.

In the meantime, poor, disappointed Peace had jerked Allee back across the street, helped her into the buggy and had just got nicely settled when Mrs. Grinnell bustled out of Darnell's Department Store, ready for the homeward journey. She eyed the sober faces keenly for an instant, undecided whether the frowns were due to impatience at her long absence, or because of some childish quarrel, but soon forgot all about the matter in planning how she should make up her new print dress, so the return trip was made in absolute silence.

But Peace had by no means given up hope in the matter of the mortgage and, feeling better after the warm dinner had been eaten, she wandered away to the barn to hatch some other impossible plan. Finding Hope in the loft sorting out rubbish to be burned, she threw herself on an old bench behind the building, where the bright sunlight shone invitingly, and here she was soon so completely wrapped up in her own thoughts that she did not hear the sound of approaching steps, and was startled when a firm hand caught her by the shoulder and a merry voice demanded, "Why so pensive, little maid? That face would scare the tramps away."

"Oh, Mr. Strong," she cried, catching his hand and pulling him down beside her, "we are in the worst fix you ever heard. I knocked old Skinflint's bull's horn off pawing red rags in the raspberry patch so Faith could have some sour jelly for her jelly rolls, and to pay me for that he won't give us back our mordige. Gail cried and Faith cried and we all cried. In a month we must break up this house and go to live with different people unless we can get some money somewhere. I tried this morning to borrow some in Martindale, but they wouldn't believe we needed it. I know we do, 'cause Gail said so the night I hid in the closet when she didn't know I was there."

She paused for breath, and Mr. Strong said cheerily, "Yes, dear, I know all about it. Gail told me, but I think maybe everything is coming out all right in the end. Don't you fret! But if I were you, I wouldn't try any more to borrow the money – "

"How are we to get it, then? Gail doesn't know of anybody."

"Gail was meant for a little mother instead of a business woman. Now that she has asked some of us older folks for advice, I think we can manage matters beautifully. Gail is just a girl herself, you know. She understands the situation a little better now, but the burden is too heavy for her young shoulders. We must make it lighter, lots lighter. She wants to go to college, and Faith wants music lessons, and Hope ought to study drawing, and what would you like to study?"

"Pigs! I want a pig farm," was the unexpected answer. "Ain't baby pigs the dearest things you ever saw?"

His shout of derision stopped her, and she sat twisting her brown hands in hurt and embarrassed silence.

Her mournful attitude brought the young preacher to his senses, and he pinched her cheek playfully, saying, "Oh, what a doleful face! See if we can't make it smile a little. No? Why, Peace, this is the way it looks. Supposing it should freeze that way." He drew his face down into a comically mournful grimace, and Peace laughed outright. "I heard that you won the prize at Annette's party for making the worst looking face," he continued, "but I didn't suppose it was as bad as that."

"That isn't half bad," cried Peace scornfully. "Why, I can make the ugliest faces you ever saw."

"Bet you can't!"

"Bet I can!"

"Try it!"

Peace promptly bulged out her eyes, turned up her nose, and drew down her mouth in a hideous grimace, following it up with other horrible distortions; and then exclaimed, "How do you like that?"

"I can do as well myself," said the preacher.

"I don't b'lieve it! Let's see you do it!"

Mr. Strong laid aside his hat, rumpled up his shining black hair, and went through some fearful contortions of face, which almost paralyzed Peace for the moment. Then she screamed her delight, hopping about on one foot, and shouting boisterously, "You win, you win, Mr. Strong! If I can ever make faces like those, I shall be perfectly happy. Do you s'pose I am young enough to learn? It must have taken you all your life to do it so beautifully. Will you teach me how?"

On the other side of the fence something moved in the thick brush, and there was a sound of a man's deep chuckle, but the two contestants in the art of making faces were too much occupied to notice anything of their surroundings, and the unknown watcher enjoyed this novel entertainment for some moments.

At length the preacher said, "Well, Peace, I came over to see Gail. Where can I find her?"

"In the kitchen, most likely. Come along; I will hunt her up."

The two strolled off toward the house, and a crouching figure in the hazel thicket followed them until they entered the kitchen door, when it dropped flat on the ground again and remained there alert and listening during the conference in the little brown house.

When at last, as dusk was falling, the minister strode down the path to the gate, a shabby, gray-haired man emerged from the shadows along the roadside and hurried after him. Hearing footsteps so close by, the young man halted, expecting to see some of his parishioners or acquaintances of the village trying to overtake him, and was naturally somewhat startled when accosted by a stranger.

"I beg your pardon," said Mr. Strong. "I thought it was someone who wanted me."

"It is," replied the shabby man. "I take it that you are pastor of the Parker Church, – Mr. Strong, I believe?"

"Yes, sir," answered the preacher, still a little bewildered.

"My name is Donald Campbell – "

"President Campbell of the University?" gasped Mr. Strong in surprise, involuntarily looking down at the stranger's threadbare clothes.

"As you prefer. Oh, I am in disguise! I will make explanations as we walk along if you can give me a few moments of your time. I should like to interview you in regard to our late Brother Peter Greenfield's family."

CHAPTER XXI

Surprises

"Why, Gail, what are you doing?" asked Faith one cold, dull November day, as she hurried into the kitchen from her village trip, and found the older sister picking two plump hens.

"Can't you see?" smiled the girl, glancing up from her task with an excited, happy sparkle in her eyes.

"Yes, I can see, but what is the occasion? Has Peace made another raid on the hen-house with poison or rat-traps? I shouldn't suppose we could afford chicken unless by accident. Thanksgiving is more than two weeks off."

"What day is tomorrow? Am I the only one who remembers?"

"November tenth – your birthday! Oh, Gail, it had slipped my mind for the minute! No wonder you are getting up a celebration if everyone forgets like that."

"Oh, it isn't on account of the birthday, Faith; that just happened. It's the mortgage – "

"Of course, I knew it was due soon, but the relief at being able to get the money made me overlook the exact date, I guess. So that is the cause of your excitement!"

"Partly, and then we are to have company for dinner, too."

"Who?" demanded Faith, again surprised.

"Mr. and Mrs. Strong and Glen and Mrs. Grinnell."

"What in the world will we do with them all? Eight is a tight fit for our dining-room."

"It will crowd us a little, but I have it all planned nicely. Glen must sit in his daddy's lap – he often does at home when they have company and haven't room at the table for his high-chair – and of course I will wait on the people, so there will be room for all."

"Of course you won't wait on the people! What waiting there is to attend to I shall look after. You are mistress of this house. Oh, I can't help hugging myself every other minute to think Mr. Strong was able to get the money for the mortgage and we won't have to leave this dear little brown house after all."

"Do you care so much?" asked Gail, with such a curious wistfulness in her voice that Faith stopped her ecstatic prancing to study the thin, flushed face.

"I should say I do!" she exclaimed emphatically. "Someway, in these last six months it has grown ever so much dearer than I ever dreamed it could. I used to think I hated farm life, and it fretted me because we couldn't live in Pendennis or Martindale, and have things like other folks. I did want a piano so much, instead of a worn-out, wheezy old organ."

"Wouldn't you still like all that?" questioned the older girl, keeping her eyes fixed on the half-picked fowl in her lap, as if afraid of betraying some delightful secret.

"Oh, yes, indeed! But I gave up thinking about such things a long time ago. The farm is all we have, and there is the mortgage to pay on that; so I just shut up my high-falutin notions, as Mrs. Grinnell calls them, and mean to be happy doing my part in the home. I have wasted too much time already."

"You have done your part splendidly," cried Gail with brimming eyes, letting the chicken slip unnoticed from her hands as she threw one arm around Faith's waist; "and now that – " She bit her tongue just in time to keep the wonderful secret from tumbling off, and flushed furiously.

"And now that what?" questioned the other girl, without the faintest trace of suspicion in her voice.

"Now that this hard year is over, we are going to do a little celebrating even if we can't afford it," answered Gail, thinking rapidly. "Will you make a caramel cake for our dinner? Mrs. Grinnell is so fond of it, and I know it will hit the right spot with the minister. It was his suggestion that he tell – " Again she stopped in confusion.

"About the mortgage money," Faith finished. "Well, he certainly has earned the right. We have a lot to thank him for. Do you know who is loaning the money, or is that still a secret from you, too?"

"No, Mr. Strong told me, but he wants the privilege of telling the rest of you, so I promised to keep still."

"Oh!" There was a long pause, during which both girls busied themselves with the chickens; and then Faith ventured the question, "Is it Judge Abbott?" Gail smilingly shook her head. "Nor Dr. Bainbridge?" Again the brown head shook. "Then it is Mrs. Grinnell. I thought of her in the first place – "

"You are wrong again. All the money she has is tied up in her farm and in the house in Martindale."

"Is it anyone in town?"

"No."

Faith was plainly puzzled. "Man or woman?"

"Both," answered Gail after a slight hesitation.

"Do I know them?"

"About as well as I do."

"Where do they live?"

"In Martindale."

"Who can it be?" pondered the girl.

"You might guess all night and never get it right," laughed Gail. "You better give it up. Tomorrow is time enough for little girls to know."

"For little girls to know what?" demanded Peace, as the noisy quartette burst breathlessly in from school.

"What we are to have for dinner tomorrow night," answered Gail, glancing warningly at Faith.

"Tomorrow night? We have dinner at noon."

"Tomorrow we don't. We'll have lunch at noon and dinner in the evening."

"Bet there's comp'ny coming!" shouted the smaller girls.

"Who?" asked Hope, almost as much excited.

"The minister and his family, and Mrs. Grinnell."

"What for?" questioned Cherry, for company was rare at the little brown house.

"Why, to eat up those chickens, of course," answered Peace. "Will there be enough to go around? Hadn't I better hack the head off from another?"

"Don't you fret! Mike weighed the hens after he killed them, and one is a seven-pounder, and the other weighs eight. That surely ought to be enough to satisfy your appetites."

"Well, I bony a drumstick! There'll be four this time."

"Yes, but suppose we have to wait," suggested Cherry. "The others may eat them all up."

"Oh, Gail, must we wait?" cried Peace in alarm, suddenly remembering how tiny the dining-room was.

"No, dear, there will be room for all," answered the mother-sister. "But I shall expect all of you to be little ladies and not quarrel over drumsticks or wishbones. One's guests must always be served first, you know."

"Isn't it too bad," sighed the child pensively, "that we can't be our own guests sometimes and have just the piece we want?"

"You ought to be thankful to have any part of it," Faith spoke up. "If company wasn't coming, we shouldn't have killed the hens."

"I am as thankful as I can be," answered Peace, brightening visibly. "Cherry, come help me scour the silver. I forgot it last night, and if comp'ny is coming, we want everything fine. Besides, the time goes faster when you're busy, and already I can hardly wait for tomorrow night to come. Seems 's if it never would get here with those roasted hens."

But in due time the eventful night arrived, and with it the select company who were to join in the little celebration. With eager, shining eyes, Peace ushered in the guests, who chanced to come all together, and as she relieved them of their wraps and led them into the shabby parlor, she chattered excitedly.

"You don't like drumsticks the best, do you, Mr. Strong? And neither does Mrs. Grinnell. I heard her say so lots of times. She likes the wings. I want something that ain't so skinny. That's why I always choose drumsticks. There are four in this affair – four drumsticks, I mean. You didn't think I meant comp'ny, did you? Each hen had two legs, you know; but there are nine people to eat, counting Glen, though, of course, he is too little for such things yet; and the drumsticks won't anywhere near go around, s'posing every one of you should want one. When we have only one hen, Cherry and Allee and me always fight over who is to have the drumsticks. Last time Gail settled it by eating one herself, and giving the other to Hope. That won't happen today, though, 'cause there is company."

"Aren't you giving away family secrets?" interrupted Mrs. Grinnell, trying to look severe.

"Oh, no! You already know about it, and the minister ain't s'prised at anything. I just thought I'd speak about it, 'cause I've bonied one drumstick myself, if someone else doesn't eat them all up first. And say, folks, if any of you get a wishbone in your meat, will you save it for me? Cherry's making a c'lection and has six already. I haven't but the one I asked Mr. Hartman for, and they make the cutest penwipers for Christmas. Supper – dinner is 'most ready, I guess. Gail made lots of stuffing – dressing, I mean. And Faith's cake is just fine, and the custard pies are the beautifulest she ever made. They are all extra, 'cause you are here. We don't often get such nice things to eat, but this is a special 'casion. When supper is over the rest of the girls will help me do the talking, but now they are every one busy except Allee and me, and Allee's getting dressed. There's someone at the door. I hope it ain't more comp'ny. S'posing it is, wouldn't that be the worst luck, – the very night we have roast chicken!"

Before Peace could reach the door to see who was there, however, Mr. Strong swung it wide open, and reaching out into the dusk, drew in a sweet-faced, motherly, old lady with silvery hair, and the familiar tall, gray man of the broker's office, exclaiming in his hearty, boyish fashion, "Mrs. Campbell, Doctor, I am so glad you have come! I was beginning to fear you had missed the place."

"Missed the place? Now, **Brother Strong**, I am insulted, – after the number of times I have been **here! Good** evening, ladies. Mother, I want you to meet Mrs. Strong and Mrs. Grinnell. Hello, Peace, where is – "

"Have you come for dinner?" demanded that young lady, with frigid dignity, wondering where she had seen that kindly face before, and secretly wishing they had delayed their coming until a more convenient time.

"Yes, I have," he answered decidedly, "and I am as hungry as a bear!"

"Oh, dear," thought Peace, "there goes a drumstick! Hungry folks always want them." But though her face lengthened, she did not voice such sentiments, and started for the kitchen, saying, "I must tell Gail, so's she'll set you a plate for sup – dinner. Is that lady going to stay?"

"That lady is my wife. If you have any fault to find with us for dropping in unannounced, just scrap it out with Brother Strong, for he invited us."

"I'm not finding fault," Peace answered haughtily, turning once more toward the door, "but there's no telling what Faith will do. I better warn them now."

"And at the same time you might tell Abigail that someone in the parlor wants to see her," laughed the genial voice.

Peace disappeared through the door like a flash, and they heard her shrill voice call, "Oh, Gail, Faith, there are some folks here for supper what weren't invited. Do you s'pose there is hen enough now? And, oh, yes, he wants to see you right away, Gail!"

The oldest sister paused in the act of lifting the beautifully browned birds from their nest of dressing, dropped the carving set, shoved the pan back into the oven, and with flushed cheeks and glowing eyes, hurried for the parlor with such a buoyant step that the other sisters followed wonderingly. She paused an instant in the doorway, smiled at the little company within, and then straight to the white-haired lady she went, and kissed her, saying happily, "I have never seen you before, Mrs. Campbell, but I shall love you dearly."

"Not that, Gail," tenderly answered the stranger, holding the tall girl close. "Call me Grandma."

"And me Grandpa," added the gray man, drawing Gail out of the woman's arms and kissing her blushing cheek.

"Now she'll give him a drumstick sure," sighed Peace; "and s'posing he should ask for four!"

"This is Faith, the baker and my right-hand man," she heard Gail saying, "and Hope, our sunbeam; Charity, the scholar; and Peace, the – "

"Mischief-maker, heart captivator, and worth her weight in gold," finished the familiar voice which Peace could not quite place in her memory. "Kiss me!"

Passively she allowed him to embrace her as he had greeted the other sisters, and then squirming out of his arms, she backed into a corner, where she frowned impartially on the excited group, all talking at once, while she tried to puzzle out how this man could be "Grandpa" when all her own relatives had long since been carried away by the angels.

"I'll bet he is a make-believe," she told herself; "and he's got them all fooled proper. Maybe he wants the farm, seeing old Skinflint didn't get it. I am going to ask Mrs. Grinnell. She had sense enough to run when the kissing began."

Peace slipped noiselessly through the nearby door, and fled to the kitchen, where their kind neighbor was busy dishing up the forgotten dinner, demanding, "Is he really a grandpa we didn't know anything about, or is he a make-believe frog?"

"Make-believe frog!" echoed matter-of-fact Mrs. Grinnell. "Do you mean fraud? Well, he certainly ain't a fraud, Peace Greenfield! He's a big man. Everyone in the state knows him, pretty near. He is Dr. Campbell of the University. 'Tisn't every little girl that can have an adopted – Peace, I am afraid you and Cherry will have to wait until the rest are through eating."

"That's where you are mistaken," returned Peace with energy. "Gail said only last night that there was room for all."

"But she wasn't expecting the Campbells for supper."

"Oh, dear, if that ain't always the way! Gail, must I wait?"

Gail had just hurriedly entered the kitchen, fearful lest the forgotten dinner was spoiled, but seeing the great bowl of gravy on the table, and Mrs. Grinnell busy mashing the potatoes, she sighed in relief and stopped to answer, "I am afraid you must, dear."

"After you said we wouldn't have to?"

"I didn't look for Grandpa and Grandma Campbell until later, Peace. We can't ask them to wait."

"Faith and Hope might for once. They never have to!"

"Faith is to serve dinner, and Hope is needed at the table."

"Which I s'pose means Cherry and me ain't needed," cried the disappointed child.

"Peace! I am ashamed of such a little pig."

"It ain't piggishness, Gail. I don't want a whole hen, I want just a drumstick," protested Peace, with two real tears in her eyes.

"Oh, dear, now we are in for a scene," sighed the older girl, anxious to avert the storm. "Now be reasonable, Peace. If you will wait like a good little girl, you shall have a drumstick. Look at Cherry, – she doesn't make a fuss at all. You will be sorry by and by if you cry and get your eyes all red."

"Is there to be a s'prise?" asked Peace in animated curiosity.

"Yes, such a splendid one!"

"I'm not going to cry, Gail. Those two tears just got loose 'fore I knew it. I will stay in the parlor with Cherry all right, but don't take too long a time eating dinner, and don't forget my drumstick."

With this parting warning she flew back into the front room and announced, "Dinner is ready, folkses! Faith, tell them where to sit; and say, you all better eat fast, 'cause Gail says there is a big s'prise coming."

Slamming the door behind them as they filed out into the dining-room, she sat down in the nearest chair and faced Cherry with a droll look of resignation, saying, "Well, Charity Greenfield, how do you like being one of the children and having to wait every time we have comp'ny? When I have a family of my own, I'll make the visitors do the waiting."

"I don't mind it much," answered Cherry, serenely. "There is a heap of victuals cooked. Mrs. Grinnell said she guessed we must have been expecting a regiment."

Peace sniffed the air hungrily, rose with deliberation from the rocker, tiptoed to the door, opened it a crack and peeked out at the merry diners. Then she let go of the knob with a jerk, wheeled toward Cherry and whispered, "Just as I 'xpected! That man has got a drumstick and he just gave Allee one. He's stuffing her for all he's worth. First thing we know, she will be sick."

"Yes, and you banged that door, too, so they must have heard you," said Cherry indignantly.

"Maybe 'twill hurry them up. I don't see how I can wait."

"Get a book and read. Then the time will seem shorter."

Peace rocked idly back and forth a few turns, patching her companion in misery, who seemed so absorbed in her story that even the thoughts of no dinner did not disturb her; then she stalked over to the battered bookcase, drew out a big, green-covered book which evidently had been often read, for the binding was in rags, and sat down on the rug to digest its contents.

"'Bright was the summer of 1296. The war which had desolated Scotland was then at an end,'" read Peace slowly, spelling out the long, unfamiliar words and finding it dry reading. She turned the yellowed pages rapidly in search of pictures, but found none. She skipped several lines and began again to read, "'But while the courts of Edward, or of his representatives, were crowded – ' oh, dear, what does it mean? There ain't a mite of sense in using such long words. Cherry, what is this book about?"

"'Scottish Chiefs?'" said the sister, looking up indifferently. "I don't know. Ask Hope. She had to read it last year when they studied English history."

"I thought maybe 'twas about Indians. I didn't know other things were called chiefs. My, I can smell dinner awfully plain! They've been at it long enough to have finished, seems to me. I'm going to peek again."

"You better not let that door slam," warned Cherry, "or Gail will be getting after you."

"I don't intend to. It slipped the other time. There goes another drumstick!" she wailed dismally, forgetting to speak in whispers; and the amazed guests beheld a flushed, distressed face popped through the wide crack of the door, as rebellious Peace called in bitter indignation, "Remember, all the family haven't had dinner yet, and chickens don't grow on every bush!"

"Peace!" gasped poor, mortified Gail.

"Ha-ha-ha!" roared the minister, and President Campbell called after the little figure which had vanished behind the closed door once more, "That is right, Peace! You needn't stay in there another minute. Here is plenty of room for you and Cherry in my lap."

The only answer was the sound of a choking sob from the adjoining room, and the college president started to his feet with remorse in his heart, pleading, "Let me get her! It's too bad to shut them off there to wait for us older folks to eat dinner. I know from experience."

But Gail stopped him, saying firmly, "No, it was very naughty of her to do that, and she can't have any dinner at all now until she has apologized."

"You are hard on her."

"She must remember her manners. I resign my authority to you and Grandma in a few hours," she answered laughingly, "but until then she must mind me."

"Please let me bring them out here with us, anyway," he urged. "She will apologize; and around the table is a good place for the big 's'prise' she is expecting."

"Very well," she answered reluctantly.

Excusing himself to the little dinner party, he disappeared behind the parlor door, whispered a few words to the conscience-stricken culprit in the corner, and in a surprisingly short time reappeared with two smiling little girls.

Peace's eyes were red, and one lone tear stood on the rosy cheek, but she marched up to the table, bowed, and said with some embarrassment, but in all sincerity, "Ladies and gentlemen, I've already told Grandpa, and he said it was all right – I apologize. I s'pose you are hungry, same as I, and that's what has kept you busy eating for so long. I shouldn't have hollered at you from the door like I did, but if you wanted that drumstick as bad as I do, you'd have hollered, too. Now can I have my dinner? Cherry, you sit in half of Allee's chair. Faith, Hope will give you a piece of her place, and I am to have half of Grandpa's. That's all his plan, so come along, Faith. Please pass me my drumstick. You've already blessed it, haven't you?"

"Peace!"

"Now, Gail, please don't scold! This is the last day in the little brown house, you know – "

"What!" burst forth, a chorus of dismayed voices.

"Ain't that mordige settled yet?" demanded Peace.

"Oh, yes. I had a long talk with Mr. Strong, and we settled that question forever and all time, I hope. Nevertheless, you aren't going to stay here any longer."

A hush fell over the five younger girls, though Gail was smiling happily with the rest of the little company, and even Baby Glen seemed to appreciate the situation, and cooed gleefully, as he pounded the table with his spoon.

"It's just as I 'xpected," Peace blurted out at length. "I said I bet you wanted the farm yourself, seeing that old Skin – Mr. Skinflint didn't get it."

He threw back his head and laughed loud and long; then the old face sobered, and he said, "No, it isn't that, Peace. We – Grandma and I – want you to come and live with us. Gail says yes. What is your answer?"

"All of us?" whispered Hope in awestruck tones, remembering with fresh fear the midnight conference of a few weeks before.

"All of you!"

"Gail, too?"

"Yes, indeed!"

"Haven't you any children yourself?" asked Allee, not exactly understanding the drift of remarks.

"No, dear. The angels came and took away our two little girlies before they were as big as you are."

"But six is an awful many to raise at once," sighed Peace. "Do you think you can do it?"

"I will try if you will come."

"Do you live in Martindale?"

"Yes."

"Is your house big enough?"

"It has ten big rooms and an attic. Won't that do?"

"Y – es. Do you lick?"

"Do I lick?" he echoed in surprise.

"When we are bad, you know."

"Oh! Well, I can, but I don't very often. I am pretty easy to get along with; but folks have to mind. I am fond of good children."

"I'm usually good. I have been bad today, but I am ever so sorry now. I always am when it's too late to mend matters. But I don't want you to think I am always such a pig and have to 'pologize for my dinner. Yes, I'll come to live with you, and of course the others will. Mrs. Grinnell says you are an awfully nice man."

"I am sure I thank Mrs. Grinnell," he answered with twinkling eyes, bowing gravely to the embarrassed lady across the table.

"But what I can't see is how you came to pick us out to take home with you, – Mr. Tramp!" She started to her feet in astonishment, having suddenly fitted the familiar face into its place in her memory.

"At your service, ma'am."

"Ain't you my tramp?"

"Yes."

"Then you are just fooling about our going to live with, you."

"Not at all. I mean every word of it. Ask Grandma, ask Brother Strong, ask Gail, any of them."

"But what about the tramp?" she half whispered, still too dazed to understand.

"That is rather a long story," he smiled, stroking the tight ringlets of brown on one side of him, and the bright, golden curls on the other. "A year ago last spring I tried to be ill – play sick, you know; and the doctor told me a vacation of tramping was what I needed to put me in tune again. Having some pet theories in regard to the tramp problem of this country, I decided to take his words literally, so I turned tramp myself – just for a little time, you see. That is how you saw me first. I told my wife it was a case of love at first sight, and I became so much interested in this brave little family that I have kept watch ever since.

"Here was a family without any father and mother, and there were a father and mother without any family. You needed the one and we needed the other. But at first the way didn't seem clear. I was given to understand that you didn't want to be adopted, and as I found that Gail was legally old enough to take care of the family, I was just on the point of preparing to play guardian angel instead of grandfather, when I chanced upon some old church records telling about your own grandfather's death. It gave a brief account of his life, and I was astonished to find that I knew him well, – in fact, as my big brother."

"Tell us about it," pleaded Hope, as he paused reminiscently.

"When I was a little shaver my father was a seaman, captain of a ship; but his whole fortune consisted of his vessel, his wife and son. Mother and I often used to go with him on his trips, but for some reason he left me at home the last time he set sail, and he never came back. New Orleans was his port. Yellow fever broke out while he was there, and so far as I have been able to find out, every soul of his crew died of it. I had been left with a neighbor who had her hands full looking after her own children; so, when word came that my parents were both dead, she sent for the town officers, and told them I must go to the poor-farm. I was only about the size of Allee, here, but I knew that the poor-farm was a place much dreaded, and rather than be taken there, I tried to run away. Your grandfather found me. He was one of our nearest neighbors and knew me well, so when I sobbed out the whole terrible story into his sympathetic ears, he adopted me on the spot. He wasn't more than a dozen years old himself, but he had a heart big enough to take in the whole world, and when he had coaxed me home with him and told his mother about my misfortune, I knew I was safe. They would never send me away again. So Hiram Allen became my big brother, and the Allen home was mine for ten long years. Then an uncle of mine whom everyone had thought was dead put in appearance and took me to sea on a long voyage which covered the greater part of four years. When I returned, Mother and Father Allen were dead and the younger fry had gone West, – no one seemed to know where. Then and there I completely lost sight of them, and it was only by chance that I – "

"Grandpa's name wasn't Hi Allen," mused Faith aloud, with a puzzled look in her eyes. "It was Greenfield, just like ours."

"Yes; that is one reason, I suppose, why I never found my big brother of my boyhood days. You see, he had a stepfather. His own parent was drowned at sea when he was a tiny baby, and his mother married again; so he was known all over the place as Hi Allen instead of Hi Greenfield, which was his real name. When he grew to manhood and entered the ministry he decided to take his own name. But, though I dimly remembered having heard people say that Mr. Allen wasn't Hi's own father, I never heard his real name spoken, to my knowledge, and I never once thought of the possibility of his assuming it in place of his stepfather's.

"When I discovered your grandfather's identity only a few days ago, the way seemed suddenly open to me. Hi Allen had shared his home with me when I was an orphan; I would share my home with his little granddaughters, alone in the world and in trouble, – for by this time I had heard about the mortgage and the battle being fought in the little brown house to keep the family together. Mothering this big brood is too great a task for Gail. She needs mothering herself. We want to adopt you, mother and I. Will you let us; for the sake of the dear grandfather who did so much for me?"

His face was so full of yearning tenderness that tears came to the eyes of the older members of the queer little party, and even the children had to swallow hard.

"I have talked the matter over with Gail, and she agrees if the rest of you will consent. I am not a millionaire, but we are pretty well fixed in a material way and can give you a great many pleasures and advantages that the little town of Parker can never offer. There are fine schools in the city, and college for Gail. We have a piano and violin and all sorts of music, a horse and buggy, a big barn, and a splendid yard in a nice locality, with plenty of room for tennis or any other kind of gymnastics. Maybe some day there will be an automobile – "

"I don't care about pianos and nautomobiles," interrupted Peace. "It's the kind of people you are that I am thinking about. Mrs. Grinnell says you're the president of a big college and everyone knows you. If that's so, you ought to be pretty nice, I sh'd think. I like you, anyhow, and I b'lieve you'll like us, too. But I'm an awful case, even when I don't mean to be. Maybe you would rather – didn't I – weren't you – I saw you in Swift & Smart's store!"

"Yes, my lady! Twice in the city I have seen you and Allee, and both times I thought surely you knew me, but I don't believe you did."

"No, I didn't. I 'member now. It was you who gave us that gold money when we were selling flowers. But you look different with new clothes on and a clean face."

"Why, you little rascal! Wasn't my face clean when I came here to get something to eat?"

"It might have been, but it was prickly looking with the mustache all over your chin, and I like you lots better this way. I almost didn't know you the night you got supper for us, either."

"And the rice burned."

"And I broke Bossy's leg and you sent us Queenie to take her place, and Faith said I was worse than Jack of the Bean Stalk, and – I bet you are the fellow that pinned the money to the gatepost and grain sacks! Now, aren't you?"

"I am afraid I am."

"You told me once before that you weren't."

"No, I didn't. I just asked you if it wouldn't be a queer kind of tramp who could do such a thing. Isn't that what I said?"

"Y – es," she finally acknowledged. Then the puzzled frown in her forehead smoothed itself away and she wheeled toward the oldest sister with the triumphant shout, "There, Gail, didn't I tell you he was a prince in disgus – disguise? Now ain't you sorry you didn't spend the money? She has got it all saved away yet. I must kiss you for that, Grandpa, even if it didn't do us any good." She threw her arms, drumstick and all, about his neck and gave him a greasy smack, immediately rubbing her lips with the back of one hand.

"Aha! That's no fair," he protested. "You rubbed that off."

"No, I didn't. I just rubbed it in. Thank you, I don't care for any pie tonight. Somehow this drumstick filled me up full. I can't eat a bite more. Have you been waiting all this time for me? Well, let's go back into the parlor then, and do the rest of our talking. I've sat on the tip edge of nothing until I am tired. There's more space in the front room."

"Do you know, Peace Greenfield," cried Mr. Campbell, pretending to feel insulted at her intimation that he had not given her a large enough share of his chair, "the first time I ever called at your house, I found you sitting on the gatepost, – the gatepost, mind you, – about so square," measuring with his hands; "and just as I turned in from the road, you began to sing, 'The Campbells are coming, oho, oho!' What kind of a reception do you call that? And tonight you weren't even going to give me any supper."

"Oh," she hastily assured him, "I didn't mean you by that song. I used to think that the Campbells were little striped bugs that eat up the cucumber plants, and the very morning that you came here for breakfast I found two in the garden. What are you laughing at? I know better now, but I truly didn't have a notion what your name was then. You must have known I didn't. But I am awfully glad you came and that you kept coming even when I was bad and made you work so hard. I am sorry, but never mind, I am deformed now."

"Deformed, child? Where?"

"Right here in my heart! I am going to be as good as gold all the time after this. I think the angels must have sent you. We've always wanted a first-class grandfather and grandmother, but we never 'xpected to get 'em until we found our own inside the Gates some day. Just the same, I spoke to God about it, and He probably had the angels hunt you up. So I have deformed and now I'll be real good. I'm truly sorry I was such a selfish pig about wanting a drumstick tonight. I s'pose that's why the drumstick filled me up so quick and didn't leave any room for pie. Custard is my favorite."

"Perhaps that is the reason," he agreed, quite as serious as she. "We always are happiest when we are unselfish. Now, let's forget all about the badness and just remember the goodness. I have some of the most splendid plans for what we shall do when I have my six girls at home with me. What beautiful times we shall have, mother!"

"How can we ever thank them?" whispered bright-eyed Gail to Mrs. Strong, under cover of the lively conversation at the other end of the table.

"By loving them," promptly answered the little woman, offering up a prayer of thanksgiving that the brave little orphan band had found such a beautiful home. "They are noble people and have hungered all their lives for just that very thing."

"But love seems such a little thing to give for the blessings we shall enjoy from their hands."

"Ah, my dear, that is where you are mistaken, Love is everything."

THE END.

Printed in the United States
146159LV00002B/12/P